DEAD WRONG

A NOVEL

Klaus Jakelski

blue denim press

For Jane
Thanks For Reading

Klaus

Dead Wrong
Copyright © 2014 Klaus Jakelski
All rights reserved
Published by Blue Denim Press Inc.
First Edition
ISBN 978-1-927882-04-7
No part of this book may be used or reproduced in any manner whatsoever without written permission except in the case of brief quotations embodied in critical articles or reviews.

This is a work of fiction. Any resemblance to events, organizations, or to people living or dead, is entirely coincidental and beyond the intent of the author or the publisher.

Cover Design—Joanna Joseph/Typeset in Cambria and Garamond

Library and Archives Canada Cataloguing in Publication
Jakelski, Klaus, 1951-, author
    Dead wrong: a novel / Klaus Jakelski. -- First edition.

 Issued in print and electronic formats.
ISBN 978-1-927882-04-7 (pbk.).--ISBN 978-1-927882-05-4 (kindle).--
ISBN 978-1-927882-06-1 (epub)

    I. Title.

PS8619.A3695D42 2014   C813'.6   C2014-905007-0
                                                                                  C2014-905008-9

Dedication

For Edwin Owen Wyllis Knight.
Friend, mentor, and the finest heart surgeon I have ever known.

ONE

"Don't make me do this."

Roy Purvis winced and said, "Ed, I just don't understand."

"Come on Roy. I want him now." Ed Van Boren glowered at him.

Roy Purvis sat hunched, nervously twirling his pen between his fingers under the table. "I still don't understand. For Christ's sake, the only appointments outside the university are chiefs and chairmen. You're not thinking of making *him* chief of cardiac surgery? Are you?" He looked around, wanting to dismiss the idea. Silence followed.

A drop of ink escaped Roy's Montblanc pen and stained his hand.

"Heaven forbid," Van Boren finally said. He stroked his grey hair. "You're doing a great job. We can't find the kind of talent we need around here, so tradition will have to change." He turned to the man at the end of the table. "Isn't that so Abe?"

"That's right," said Frank Abel.

Roy watched Abel looking out the tall windows onto the golden evening skyline of east Boston. Long sheer curtains, fanned by soft breezes, swept at the edge of the Persian carpet.

"I agree, Roy," said Van Boren, the chief of staff. "It's not like there are no good cardiac surgeons hanging around here. But there aren't any great ones—ones you'd want to work with. Are there?"

Were Ed and Frank starting to make sense, or was Roy tiring? No!

"I've never really understood why you insist that Martins is the man for the job." Roy was bewildered. "I trained him. Groomed him." He stretched his hands out. "I can train another just like him."

"The simple truth is, Roy, we don't have the time," said Abel. "Mass Heart needs a new heart surgeon now." He clasped his hands on his lap as he tilted back in his chair with a pipe in the corner of his mouth. He watched a puff of blue smoke rise to the ceiling and slash sideways by the breeze from the open window. He suddenly sat up, looking serious and straight at Roy Purvis.

"Roy. You're the leading heart surgeon in the United States." Abel fidgeted with his pipe. "You took Peter Martins on as a fellow. You spent lots of time with him. I understand you didn't do many cases without him."

Roy waffled. "That's right."

"Is there something about Doctor Martins we don't know? Something you'd like to share with us now?" Abel's voice slipped a few octaves. "Is he unsuitable to work here? Speak freely Roy. Being the Chairman of The Board, I can guarantee your confidence."

"No, there's nothing wrong with him," said Roy. "We worked very well together."

Remembering was easy. Roy had known the moment Peter Martins scrubbed with him, the young man was a serious talent with his hands. That, and flawless judgment, a winning combination. He recalled how well they worked together. Peter reminded Roy of himself as a young man. There really wasn't anybody else. He knew that.

"There's nothing wrong with him." Roy looked around the room, feeling lost. "I just can't understand the sudden push. One day you guys phone up and say, 'Hey we're going to hire this new surgeon.' You don't even ask me if I think we need one." He sat upright. "What about me? What about *my* opinion?"

"You're right. We've been pushy," said Van Boren. "But we have a business to run—we run the best private heart hospital in the world. We've kept our distance from the university, to operate privately, for profit. We kept our affiliation with them for prestige. Mass Heart has the best doctors, the best equipment, and the best service anywhere."

He folded his arms across the double-breasted Brooks Brothers jacket that covered his considerable torso. "That business model, Roy, is what keeps your salary and benefits at their present stratospheric level."

All right. That does it. Roy stood up and cleared his throat.

"Ed. Frank. I'll hand in my resignation tomorrow."

"You will not," said Van Boren, leaning forward, popping a button. The chief of staff stood up and smoothed the spot on his shirt, as he leaned forward and tapped his right index finger hard onto the polished rosewood table. "You'll stay right where you are. Doctor A Roy Purvis is the chief of cardiac surgery of the Massachusetts Heart Institute, until *I* say otherwise."

The silence left no room for reply. Van Boren pounded his fist once on the table and continued. "May I remind you that there is nowhere in this great country or any other goddamned place where you could do as well! Is that important to you?" Beads of perspiration formed on Van Boren's brow as Roy's gaze fell. "No?"

Roy slumped to his chair; he realized his folly. His problems—all of them—were there any that Ed and Frank didn't know about? Not likely. Why else would Ed expect him to roll over like a dog and approve Martins? He was obviously their *boy*! The number one heart surgeon in the United States was their *boy*. He loathed it!

Roy thought for a moment and finally noticed the large smudge of ink on his right hand. Shocked. He surveyed his suit. Safe. He collected his thoughts.

"So what do you want me to do?" he said.

"Have Doctor Martins nominated by your department," Van Boren said in a cordial tone, as if nothing had happened. "Present it to the board as a motion from your department. The board will approve." He paused to let Roy mull it over. "Any questions?"

Roy paused a moment. "When does he start?"

A smile passed over Abel's lips. "In two months."

TWO

Doctor Peter Martins stood in the operating room of the Massachusetts Heart Institute, gloved hands folded over his gown, as he surveyed the patient.

She was a young woman, Bernice Green, pregnant for the second time, and near term. That alone shouldn't have brought her here. However, she lay, with a tear in a large artery in her abdomen, every beat of her heart, clearly visible as an undulating pulse in her belly.

Peter Martins fixated on the jiggling belly from across the room. He didn't like this sort of case with two lives at stake. If they both died, well, blame that on fate, although they had made it this far. And if only one died? That would likely be the mother. So how did you tell a man you never met before that he was a new father; oh, just one thing, the child doesn't have a mother. Assuming the child was okay. Peter was certainly the man to go into her belly to fix the torn artery, but he hadn't delivered a child in over ten years. *More like robbing the dying womb.* And there wasn't an obstetrician available to back him up. *Just the sort of case to make your reputation in a new place!*

"Blood pressure can go up in black women near term," said Ian Scott, the tall black surgeon beside Martins. "It's high enough, you know, they rupture an artery." Ian looked at Peter. "How'd you get her anyway?"

"Eugen Wittman in Emerg had her diverted here 'cause he figured neither of them would survive the trip downtown. Called me after they got here. Told me the kid was still okay in Emerg."

"Probably right about the trip to town," said Ian Scott, turning back to the patient.

Two nurses scrubbed the belly with a pink liquid and draped it under blue sheets.

"Just one thing," Peter said quietly to Ian. "Wittman bet me we wouldn't save her, or the kid."

They looked at each other.

"Ready for crash induction?" asked the anesthetist, Frank Fanconi.

"Go," said Peter.

"God save momma and God bless this child," Ian whispered.

The anesthetist unloaded two syringes into the patient's IV. She trembled imperceptibly and was paralyzed for surgery. The doctor put an airway into Bernice's throat and hooked her up to the anesthesia machine. He ran pure oxygen.

With Ian on the other side of the patient, Peter took a large blade and incised the belly from the chest to the pelvis. Hardly any bleeding. Body fat was oddly golden, not yellow. He got into the abdomen, and the large, dusky uterus popped up into view. What surprise would it hold?

"Here we go." He looked at Ian, who nodded.

Martins took a large knife and nicked the uterus until he was through. He placed his left index finger in the hole, and pushed the blunt end of a pair of scissors over his finger, which he used as a guide to avoid cutting the infant. As he cut down the length of the uterus, clear amniotic fluid welled up over the edges and splashed to the floor, soaking the surgeons' feet. A little black head with soft, curly hair came into view. Scott plucked out the limp infant and cradled it in his left arm as he cut the cord. The infant didn't stir as he was passed to a nurse.

"Gas is on," said Fanconi. "Drugs running. Patient's going to sleep now."

"I'm going to put a large clamp over the base of the uterus and amputate it, so I can get a better view of the aneurysm," said Peter. "She won't need her uterus again if she doesn't live."

"Right," said Ian.

A suctioning sound came from the far corner of the operating room.

The large clamp clicked home, and Martins transected the base of the uterus. He plucked the burst pear from its stalk, and removed the organ from the bloody cavity. He quickly searched higher in the abdomen, up at the back, sweeping some bowel out of his way.

"Can you feel the top of the aneurysm?" said Ian, as he attempted to hold loops of bowel out of the way. "Can you feel the top? Just find the top." He was suddenly breathing fast.

The two surgeons stood hunched over, oblivious to their surroundings. As quickly as Scott sucked the abdomen dry, dark blood welled up to obscure their view.

"Blood pressure's dropping," said Fanconi. "Hate to break it to you, but it's not looking good."

"I think I've got the aorta," said Peter. "The top's between my fingers." He could hear and feel Ian's breath. "It's below the kidneys so we should be all right."

"Wa ... wa ... waah!" came feebly from the corner. "Waah. Wa ... Wa ... Waaah. Waah." A staggered gasp and then a definite protesting, "Waaaaaah!"

Peter said. "Holy shit, is he glad to be out of there." He interrupted the ensuing laughter to say, "Get Junior over to Children's Hospital now."

Martins slid a long clamp, down over the back of his hand, and clicked it down over the neck of the aneurysm.

"Clamp's on," he said.

After some moments Fanconi said, "Blood pressure stopped falling, may be stable. Better get to work fast."

With the leakage of blood finally stopped, looking into the abdomen became easier. Ian and Peter confirmed that the front of the aorta had a hole in it. Over the course of the next hour and a half, they replaced the blown segment with a tubular fabric patch. The job wasn't easy. They improvised.

Finally Ian, the senior surgeon, said, "I think it's time to take the clamp off the aorta." And he did.

There were some leaks around a few needle holes where the patch was joined to human tissue, but those soon stopped. The rest was routine. Ian and Peter worked well together.

Three hours later the patient was in Post-Op Intensive Care, up on the eleventh floor.

Doctor Schwartz was in charge and received the patient.

"So, this is Bernice Green," the small man said as he looked over the chart. "Now let me see. She's a little cool at 35.1, but what do you expect when her guts have been hanging outside her body for a couple of hours? That should normalize this evening. Vital signs are good. No drugs running. I can only assume that your graft isn't leaking, gentlemen." Schwartz nodded approval. "We'll ventilate her tonight and keep her paralyzed, what with the hysterectomy and all. I don't want her coughing and loosening anything up."

"Sounds good to me Schwartzy," said Peter. "I'll check with you tomorrow."

"Yeah okay," said Schwartz. "Just one thing ..."

Peter and Ian looked at him.

"You heard about the newborn Purvis operated on two days ago? Congenital heart? Tetralogy?"

"Kid was doing well," said Peter.

"Died two hours ago," said Schwartz. "Roy took it pretty hard. Told the parents." He shook his head.

"Very high risk surgery," said Ian. "The coroner come?"

"No," said Schwartz. "Been so many of these over the years. They never find anything. I think they've given up on us."

"So," said Peter. He paused a moment, thinking. "Does anybody know where I can find Mr. Green?" He pulled off the OR cap revealing a tussle of dirty blond hair.

"Apparently he's been down in Emerg with Wittman," said Schwartz. "He called. I mean, Wittman. Said the husband was sitting in a corner of the waiting room, you know ..." He bobbed his head from side to side.

"I see," said Peter. "Guess I better find him and explain why I robbed his wife of her fertility."

"Not a bad idea," said Ian. He put his black arm on Peter's shoulder. Hugged him. "Bear in mind though, that there are redeeming aspects to what we did."

"Yeah." Peter understood. "A few minutes longer, or a few more bumps in the road, and they might both have gone."

"Exactly, you done good." said Ian. He winked at Peter. "You gonna do obstetrics now?"

"Give me a break," he said, pulling away. "But listen, Wittman lost his bet and owes us dinner. What about tomorrow, being Saturday and all?"

"Sounds good to me. I wanna see him pay big for a change."

"Pay big, he will." said Peter as he rubbed his hands together. "I'll let him know we're coming, and that we're hungry. Get back to you in the morning."

"Very well." Ian Scott bowed his head ever so slightly.

"Goodnight." Peter waved to the I.C.U. staff.

He stood in an alcove as the elevator door opened and a black man got out, looking bewildered.

"Mr. Green?" said Peter.

"Yes." The man's head wavered.

"I'm Doctor Peter Martins." The surgeon extended his hand. "I'm sorry we couldn't meet before." Green's grip was weak. "Your wife is fine."

"Oh yeah?" He took a moment, like he was measuring the words, looking for hidden meanings before letting go his fear. He spoke quickly, "Well that makes two! I just left my son at Children's Hospital and he's fine, howling up a storm."

"You've got your hands full then."

"Sure do," said Mr. Green. "This isn't one of those things where the operation is a success, but there's something wrong with the patient?"

"I really don't think so. Let me say that this was a very high risk case. You're wife is strong. She should make it now." Peter continued slowly, "There's just one thing ..."

Mr. Green looked up, alarm on his face. "What?"

"She lost her womb." Peter waited for the look in the man's eyes to change. Perhaps he didn't understand, he hadn't heard, or he had chosen not to hear. "She can't have any more children."

Mr. Green looked around the dim halls for a moment, at the windows that mirrored the corridors against the twinkling city night, and finally at the tall young man who had now given him the worst of the news. "If that's the way it is, then it is."

After a moment, Mr. Green said again, "Then it is." He put his hand on Peter Martins shoulder and choked back a tear.

"I think you should go see her. Remember that Bernice can hear you even though she can't move or speak. That's just a precaution for the first night, so don't be alarmed. She's the first door on the right through there," Peter directed him towards the closed doors of the Intensive Care Unit.

"Thank you, Doctor. I'll be talking to you."

"You sure will." Peter turned to the elevator.

A few minutes later he was changed and driving his Porsche home along Storrow Drive. He was thinking about Roy Purvis's bad news and how he must be feeling. Knowing that Roy took his failures personally, and that there had been some. That was one thing he had really liked about working with him. Roy really cared about his people.

He exited at Copley, pulled into a laneway and parked in a garage adjoining a four-storey, red brick building.

Up on the top floor, he had sublet a large, comfortable, three bedroom condo that overlooked the back bay. The place, one of those old ones with eleven-foot ceilings and high windows, had been tastefully decorated by the owner who was away on sabbatical. Traditional American furniture graced the rooms that were trimmed in deep reds with a hint of green. Art deco lighting and oriental scatter rugs complemented the oak plank floor. Peter thanked his lucky stars for finding this place while he was getting established in Boston.

On the way to the bedroom he turned on the television to catch the eleven o'clock news. He returned in pyjama bottoms just as the anchor switched to an announcer in Washington.

"Congress today started debate on the National Health Bill." The woman went on. "The objective is to standarize health care, as well as the cost, across the nation. Critics say that it echoes Bill Clinton's defeated initiative and builds on

Obama-Care. However, supporters say that standardization of care and the price of services would be a bold step toward ensuring universal access and stopping the rapidly escalating cycle of health care costs. Such a system would be more like the one in Canada. Critics have also maligned reform for paving the way towards state ownership of private health care facilities. This is Jayne Baxter at the nation's capital."

THREE

Roy Purvis sat listening to the sound of waves as they broke onto the seashore, a hundred feet below. Waves that folded into the rocks with a rush, not a roar. Waves that played with the golden morning sunlight, reflecting myriad flashes into his eyes. Long gentle waves carried by a moderate wind on a high tide. It was a good sign. Roy put down his cobalt blue coffee cup. He loved the sea.

The patio trellis offered no protection from the six o'clock sun. No traffic could be heard. Neither had the planes started their noisy assault on Logan Airport to the south.

Roy, a thin man of fifty-eight, sported aviator glasses as he looked out and happily contemplated his position. As he stared east, intoxicated by the hypnotic sight and smell of the sea, a gentle wind ruffled his salt and pepper hair and tugged at the lapels of his burgundy terrycloth house coat.

On his right, about a mile south, sat the town of Winthrop with the landmark red, white and blue water tower perched atop the knoll of Ocean Point. Front Street followed the straight shoreline back toward his house and could have been borrowed from any southern seaside town. Roy's house was situated atop a steep, unkempt embankment. A wooden step, almost lost from view in the sunburnt grass and weeds, connected Seaside Avenue to the breakwater below.

The rocky shore continued north, past a few houses to the Bar Harbor condominium complex. Far on the northern horizon, stood the island of Nahant.

Roy finished his coffee and returned his thoughts to the present. He entered the Cape Cod house by the storm door to the kitchen.

He and Patricia had renovated the large old house. Here was a quiet seaside location close to downtown Boston, with the added benefit of modest realty prices, a good fit for a man with his marital history.

The kitchen, where he left his cup, was now thoroughly modern. The rest of the main floor was decorated chinois, with floors of dark herringbone oak.

Roy strode up the beige carpeted stairway, two at a time.

He peered inside the darkened, Italian lacquer bedroom to see his wife still sleeping, only a luxurious tussle of auburn hair showing on the pillow. He remembered the sensuous feel and smell of her hair, the taste of her lips—that was years ago—when he was still married to his second wife. Roy was saddened that Patricia had never shared his keenness for sailing. She had briefly, early in their relationship, but was now immersed in bridge games with her friends and in membership in this or that society. Ah well, at least he hadn't forgotten how to enjoy himself.

In the bathroom, he quickly changed into khaki safari pants and tunic which he had laid out the night before. He turned out the lights, grabbed his small overnight bag, took one last look around the room, and headed for the garage.

The high pitched whine of the starter surged the Jaguar to life. Roy backed out of the garage, leaving behind his wife's Mercedes SL. He jabbed the throttle and easily merged onto the coast road at Revere Beach. He adjusted the sun visor as the road took a more easterly heading past a lift bridge.

Revere beach stretched wide for a few miles with the gently sloped sand marked here and there with park benches, life guard posts and ornate metal cabanas. The sea rolled in on slow shimmering waves, lapping up onto shore in crescents. A good sign.

He still felt bad about the little boy who had died that week. Couldn't get him off his mind. Christopher Charles Spekkens. The operation had gone without a hitch, and then on day two everything went south. There was nothing he could do. Roy still had that horrible feeling in the pit of his stomach. Then the coroner didn't come, again. *Get it out of your mind.*

For some reason he thought of Peter Martins.

Only two years ago, Martins used to be his fellow, his *kid*, and Roy had guided him like a true protégé. Almost like a son for Christ's sake. And now, here's Martins knocking on his door, pissing him off. Taking cases that only he could have done. Taking them from that German working in Emerg without even examining the patient! He, not Martins, was after all the best cardio-vascular surgeon in the United States. No American could compete with him, and certainly no Canadian. Who else? Chapuis in Paris? Fraser in Edinburgh?

Roy dismissed the idea. *I'm the best in the world.*

So yesterday, the *kid* did the operation everyone was talking about, without even asking him to come in. No nod, no kudos, no nothing. Instead he got Ian Scott to help him. But then, Martins had pulled it off. *Can't argue with that. So. What the hell are these guys doing?*

All of which begged the central issue. Why did Van Boren and Abel get these two in the first place? Wittman was easier to understand because the joint needed somebody first rate in Emerg. But Martins? The cardiac surgical staff was already the best in the world. *Why appoint him without even asking me?*

Roy couldn't imagine what the board was up to, promoting minor people from outside. The university always promoted from within. Only the highest positions were recruited from outside the system, for obvious reasons. *What the hell's happening around here?*

Roy steered out of the miracle mile, a piece of north coast beach littered with car dealers, and businesses that clung to them like barnacles to a boat. The clock in the burled walnut console showed 6:30.

Just a little further, and she'd join him. *Ah Janet.*

He had met her a year ago while doing rounds with the residents. The fire started a moment after, first in their eyes, then in their loins. They had been inseparable since. Well, almost inseparable. Even Roy had to go home some nights!

And when Patricia had asked, "Why does the recruiting committee for the university take so much of your time," he had answered, "because it's a big school, dear, and we're in an expansion phase." She seemed to accept that with the blind faith of so many medical wives. Meaning, it had been a cinch.

Wasn't that when Patricia started "finding" herself on the board of the science museum? He couldn't remember.

But Janet, with her blond hair, blue eyes, peerless skin, and centre fold body made him feel young again.

He was on the causeway to Nahant; the damned thing was almost a bloody mile long. At the fork in the road he turned right, past the quaint little pharmacy located half way out to the beach. Probably turned a fortune in Coca-Cola and suntan oil.

Nahant was where he should have been. He could have had any of a number of big homes on this island of rolling hills, huge trees, and beautifully varied shoreline.

Jimmy Boyle's Marina stood next on the right, at the far side of a picture perfect bay. Dozens of boats lay moored to orange balls in the quiet, crescent-shaped bay that pointed south toward Winthrop and Boston. Jungle green trees skirted the bay on the island's hillside. Houses were built Cape Cod style, some on stilts, right up to the water's edge. Their clapboard siding captured the orange glow of the morning sun in splendored contrast to the sheltering trees.

Roy parked the Jaguar near the concrete end of the dock. He picked up his overnight bag and left the car. He walked towards the harbor master's office, onto the dock.

Roy took in a breath of sea air and surveyed the sleeping harbor. Boyle was probably right around somewhere.

He appeared almost immediately.

"Doc. How ya doing?"

"Just fine, thank you. How is she?"

"Ready."

Boyle turned and walked back to another man. When Boyle said "ready," nothing else needed saying.

Roy quickly surveyed his forty-seven-foot Hinckley with the eyes of a veteran sailor. She was the only boat secured at the end of the dock. The stern pointed to sea, no problem. Fresh water. Lots of fuel. Tanks pumped out. The sail covers were even off.

God bless Jimmy Boyle.

Once on board he let himself down the companionway and looked around. The interior was in order. He walked to the forward stateroom and threw his overnight bag onto the gigantic V-berth.

Janet obviously hadn't arrived yet. The sheets were unruffled and no other luggage was about.

Roy smoked secretly on weekends, and he needed one now. He poked in the side compartment of his overnight bag where he always kept a packet of Kools, and pulled it out. There, taped onto the front of the pack was a message in his wife's handwriting.

It read, "Have fun with your baby doll."

FOUR

Governor Willard Duke sat in his study, gazing into his cup of tea, ruminating over the last hectic week.

He had been to Washington to lobby the president for a bigger slice of the transfer payment pie. Unemployment was still high in Massachusetts. The recession had seen the failure of some high tech arms contractors in the suburbs. Then, the domino effect: the whole stinking thing because of bad real estate and bank failures.

So, the president printed trillions of dollars to bail out banks that should have known better. And the bankers? They'd bonused themselves with bailout bucks. *Damn!* And then the car manufacturers! *Double damn!*

But why did the president have to mess with defense? *The taxes it's costing me!*

Massachusetts still had unemployment lines *he* had to pay for! That was inflationary. Jim-Boy, his Secretary of Finance, had explained the whole thing to him once.

Duke stared into his cup of tea. The leaves from Sri Lanka. Public office had afforded him the luxury of such a splendid cup of tea for entertaining, even if he was only entertaining himself. Milk he poured from an ornate creamer into his cup seemed to explode like the mushroom cloud of an atom bomb.

The president had made lots of promises, even though the whole country had gone for a crap. Privately, the president once said he'd remember anybody who supported *his* health bill. His new health bill. What about the old one?

Time to call in the markers he'd thought. So, Duke had gone to speak to the president personally, but got little more than a group address. Had to look the bill up on the internet. Willard Duke, a governor, had to look it up on the internet. Well. Wasn't that just like a modern president?

Duke stirred his tea and sipped. Ah, the simple pleasures. Now why didn't more of the electorate appreciate them?

He panned his dark paneled library from the east wall with its tight grid of bookshelves and rolling wood ladder, just to the side of the tall entry, to the opposite wall of colonial windows covered in the whitest of ornate sheers. The wall in between was hung with a huge Persian carpet, a bestowment from some sheik he couldn't remember, which served as a focal point for a sitting area. Surrounding the great south wall fireplace were signed pictures of every president back to George Washington.

He wondered what sedition had passed through this place, all in the name of the common good. Signed, sealed, and delivered over coffee, tea, or bourbon. This old walnut table he was sitting at would have been party to those deals. He stared deeply into the shine but saw only his reflection.

He looked for a minute at the morning sun playing on the rose garden.

Duke rested his cherubic cheek on his palm, and with his small mouth tightly pursed to the edge of the cup, sipped more tea. He had a rosy complexion capped with thinning red hair that had tightened to a curl by the summer heat. His nose, hardly big enough to get a decent whiff from the tea, was subordinate to wide eyes of an indeterminate color. In fact, since childhood, people had told him that his eyes seemed to take on the predominant color of their surroundings. The underpinning of this was clad in a red and blue silk bathrobe which clung to every extra ounce of flesh that made up the governor's rotund body. Willard Duke didn't owe his ancestors any thanks for his physical habitus. Fortunately, his mind was another matter, and it was on the National Health Bill again.

Somehow, Duke had a gut feeling that the Bill was going to touch him, or that he was going to touch the Bill in a big way, with something more than the taxes he was going to have to collect to run the damned hospitals of Massachusetts.

He had been right about such feelings before. Oh yes, part of his intuition.

Duke took another sip of tea and pondered the bottom of his cup where the leaves had come to rest in a pattern like a cross. *Rubbish.* He gazed at the two telephones on the table, one black and one white. They were plain telephones with neither dials nor buttons. He picked up the black phone's receiver.

"Paula. Find me Frank Abel of Mass Heart." A pause. "Yeah, the chairman of the board."

He hung up and poured himself another cup of tea from the English service. As the milk mushroomed into the tea, he wondered for a moment, what being the president might feel like. He had no idea what he would say to Frank Abel. For a moment he crossed his bare feet which were cold from the plank hardwood floor.

A subdued ping pong came from the phone. Duke picked up the receiver.

"Frank, Frank Abel?" asked the governor, giving away a slight southern drawl.

"Yes," came the answer.

"This is Willard Duke, Governor Willard Duke."

"Oh, Governor! What a pleasant surprise. What may I do for you, sir?"

"Well now, I was just sitting here admiring the garden on this fine mornin', when it occurred to me that we had something in common. Yes, indeed. We have the health care of the people of this state in common. The National Health Bill has been tabled, you know."

"I heard," said Abel. "But that sort of thing's been tried before."

"Not quite like this, Mr. Abel. You see, the idea is to stabilize the cost of medical care across the country. So that something that costs a certain amount in Massachusetts costs the same fair amount in Seattle or LA."

"But Governor Duke, surely your charge will be the public hospitals of this state, the hospitals that serve the vast majority of our residents. Massachusetts Heart Institute is a private facility and most of our patients come from outside the state, if not from outside the country. Our role is not as a primary care giver, but as an institution of last resort, an institution of unparalleled expertise."

"That's true." Duke thought for a moment. "I just wanted you to know that I now consider us to be on the same team, workin' together toward the same goal, if you know what I mean. Right, Mr. Abel?" After a moment, Duke looked at the phone. "Are you still there, Mr. Abel?"

"Yes, yes, that's very true, sir, and I want you to know that I'm proud to be part of that team." said Abel. "Yes, very proud."

"You see, I think some of this politicking will become quite sensational. There may be some pressure on certain institutions, like yours," said Duke. He reminded himself of the taxes Massachusetts Heart Institute generated. He lowered his voice a little. "In your case, we want to try and maintain the status quo. Don't we?"

"I'm delighted at your point of view, Governor," said Abel. "You can rest assured this institution will back your efforts in the public domain."

"Why that's ... that's just what I wanted to hear." said Duke. Thinking he had made a good point, he was going to follow it through like a professional golf swing. His voice became serious, wavering a bit. "The next little while may be difficult, but if there's anything I can do for you or your institution, I hope you won't be afraid to call on me."

"Not at all, sir. In fact you can count on it. And thank you for taking the time to call. Goodbye, sir."

"The pleasure was all mine. Goodbye."

Duke was pleased for having introduced himself to Abel on a positive, cooperative note. Private enterprise always rallied around an open, receptive administration. He was glad he had shown the initiative. Who knew what might follow?

Duke looked out at the rose garden, and felt a smug satisfaction. He drained his cup. Another idea was coming to him.

Picking up the phone he said, "Paula, get me Jim-Boy."

With the next ping pong, he picked up the black receiver.

"Hello Jimmy? Willard here. Tell me something. How much money is in the current account? Nine hundred and fifty million. I see. How much of that is committed? That only leaves seven hundred and twenty-five million dollars! Shit!" He nervously tapped the dark tabletop with a pencil he had picked up. Then he had it.

"Think we should raise the gasoline tax again?"

FIVE

The little old man quickly walked up to the side of the car and reached into his jacket. He pulled out an automatic pistol. The Walther P-9 was almost too big for him to hold. He racked it and stuck the piece right under Ian Scott's nose.

Peter slouched in under the dash as much as he could, and covered his head with his arms. That was when he became oblivious. Expecting an explosion, there was none.

Instead he remembered the morning. Leaving the hospital with Mel Finegold and going shopping downtown. A hundred and one degree day where even molasses would have flowed on the sidewalk. Cars crawling around the back bay, some honking maliciously. Some pulled over steaming. People beside the Charles River dressed to the minimum. Lounging. Smoking. Drinking. Sailboats laboring under power on the glassy water.

Shopping in the almost empty downtown core, Mel had found a lens for a telescope he owned at a dealer in a stifling historic building on Tremont Street. Peter had bought a gold, red and green paisley tie that he liked so much, he said he'd get a suit to match.

They had driven up to Mel's place in Winthrop, past Logan airport. Past the sunburned colors of the brackish portion of the outer harbor, up to the Bar Harbor condominium complex which was just a stone's throw away from Roy Purvis's house.

Mel showed him his apartment which was two stories and beautifully decorated with plenty of Italian lacquer. He played for him on his Steinway Grand. A little Rachmaninov and then a quick Golliwog's Cakewalk. He was really good! They had a few drinks, and Mel showed him the glass conservatory on the north end where he had a sixteen-inch Meade reflector telescope on an electric base.

Mel had trained the thing on Revere Beach, about four miles away, and you could make out the faces!

Peter had thought it crazy that Mel's parents had given him the condo, and the Steinway! He'd figured he should choose better parents in his next life.

The time had come for Ian to pick him up. He had his clothes with him and changed. Unfortunately, Mel had other plans.

Peter and Ian were quite the sight! One white and one black, smoking, and driving the white BMW convertible with the red interior. The engine screaming as Ian worked the gears, ashes spraying off his cigarette. The salty air tumbling over the windshield and around the side pillars. But it all came to a stop just short of the Tobin Bridge.

There in front and below them, in the mile long sweeping right hand turn and over the spine of the Tobin Bridge, were thousands of stopped cars, looking like three long strings of pearls lit by the evening sun that illuminated the haze around the centre of Boston.

That was when a red metallic Benz 500 E inched past them on the right. Peter thought he recognized the woman driving. A good looking girl with wavy, long black hair. She worked her way to the on ramp from Chelsea and backed down. Ian jockeyed into position and followed, backing down the long dizzying ramp as quickly as he could. They followed the speeding Benz through Chelsea's industrial area right to the Sumner Tunnel, and Peter tried to figure how he knew her. But she was ahead of them, and Ian turned up the stereo, making Luciano Pavarotti's rendition of Verdi's Vesti La Giubba reverberate through the tunnel. Peter saw the woman eyeing them in her rear view mirror, victory in her smile.

When they reached the North End, Ian turned down the stereo, and they began inching along toward the waterfront. The buildings even looked like they came from old Italy.

The first honk sounded like a diesel locomotive. Then another.

Ian motioned with a cock of his head for Peter to look back.

He stared over his shoulder at a big old, white Cadillac. A little man sat behind the wheel, barely able to see over the dash. He rewarded Peter's interest with two more honks.

"Jesus Christ!" said Ian, not going any faster as he searched for street signs.

Peter looked back with his hand draped over the seat.

The man had straight white hair and deep dimples. Cuddled beside him was a good looking blonde a fraction of his age. She had an unwavering smile and wore a black evening dress. But what really held Peter's attention was the pair of bullhorns mounted on the grill! The old man scowled at Peter.

"Jesus Christ!" said Ian. "Boston drivers. Here he goes."

The road widened out, and the little old man roared past in his Eldorado.

A quick glance showed the woman to be very attractive, and the old man wore a dark pinstripe suit.

The old fellow let go one long honk as he roared by.

Somehow that hooked Ian. In some unconsidered way he smiled smugly, raised his left hand, and gave the old man the finger.

The Eldorado cut right in front of them and screeched to a halt. The old man left his door open to run to Ian. The street cleared of onlookers. Ian, silent, had a puzzled look on his face.

Then the little man reached into his jacket and pulled out a Walther P-9. He racked it and held it under Ian's nose.

Peter slumped in close to the dash and covered his head.

Ian looked at the man with his mouth open and raised his hands. "Don't shoot! Don't shoot!" he pleaded. "Ah'm Italian too."

The little man sighed, shrugged his shoulders, and said in a heavy accent, "You don't do that in the North End, sonny."

SIX

Eugen Wittman stood outside the entrance to Restaurant Giorgio with his hands in his pockets, tapping his toes. He surveyed the gentle curve of the street for any sign of a white BMW convertible. Old buildings that had been renovated stood in front of him, flanked by half empty warehouses, on a ribbon of land that skirted the waterfront.

The hot street was quiet enough that he could safely have watched from the middle—very unusual. He noticed distant sounds from the stifled city cascade over the rooftops of harbor buildings. A pervasive din of city noise, a mixture of traffic, horns, music, and children's screams. Beyond that, if he listened carefully, the fog horns were starting their haunt, coloring the golden hues of the evening sky with their rhythmic blue notes.

Eugen noticed the languid aromas of sweet salt air, which were reminiscent of south sea evenings. St Tropez. Majorca. Gandia.

The valet, who had just returned from parking his car, sat down on a metal chair beside a blue and white sign that announced, "Valet Parking. $40." He was sweating in black trousers, white shirt, and a bow tie. The black haired valet studied the Aryan who hadn't said a word to him when he had given him his car, and forty dollars.

Eugen knew he was being sized up. He knew he was thin and carried himself with a slight stoop. That could look weary, contemplative, or just plain bored. He parted his hair to the left. His nose was prominent but not large and his eyes were blue. He wore a light weight grey and blue striped suit, showing off a dark patterned tie. It was fashionably tight. Too tight to hide a gun. Eugen stood there jingling the coins in his trouser pockets as he tapped his right foot, shifting his gaze between the valet and the street. He figured the guy likely had him pegged as a Friuli. Maybe a nervous mortician.

A drop of moisture condensed on his forehead. Suddenly, he felt impatient and tired of the attention. He motioned to the door and said to the valet, "Think I will wait inside, *ja?*"

The valet dropped his jaw just enough.

Got ya! He smiled.

Just as Eugen took his first step, he heard a car coming. A car with steady high exhaust note. He turned on a heel, looking toward the North End.

Ian Scott drove over to the valet parking sign, where he stopped with a heavy squeal. The engine relaxed to an idle. The pair in the Bimmer looked motionless at Wittmann with fixed stares.

Eugen, pleased to finally see his friends, walked to the car with an enthusiastic bounce in his step, smiled, rubbed his hands and asked, "So, how was your drive into town?"

Ian Scott gave the valet his keys, and forty dollars.

With the valet gone, Eugen got the low down, and howled until he held his sides.

"I'm glad the little man didn't blow you away." He made a show of giving the tall, black man a hug.

With that he opened the outer glass door to the restaurant and let his shaken friends in.

***

Peter knew this restaurant was Eugen's favorite spot, and he was warming to it too. He liked the feel of the entry, up some stone steps. Inside, dark oak balustrade covering the lower half of old masonry walls. Antique arched windows. Linen set tables were neatly arranged around the room.

The Maitre d', a bald tuxedo of some presumption, with a European accent, asked the name.

"Wittman."

He made a fuss checking the register. "Ah yes. Table for three." He motioned to the back and said, "Follow me."

Peter followed behind, into the far side of the restaurant. There were booths like conch shells, covered with deeply pleated, dark leather, against the outer wall.

The place was full.

The Maitre pulled out the table which had been set and politely motioned the party to sit down. Peter sat in the middle.

Ian Scott said, "JB and soda," as the table was being pushed in.

The Maitre looked a bit surprised, but nodded.

"Double."

Peter said, "Tanqueray and Noilly Prat. Double, ice and a twist."

The Maitre seemed ruffled. He puffed his chest noticeably as he held his menus close and looked at Eugen. "Well?"

"My usual," said the German with a throw away gesture. "In deference to my alcoholic friends, make it a double."

"Graci signore." With the menus on the table, the Maitre hurried away.

Ian said, "The only thing that would make a scotch better is a nice smoke."

"After that drive," said Peter.

"That would be a pretty sight." said Eugen. "Two heart surgeons smoking. Ya. That would look good on Mass Heart! You could make a poster." He slapped Ian on the wrist.

"The hell with you Wittman!" Ian laughed and said, "I remember when it wasn't illegal. Besides, who really cares about a little bit of smoke. It's a lot of smoke that kills you."

"It's all part of this modern Puritanism that's creeping into society," said Peter. "Pretty soon you won't even be able to have a drink."

"Worse than that," said Ian, "it's creeping into everything." He looked around the table, as if to speak in confidence. "You see all this prayer getting into American politics." He nodded his head. "Uh-huh."

Eugen looked at Ian with a pout. "Well," he said, "I guess that settles the 'puritanical American fundamentalists against smoking argument."

"Get lost."

They both laughed.

The regular waiter, a shorter, slighter fellow with straight black hair, brought the drinks, sized up the chortling diners. "I'm Alberto. Let me tell you my life story."

He got their attention.

"In the beginning there was calamari salad and risotto. Then came spinach tortellini stuffed with spiced pecorino cheese in a creamy pesto sauce, or a polo primavera on linguini. Naturally this was followed by veal scaloppini in a light lemon oil served with pan fried potatoes and *al dante* house vegetables. The pinnacle of my career came with pan fried sweetbreads on garlic and hot pepper oil fusilli. For close friends we kept duck confit with gourmet poutine. In the end came white chocolate ice cream on a plate of vodka strawberry sauce, or custard kiwi torte, or sinfully sweet pecan pie—the recipe for which is a closely guarded family secret."

"Which family?" said Ian, trying to look serious.

Peter kicked him discreetly and said to the waiter, "Do you mind if we smoke?"

"Sir." The waiter cocked his head.

"All right, all right," said Peter, waving his left hand and taking a gulp of his drink.

The waiter smiled benignly. "The rest, as they say, is history, and can be found in the book." He looked at Eugen. "Will you be needing the wine list tonight?"

The German nodded toward the heart surgeon.

Peter took one more swig of his martini and answered, "Yeah, but first bring another round of these."

"Yes, sir." The waiter left.

"I can see you fit in well," said Eugen, looking at Peter.

"Enjoying myself." He shot a glance back. "Been here a while and enjoying myself."

"It's simply a question of propriety."

"Relax. You're in America," said Ian.

The second round came and some drained glasses were quickly traded.

"You know Peter, I've been meaning to ask, how you got to Mass Heart?" said Eugen.

"Same way you did—Abel picked me—made me an offer I couldn't refuse." He shook his head knowingly. He remembered how easy the trial had made leaving Toronto. No wrong done, but everybody who had anything to do with it, was all shook up. Peter decided to shelve the topic.

"Tell me all about it." Eugen looking at him, as if he knew Peter's thoughts.

Ian looked up from his open menu and said in his southern drawl, "Might not be a bad idea to ordah before we get going, or get too high."

"Right." Peter picked up his menu for closer inspection. He muttered, "Going to be lots of spice, cheese, and pepper. Going to need a big wine." He eyed Ian and Eugen over the top of the menu.

"An Italian wine?" said Eugen, with mock discretion.

"Exactly."

The waiter returned with a pad and pen. "Gentlemen?"

The order was placed, but the choice of wine was deferred to Martins, this being his night.

He said, "We'll start with a bottle of Tignanello '71."

"Nice choice," said the waiter. "First year it was made." He turned and left.

"So, how did Abel recruit you?" Eugen changed the subject. "Ian has been in the university system since the word go."

"I did a fellowship here, before you arrived," said Peter. "Did it because I wanted to be around Purvis, and I got it. Surprised me. Then I did lots of cases. Roy let me pinch hit whenever I wanted, and then some! Then my visa ran out, and I had to go back to Canada. Next, I went on staff in Toronto and got into the laser research program."

"Yes, but you wouldn't be eligible to re-apply for a work visa to the United States for at least another four years, under the rules?" said Eugen. "The only other way, would have been to marry an American, which you did not, or you would have had to be a physician of international renown—for which we are all too young."

"Sure," said Peter, reflecting on his second martini. "Well, all I can say is Abel showed up one day after a meeting. He came to my office unannounced. Said he was checking up on me to see how happy I was after leaving Boston. Told me Roy Purvis wanted me back in Boston—badly! Next thing I know I get a visa." He looked at Eugen. "What about you?"

"Well! I was working at the emergency receiving hospital in Bonn when Abel showed up. He was there to try to get some liaison going for his company in Germany. There was some nonsense about private hospitals going into the old eastern sector and contracting work for the Kranken Sparkasse, the department of health." He cleared the phrase from the air with a broad stroke of his right hand. "Nonsense. Anyway, somehow he came to the emergency room just after we got patients from an autobahn accident. You know, one of those where there are thirty or forty cars involved, all going over one hundred miles an hour, ya. We talked afterwards. Then I got a phone call. Then I got a visa."

"That simple to leave Europe?" said Peter.

"Over there you get only a salary from the hospital. Here things are different. Besides European politicians are becoming increasingly feudal again, in case you don't follow the news."

"Look it's simple," said Ian. Abel has a pocketbook big enough to contribute to any cause, political or othahwise." He finished with his palms open. "He gets what he wants."

The waiter arrived with the appetizers. Mussels for Ian. Garlic soup for Peter, and three tureens for Eugen. And of course, the bottle of wine.

The waiter uncorked the bottle, and offered Peter the first taste.

The wine was full, plumy, and tarry.

"Good choice fellows, if I do say so," Peter said as he ceremoniously nodded to the waiter.

They got down to some soulful eating.

The waiter returned to ask if everything was all right. He got three nods and instructions to pour the wine. The aroma of alcoholic fruit engulfed the table like a cloud.

"Alberto," said Peter. "Bring a bottle of Barolo Mascarello Monprivato 1985. Open it and leave it for later."

"Yes, sir." He gave a short bow before leaving.

"You spend my money very well," said Eugen as he picked up his glass and buried his nose inside the wide brim. He took a sip. "Very, very nice." He nodded appreciatively to Peter. "I will remember this one. My compliments!"

Ian gave his approval before returning to the talk. "You know, it's unusual for the university to recruit a member from outside. And heah I sit with two of you."

"As you said, Abel gets what he wants," said Eugen. "And Mass Heart is private. So why should they follow the rules?"

"Now I've been at Mass Heart for fifteen years. I've been here since I started twenty-three years ago. It's only the last few years Mass Heart started bringing people in from outside. The university, not so much. But even that's changin'. That's a fact." Ian emphasized with his fork. He paused in contemplation before going on. "A new chairman of a department always comes from outside, for the obvious reason. And on rare occasions, so does a department head, but the hospital has to be pretty damn hard up for that to happen." He shook his head slowly as he finished his last mussel. "No. I don't understand."

"Take emergency," said Eugen, after sipping his wine. "There really was no department before. I came not only to head the place, but to man it." His friends nodded. "The idea of an emergency department at Mass Heart is something a little foreign. You know, it's so expensive, and the place just around the corner accepts Blue Cross. Emergency at Mass Heart acts as a stabilizing and receiving area."

The waiter returned for the empty dishes. He whisked off the table with a small hand brush.

Peter took his turn explaining. "I just did my cases with Roy. Often I did them without him. After that I went home, and you know the rest."

"But there were other guys here Peter, other guys they could have appointed." Ian held up his hand against a retort. "I'm not saying you aren't good. You are good, damn good. In fact, you're catching up to old Roy pretty fast."

"Thanks, Ian."

"It just makes me wonder if there isn't some master plan," said Ian. "You aren't hiding anything from me, are you?"

"Not a thing." Martins raised his voice. "Hell, I've been here almost seven months and I'm not the chief yet!"

They laughed.

Peter asked Ian, "How long has gynecology been this big at Mass Heart? Seems rather strange that it's even here."

"Not at all." said Ian. "The department has been active for almost five years. But it really got going in the last two. You know, word got around."

"But why did it get started at all? I mean, it's the Massachusetts Heart Institute."

"It started with cases like yours, years ago. Roy's done one or two of those. But then I think Abel figured out that elective gyne could be a highly profitable side line. Lots of new stuff you can't get outside of New York. You know ... in-Vitro ... gender selection ... you name it, and we got someone very famous on staff who can do it! And insurance doesn't cover any of this, so it's an open market."

Peter nodded.

The waiter returned with the Barolo and showed him the bottle.

Peter approved and reminded himself to tip extra.

The bottle of rare 1985 Barolo was uncorked just as carefully as the Tignanello before, and set aside.

"There's the thing," said Eugen after the waiter was gone, "to have Roy's job. And his money."

"True," said Ian.

The waiter returned with a trolley and proceeded to make Caesar salad, tableside. The illuminated friends watched the waiter perform his ceremonial task as they took sips.

"First time I've ever had a wine taste explode like this," said Ian.

With the ingredients at the bottom of a great wooden bowl, the waiter combined the mixture with a practiced whip of his fork, which made a sound over the gentle din of the restaurant like a busy woodpecker.

"I love this. Same way Caesar Ritz made it. You can't get that any more. Except here." Eugen smiled and had his approval returned by the waiter.

"Very good, Albert." His German and the wine getting in the way. "Very, very, good."

The waiter seemed pleased as he added the deveined romaine, croutons, and cheese before serving the salad into huge portions.

"Fresh ground pepper?"

"Yes, of course," said Eugen.

As the three salads were peppered, it occurred to Peter that the drunker Eugen sat there the longer his German accent got—or some such thing.

About half way through his salad, Peter decided to ask a difficult question. "So what am I to expect in a salary offer next year?"

"What does Abel pay you now?" said Ian.

"Two hundred and fifty."

"No stocks?"

"No. No stocks yet. Explain that one to me."

"Well, look," Ian said flatly, "I've been here fifteen years and I earn three hundred and twenty-five, plus the same benefits as you. Howevah," he pointed his loaded fork at Peter, "I get an incremental increase in Mass Heart stock every year. What I get is based on my productivity, my research, and my drawing power for the hospital. The amount is strictly my business. But I will say that it has only become significant the last few years. The stock is pegged at ten-to-one for U.S.

Medical Hospital Enterprises shares, so there's its intrinsic value."

"You will find no one here who earns more than four hundred, but their stock options vary widely," said Eugen.

"If you weren't that interested in the money, what brought you here?" said Ian.

"The idea of being here, getting a bit more than the usual starting surgeon, working with some of the greatest names in the business, the opportunity of advancement, however vague that concept might be." He paused for a moment. Then looked in his glass and said, "I think that about sums it up. Sure hope dinner comes soon! I think I'm seeing double."

"Me too," said Ian. "Let me tell you though, a time will come when Abel sits down with you to discuss something very earnest 'round about the time your contract comes up for renewal. When that happens, don't cut yourself short."

"My problem is, I've no basis for comparison."

"Don't worry. Abel will open the discussion in the proper ballpark. Just do what every other self respecting doctor does." Ian said smugly, as if he had let a secret.

"And what's that?"

Ian raised his eyebrows as he sat bolt upright. "Just tell him you want more."

"Oh! That."

"Peter. Just think, I bring in one very sick black woman with a baby in her belly und a ruptured aneurysm. You save them both. Of course we publish! And remember too, when you, Ian or Roy do a bypass, the cross-clamp time is twenty-five, maybe thirty-two minutes. Not like Downtown General where it's sixty minutes or more to do the same thing." Eugen didn't wait for the implication to sink in. "People look this up. They understand the significance. That's why they come here."

"Can't say I never saw it that way," said Peter.

"Y'ur problem is that you grew up in a socialist medical system where everybody got the same thing. But the fact of the matter is that everybody can't have the same treatment and drugs, just like everybody can't drive the same fancy car.

Capiche?" Ian paused. "You, sir, are becoming a drawing card."

The waiter arrived with a large bowl and three plates. With a smile of increased familiarity, he cleaned the table that had suddenly fallen mute, and just as quickly served out a penne puttanesca. He poured the rest of the Tignanello. When he was done, he looked over the three mum faces and asked with a smile, "Is everything okay tonight, gentlemen?"

"Albert." Eugen practised perfect German. "Everything is fantastisch."

"Buon appetito!" He left, smiling, with a pleased lightness in his step.

"Thanks for the vote of confidence fellows. I won't mention a word. And bon appetite." Peter Martins held up his glass and touched rims with his friends.

The table fell quiet to some thoughtful eating.

Alberto showed up just as the three diners had relaxed deep into the back of their sofa.

The dishes were gone and three fresh wine glasses were on the table before he said, "Main course in three or four minutes. The Monprivato now?"

"Please," said Eugen.

The waiter poured him a taste.

He held the glass up to the light, then passed his bent nose thoughtfully over the rim before sampling. "*Mein Gott!* Nice."

Alberto poured proudly, and left.

Peter tried the wine. He turned to Eugen and said, "Thank you."

He shrugged contentedly.

"Okay, Mr. Oenophile," said Ian. "This one made of anything special?"

"Grapes."

Eugen and Peter laughed shamelessly, catching too much attention from the surrounding tables. Getting Ian embarrassed.

Alberto arrived at that moment, with an uncertain smile on his face. The three diners fell silent again and watched him serve the main course. Rack of lamb for Ian. For Peter, blackened red snapper; Eugen got veal marsala. He peppered each dish and asked if there would be anything else.

Peter knew the look on his face. The look that betrayed either an understanding of three grown men having a good time in each other's company, or a deeper suspicion that neither one of them was capable of paying the rapidly escalating bill. He said, "Everything looks great."

Alberto smiled, raised his brows, and left with his hands clasped rigidly behind his back.

"We've got to stop acting paranoid around the waiter," said Peter.

"Nevah mind. Hospital business is no one's business."

"Aren't you worried about what they'll think?"

Ian looked deadpan at Eugen. He shrugged. "No."

The table became busy with the sounds of eating.

Near the end of the main course, Peter asked Eugen, "You dating anybody?"

"Ya. Sally Watson. Nice girl from the post surgical intensive care unit." He went on to talk about her.

Finally Eugen said, "What about you?"

"Nobody yet. Too busy getting into the new place."

Ian being married didn't have a story to tell. His marriage was solid. But he did have a lot to say about his research.

At one point the Maitre went by and cast an eye upon them. They fell silent and watched him pass. The Maitre said nothing and momentarily walked by in the other direction. The three diners looked like spectators at a replay of a tennis match.

Ian returned his attention to his food before going on.

His research had started with pig and dog valves, but was now going into the realm of 3-D printing. He explained in minute detail. He concluded with, "We're going to genetically engineer and print a patient's personal replacement heart valve."

"Impressive." said Peter.

Alberto appeared, and the table fell silent.

They looked at him.

Peter turned and said to Eugen, "You know this man publishes fifteen papers a year and has a new chapter in a textbook?"

"Ya?"

Ian's eyes shifting from Peter to Eugen to Alberto.

"Ask him who actually writes this."

"Peter!" Ian looking from Peter to Alberto.

"Ask him."

"Peter?"

SEVEN

Roy Purvis got out of the Jaguar and slipped under the closing garage door.

The house, lit by the glow of one lamp from up the street, was awash in the moving shadows of great trees. Their leaves rustled rhythmically in the hot, light wind. Some lights glowed dimly inside.

Roy looked past the house and noticed that a harvest moon was rising out of the ocean in the east. Noisy crickets on the grassy embankment beyond his house added a chorus to the sound of the lightly rolling waves folding themselves into the rocky shore below.

He realized that he could not stand there forever, and he knew that he had handled such situations before. Lastly, he needn't remind himself that he had been divorced before, all over similar issues.

So, he let himself in and went upstairs. His wife was not in the bedroom. He quickly unpacked his overnight bag.

The house was quiet. Too quiet.

He heard his breath as he walked down the stairs.

A dim table lamp in the far corner of the living room cast irregular shadows over the furniture and the carpet that covered the hardwood floor.

He went to the kitchen. Dark. The door to the balcony was open. He looked outside. No lights.

Under the umbrella he saw Patricia, silhouetted darkly against the reflections of the moon twinkling on the water. She had her feet curled up beneath her bottom and rested her head on her left hand. There was a half empty martini pitcher beside her and a full glass on the patio table to her left. Roy could see that there was still some ice in the pitcher. That could be good or bad. It could mean that she had just sat down and the ice in the pitcher had not yet had a chance to melt. On the other hand, it could mean that at 10:45 at night, Patricia was on her second pitcher. Knowing his wife, the latter was more likely.

Roy opened the storm door carefully, stepped outside, and closed the door just as quietly.

Patricia's silhouette did not stir. She said, "Hello Roy. How was your sailing?" She didn't speak in an unfriendly tone.

"The sailing was very nice, thank you, dear." He held still.

"I'm having a little martini. Get yourself a glass if you care to join me." She spoke clearly, distinctly.

"No thank you. I think I'll pass." He walked up to the table and took a seat opposite his wife. She didn't take her eyes off the sea. "That is our problem isn't it?"

"What, dear?" He felt his heart miss a beat.

"We're forever passing each other." She paused a moment. "Did your heart skip a beat just now?"

"No, dear." He said politely.

"You're lying," Patricia said in a flat, even tone. "I'd say you're scared practically shitless, and right now your heart's skipping plenty of beats." She finally turned to face him.

Roy felt his heart racing in his throat. He wanted to grab his neck, but instead he sat perfectly still, concentrating on his composure. He swallowed deeply. *Be calm. Be calm!*

"That's more like it," she said soothingly. "Now we both know what we're talking about." He could see her face melt into a moonlit smile.

Why didn't he know that Patricia knew? Why hadn't he seen this side of her before? He asked, "What do you mean, dear?"

"Don't take me for a fool, Roy Purvis." Her voice was hoarse.

"Darling, the neighbors—"

"The hell with the neighbors. Let's talk."

"Yes, dear."

"Have a martini. It'll help you relax."

"Thanks, no."

"Get enough this weekend? And I don't mean drink, Roy. I mean enough of baby doll?" She cocked her head and smiled.

Roy remembered advice a lawyer had once given him about situations like this—deny, deny, deny. Patricia might be a little beyond that point. He decided he had better come clean rather than incur a wrath worse than this.

"We had a good time, yes," he said.

"Well, I for one am glad to hear that," she said. "I'm glad to hear that, because we certainly haven't had *that* in a long time, have we?"

"If you say so."

"I do say so," she said hoarsely.

Roy immediately regretted admitting to anything. But she knew. Was he being watched? Had somebody told her? He had never had this kind of disagreement with her before. In the past she had been angry about things, but she had never acted like this. She had been drinking but wasn't drunk.

"Well I think it's sad that we can't have a little bit of fun together. We don't spend much time together. I think it's sad that we see other people. Don't you think so?"

Roy knew that the "we see other people" she referred to, in fact, meant him. Yes their relationship was sad and dishonest. It had gone astray. Was there something in him that had wanted to get caught? He said, "Yes I think so."

"Well, Roy." She lightened up. "It's sad but it isn't." She picked up her drink, took a long sip and looked out to sea. "I think there are many redeeming qualities in just about any social arrangement. Don't you?"

Oh, she was clever. She'd worked him right into a corner from which she could extract almost anything. "Yes." He'd be cautious. "Sometimes."

"Well, what do you think I was doing, while you were screwing the ass off baby doll?" She played with her drink, and looked at him, quietly awaiting his reply. She held up her left hand. "Before you tell me, answer this. I've often wondered what you do with the boat while you're screwing. I mean, it's a fucking million dollar boat—a literal million dollar fucking boat! Do you put it on auto-helm and hope to God you don't bump into anything that crosses your path? Do you take the sails down and just drift? I mean, I hear of people in airplanes who turn on the auto-pilot and go at it. At least they get a radar alarm before they crash." She laughed hoarsely. "Just what do you do?"

He was shocked into admission. "Something like that."

"Radar? I knew it." She smiled smugly. "So what do you suppose I did this weekend? Or do you care?"

"Of course I care, dear, but how should I know?"

"Roy," she said eagerly, "this weekend I got supremely and royally fucked!" She smiled at him triumphantly.

I got supremely and royally fucked! The reality of the words tore at him like a knife entering his stomach and being twisted around maliciously. The idea had never crossed his mind.

"So what do you think?"

"I ... I ... uh ..." He collected his thoughts. "Who?"

"Never thought of that possibility, did you?" She laughed and slapped the arm of her chair.

Roy felt his stomach burn. "No."

"Ignorance is bliss, Roy. All the time that you were out on your boat, with Janet, what did you think I was doing? Waiting for you to come home?" She waited, seeming to expect an answer. "Hah. Don't think for one minute that I went to all those board meetings at the museum for nothing. There are some men who recognize a class act, Roy. I know a few."

"I ... I ... Who?" He tensed to get up, but then sat back as quietly as he could. He was certain she saw his trembling.

"I'm not going to compare notes with you like a couple of school kids. Just remember that the man you meet at the next cocktail party, or at a foundation reception, may have been one of several who appreciated your wife's finer qualities while you were out of town. Think of it as pinch hitting—like in base ball." She emphasized the base, and the ball.

"I had no idea."

"That's too bad, Roy. But then what's good for goosie ... Besides, I remember how I got you from Rachel. Nothing has really changed, has it?"

Roy sat there, thinking how stupid he had been, playing his game. Hadn't fooled anyone but himself. God, he felt awful!

"Got nothing to say, Roy? No need to apologize. We're both in the same boat—once a runner, always a runner." She waited for a moment, but when Roy failed to answer, she continued. "That was all I had to say—kind of like I wanted to come clean—if you know what I mean." She sighed. "Anyway, no hard feelings. I'm going to bed now. Such a beautiful night." She studied the face of the moon.

How could she make such a fool of me?

Patricia unfolded her shapely legs and got up. It was then that Roy noticed she had no underwear on under her black tee-shirt. She stretched slowly, revealing her pubic hair in the moonlight.

"You should really finish my martini—there's half a pitcher left—you'll feel better." She walked over and kissed him lightly on the cheek. She said, "Goodnight," and walked over to the door. With the door half open she looked back. "Oh, Ed called from the hospital."

He turned and faced her. "Ed?"

"Ed Van Boren. Who else? He said to tell you there's an emergency board meeting at 07:00 hours tomorrow morning. And I quote, 'Attendance is not optional.'"

"Night." She went in and let the storm door slam shut behind her.

He picked up her empty martini glass and wanted to hurl it down the embankment, to smash it on the rocks. She had been with several men, and he would never know who.

Then a glimmer came to him. He decided to have a drink instead and think things over logically. He poured the rest of the pitcher into his glass and walked over to the railing at the highest point of the balcony.

Where to begin. This couldn't be the end of the war with her. This had only been a minor skirmish. *You bitch. You took me to the slaughter.* There had to be more coming. There had to be demands. Or did there? Of course there were. He had never known a woman to operate differently.

He sipped long and hard at the martini. He swallowed awkwardly and sipped again.

Plus, his young patient had died. Peter Martins was knocking at his door. And Ed Van Boren had called a meeting for 7 a.m. *Jesus Christ! Is that young bastard taking my job?*

He took another long pull from the martini. The moon was now about twenty degrees above the horizon, smaller than before and silvery white. The reflection in the ocean extended to the shoreline below like a giant shimmering tear drop. Myriad silver reflections danced on gentle black waves. Soon the great mass of the moon would exert its pull on the ocean, gather up the great water, and wash out the next high tide.

Fog lights glimmered here and there, pale compared to the moon. The red beacon on the water tower at the end of Winthrop Shore Drive blinked on and off.

Momentarily, Roy realized that there was more than one solution to his problems. Slowly, the sickness left the pit of his stomach. His senses sharpened.

Far beneath him, the gentle ocean waves folded into the rocky shore with a subdued rush. The crickets in the weeds of the embankment lent an almost triumphant chorus to the sound of the waves.

Reveling with his thoughts in the silver moonlight, A. Roy Purvis finally rejoiced in the music of the night.

EIGHT

"I'm sorry, Doctor Young, they're in camera and can't be disturbed," said the pretty receptionist. An arrangement of pink and violet chrysanthemums set off the right side of her dark desk with a phone, the computer terminal and the dark green, registry ledger at the close end.

The pixie blond turned to Roy, who had been waiting. "They'll see you now, Doctor Purvis. No package today."

"Thank you Penny," said Roy courteously, as he signed the ledger. "Good morning, James. Nice to see you."

"Roy," Doctor Young nodded.

The master heart surgeon had no idea why he had been asked to this early morning emergency board meeting. He just as plainly had no idea why James Young, a senior cardiologist, was being turned away at a door that was normally open to him.

He let himself in through the right of a pair of oversize cherry wood doors he had passed through so many times before, that he remembered the pattern of the grain. The heavy door closed silently into its padded jamb. The smell of fresh coffee pervaded the boardroom.

"Good morning, and welcome, Roy," said Ed Van Boren, as Roy walked over to the long boardroom table.

"Good morning." Roy took an empty seat with his back to the windows, which were shaded against the early morning sun. He unbuttoned his grey suit and smoothed the skirts aside, revealing a handsome grey and red, candy cane striped tie.

"This isn't a full board meeting," said Van Boren. "All members couldn't be assembled on such short notice. You," he looked at Roy, "Doctor Maranghi and Doctor Williams have been invited because we feel that your departments may be particularly affected by recent and coming events concerning this hospital. Before I forget, you do know Mr. Brian Moody and Mr. Charles Bond, members of the board?"

"Yes of course. Good morning, Brian, Chuck." Roy waved with casual courtesy before folding his hands over his chest, a carryover from years of waiting in the OR.

His greeting was returned cordially.

There were three trays loaded with food, coffee, and dishes in the middle of the table.

"Gentlemen," said Frank Abel. "The reason I have called this meeting, is to apprise you all of a communication I received from the governor, Willard Duke. Last Saturday morning, the governor surprised me with a phone call." He looked around, seeming to wait for some reaction. The assembled faces remained blank. He went on. "The governor wasn't entirely clear about what he meant to say. I suppose that's where I have my difficulty with the conversation."

Van Boren said amicably, "Why don't you begin by telling us what he said?"

The smell of fresh coffee had been tugging at Roy's nose since his arrival, but now it overpowered him. He poured himself a cup of black Columbian.

"He said, and I quote, more or less, 'That if there was anything he could do to help us smooth out our transition in this troubled time, that I should call him.' "

"Oh?" said Roy, frowning. "What troubled time?"

Moody, a big man in a dark grey suit with hooded eyes and a bald head, said, "I think he may be referring to the passage of the National Health Bill."

"Oh yes. That." Roy paused. "Why should that bother us?" He sipped thoughtfully on the thick, black coffee.

"Doctor Purvis." Frank Abel held his smoking pipe in his hand. "There doesn't seem to be any direct effect on this institution or on U.S. Medical Hospital Enterprises for that matter, but we're interested in any thoughts or comments, concerning the possible future ramifications of this Bill."

"Oh my god!" Harold Williams suddenly became agitated. He spoke with the pressured speech of a school boy making some momentous discovery. "Do you think the government will force us to accept health insurance?"

The table erupted into spontaneous, uncoordinated discussion.

"Gentlemen," said Van Boren. "Gentlemen, please!" The room fell silent again. "Frank. Can you give us any more background into this?"

"Certainly." The Chairman of The Board relaxed into his seat and rested his chins on his chest. "Our legal department has taken an extensive look at this. In fact, we've been following the evolution of the bill, right along from the beginning. As you know, Ed and I are very well known in Washington." He inhaled deeply on his pipe. "In addition to this we subscribe to the industry lobby. And of course, U.S. Medical Hospital Enterprises has its own private lobby."

Roy eyed the pastry tray. Frank Abel had always prided himself on the food served at the hospital. He had even brought over a Parisian pastry chef for the kitchen. If he knew anything, it was that the gorgeous golden croissants on the tray were chef Louis's own.

"Where does the lobby put us?" said Van Boren.

"The lobby doesn't put us anywhere, as you well know, since the National Health Bill hasn't become law, nor has it been defeated." Abel raised his hands and waved passively.

Nervous murmuring started around the table.

Abel sat up, straightened himself out, and went on forcefully. "That however is not the crux of the matter. Our legal department has been following the situation and reports that they feel the National Health Bill is an act which empowers government in practically any jurisdiction, to go into the business of issuing health insurance. This is in addition to recently legislated care. Moreover, it paves the way to standardise the cost of care across the country. Who will end up issuing this insurance remains to be seen. In fact, I understand that government might end up underwriting the costs of previously uninsurable individuals. The central drive of this thrust is to give availability of medical care to everybody, so called universal access."

Roy finished his sinful, buttered croissant. As he reached for another, he remembered the well-stocked wine cellar Abel kept in the basement. If you happened to want Dom '71, after a board meeting or to seal a contract, well, so be it! What a hospital!

Doctor Maranghi was first to speak up. "What does this mean for us?"

"There are two ways of looking at this," said Abel. "The first is to envisage a scenario in which government realizes the enormous cost of its undertaking, and acts in a minimalistic fashion. That would likely encompass the underwriting of basic health insurance. The second is a scenario in which government doesn't fully appreciate the magnitude of its mistake. In this case government could either take it upon itself to run health care voluntarily, or for some other reason, stumble unwittingly into managing this whole mess. I tend to think more favorably on the first case. We'll have to see how it standardises the cost of care."

Maranghi bobbed his big Adam's apple. "So they, I mean the government, could conceivably take us over?"

Roy sipped some more coffee.

Van Boren turned slowly to Brian Moody. "Perhaps one of the distinguished members of the legal fraternity could shed some light here?"

Moody sat straight up and spoke matter-of-factly. "This is an interesting problem, but let me assure you of a few things. In this country, it has become increasingly difficult to expropriate property from private hands over the last forty or fifty years, and especially so in the last twenty. Why, today expropriation is almost impossible without paying fair market value. I mean, a government could buy a small piece of real estate to extend a highway or some such thing, but a major institution, I think not." He looked at Van Boren.

"Go on." Ed looked curious too.

"There has been no history of such a takeover that I can remember. The closest thing that comes to mind is the contracting of military hardware to peacetime industries in the Second World War. This just isn't the same."

Maranghi said. "What would an agency or a government have to do to take over this or any other private health care institution?"

Moody furrowed his brow over his hooded eyes. "I can't see any other way than buying a fifty-one percent majority of the stock."

"Charles?" said Aldo Calabrese, the hospital administrator, sitting at the far end of the table. "Do you know the approximate value of the outstanding shares in Mass Heart?"

Charles Bond, a slender man with glasses, sat up slowly in his chair and answered. "I can't say exactly. However, I think that a figure somewhere in the neighborhood of six hundred and forty million dollars would be about right."

Calabrese nodded, sitting there only in shirt sleeves. "That sounds close to me."

"What I don't understand is," said Harold Williams, pushing back his mane of white hair, "if this is an impossibility, then why are we worried about Duke's phone call?"

"I'm not certain that we have to be worried about Duke," said Van Boren. "But we should have these facts out on the table."

Brian Moody went on as he stirred his coffee, staring all the while at the swirling liquid in his clinking cup. "Well if none of this is terribly important," he paused thoughtfully before looking around the table, "then why did the governor make the call? Hardly a social call." He looked again slowly around the table. "The question is, gentlemen, does the governor know something we don't?" He raised his brows.

Roy was beginning to sense the seeds of paranoia. Oddly, his mind wandered. He looked at Harold Williams, and realized for the first time that he had a remarkable resemblance to the crazy professor in the movie, *Back To The Future*.

"That is precisely my point." Maranghi waved a finger around the room. "Perhaps the governor has his own agenda."

"Can't imagine how we'd find that out," said Roy.

Frank Abel surveyed the table, silently working his pipe.

There were no suggestions from Van Boren's end of the table.

After a moment, Williams said, "Let's put ourselves in the governor's shoes. What could he gain from taking us over?"

"Prestige," said Calabrese.

"Possibly." said Williams. "But we're already part of the University Group. Our members could be shuffled around the other hospitals if this one closed."

"What if the medical staff all left?" said Roy. "Surely they can't pass a law making us stay in the States."

"Where would you go Roy?" asked Calabrese. "This is the highest paying country in the world."

"I'd retire immediately." He chortled with satisfaction.

"Oh my god! Oh my god! I couldn't go back to ..."

Harold can't even finish a limp sentence. Thinks the same way he operates. Why did they let him in here anyway?

Roy went on to say, "For my friend's benefit, he should know that he could work anywhere in the world after working here. Anywhere."

"Sure." Williams continued as his eye brows twitched. "If the governor wanted this place, he'd have to do one of two things. He would either have to pass a law of expropriation and pay up, or he would have to buy fifty-one percent of the stock. There really is no other way." He looked around the table and smiled.

"In my opinion, expropriation would be very unpopular politically, and buying the stock would look fiscally irresponsible," said Calabrese. "Especially since there are so many other perfectly good hospitals in the area." He shrugged his shoulders. "Not to mention that we're in one hell of a recession."

"I agree," said Van Boren. "This man wants to get re-elected. To do that he doesn't want to look like a fool in front of the public."

"Gentlemen, this is still a country based on free enterprise, I don't see that we have much to worry about." Roy looked deliberately at Maranghi.

"Except for the issue of making us take insurance. My mind is still not made up. I hope that you are right." Maranghi still looking worried.

Van Boren smiled. "We should agree amongst ourselves that this meeting will remain completely private." He looked sternly around the table until he felt that everyone was in accord. "We should also agree, that if any one of us hear from the governor or any other senior state official, that we will immediately inform my office." He got nods on that all around. "May I have a motion?"

"Motion to adjourn," said Williams quickly.

Frank Abel said, "Seconded."

"Passed." Van Boren didn't wait for a vote.

The meeting broke up. Williams rushed out of the room, probably to get to his next case. The others started a hushed discussion and were joined by Maranghi. Roy finished his coffee.

Much later, after finishing his discussion, Maranghi said to Roy, "I've got the idea now," and left.

Roy rode the elevator down to the operating room alone. He had made up his mind.

NINE

Lieutenant Rick Malloy strode along the corridor with a knowing confidence. He was a cop who had worked his entire life on the unplanned, unpredictable streets of Boston.

As he walked he slapped the official envelope he had brought three times into the palm of his left hand. A little man carrying a leather valise followed along.

Malloy was not a nervous man. Nor was he wary about his duty. The only time he got really anxious was when he had to pull his gun, or when he had to answer for pulling it. Like at an inquiry. There was always some smartass who'd sacrifice a good cop to make a point, even if it was only political.

The memory of his worst moment ever still hung around his neck, like a great weight. It had come on the day he and his partner, Gil Malette, answered that call to a North End flat regarding a noisy domestic quarrel. They had gone to the door, knocked, and when the door opened, had found the lady of the house beaten to shreds. They went to arrest her man if only to stop him beating his wife until he was sprung on bail, and give his wife a chance to get some stitches and pull herself together. Rick remembered the sinking feeling which overcame him as he turned around to face the barrel of the wife's twelve-gauge shotgun. He remembered the warm sweat suddenly bursting out of the middle of his scalp, his heart coming to a full stop, the eternity he took to fall to the floor, and then the blast that left Gil's brains splattered all over the walls.

At the inquiry, the State's Attorney tried to hang him on the fact that he had unloaded three out of nine shots into the woman's head before she could rack her shotgun. Then he pumped three shots into her husband and felled him before he could lunge across the floor with a butcher knife. He had thoughtfully saved his last three rounds for safety. That was his greatest sin. Saving three shots! They would have accepted panic. His clear thinking and his sense of survival went against him. The entire issue got turned around and the media portrayed him as the villain after the fact, particularly because the couple was black. The headline read, "Police Ethnic Purge."

Yes, Rick Malloy, you've known all the faces of fear. He walked along chewing his spearmint gum. He had smoked up until the time of the inquest. *Gave it up for Gil.*

A recommendation of the inquest had been that he didn't carry a gun for one year. Was that in the true interest of public safety, or political pandering to interest group pressures? It wasn't an enigma for Malloy. He had served various clerical and court postings.

He strode confidently, the Beretta automatic back with him in its proper place, under his left arm for eight months now. God, he missed Gil!

He stopped and looked up. The sign on the door read. "Medical Records."

He walked in. The little man followed.

They stood in the small room with a table in the middle. There were a few old style manila charts on it. The right wall had four dictating stations with computer terminals. The far end had a large security window with an open slot at the bottom, to pass documents back and forth. A grey metal security door stood to the left of the window. The lighting was cool white fluorescent.

Momentarily, a short, rotund woman in a blue sleeveless dress appeared behind the glass. Her eyes, framed behind black horn-rimmed glasses, betrayed their curiosity as she clutched some papers to her chest, and looked over the two strangers in the dictating room.

"May I help you, gentlemen?" She said with her soft, even voice.

"Thank you. I'm Lieutenant Rick Malloy. He showed her his badge. This is Doctor Samuel Attersly of the district coroner's office." He motioned to the frail man with the thin brown hair and beard, who wore a Harris Tweed jacket. "I have a warrant," he said as he held up the official State envelope.

"Of course, gentlemen, I've been expecting you. Won't you please come in and sit down. I'm Vaida Janz, Director of Medical Records."

A buzzer sounded as she opened the door for the two men and let them into the work room.

The large inner area contained more computer work stations. Women worked at their desks, eyes occasionally darting to the strangers.

"You will want the warrant Mrs. Janz," said Malloy as he handed her the envelope.

She opened the envelope, began to read, and said, "It's Miss Janz."

Rick Malloy thought the colour of Miss Janz's dress reflected her personality.

"I'll have to call the administrator, of course."

"Of course, Miss," said Malloy.

"Won't you sit down?"

"Thank you."

The policeman busied himself, looking about the workings of the room from a far corner chair. The girls worked very efficiently. The computer system was Rantech, as he had been told. There were lockable cabinets for backups.

No wires. All clean and modern. No place for the short trip. In other words, a professional computer room.

Should be a piece of cake.

"Hello. I'm Aldo Calabrese, the Hospital Administrator." The big, dark man in the light grey suit held out his hand, as he approached Malloy. "Welcome to Massachusetts Heart Institute."

The investigators shook in turn and said, "Hello."

Vaida Janz joined them.

"I understand you've come here to look into something," said Calabrese. "I was called about it yesterday."

Malloy held up his badge. "Would you care to see the warrant?"

He caught Calabrese checking Miss Janz's response without taking his eyes off of the lieutenant.

She shook her head almost imperceptibly.

"That won't be necessary, gentlemen." Calabrese smiled. "I was contacted by the chief yesterday, personally. He assured me that everything was on the up and up." He paused a moment and looked at the two investigators. "Now what exactly is it you want?"

"Mr. Calabrese. I hope you don't take offence to our questions. However, State Superior Court Judge David Loewenstein has issued a warrant, enabling us to enter your computer system for the retrieval of certain data."

Calabrese crossed his arms. "Go on."

Malloy recognised the gesture of a nervous man. Perhaps a man with something to hide ... No. Just nervous. "We need a list of names."

"Yes?"

"And some data on those names."

"Yes, go on."

"Sir, what kind of computer system is this?" Malloy taking him through the whole spiel.

"Rantech."

"And does it have a full software complement?"

"Of course." Calabrese smiled thinly.

"Then this should take no time at all."

Calabrese looked increasingly impatient. "Right. Now if you'll just tell me what you want to know, I'll get Miss Janz to pull up the data." He tried to smile.

"Right." Malloy realised he had echoed Calabrese's word. Even he was beginning to strain. The effrontery of thinking these people had done something wrong. "We want to know the names of all pediatric heart surgery cases that died post-operatively at this institution, in the last five years, with a specified laboratory parameter of serum digoxin greater than 2.5."

"Why?" Calabrese let his crossed arms down.

"Sir, I'm not sure. I've only been sent here to do a job. In addition, we'd like the biochemistry laboratory results of the last three days of their lives, as well as their med sheets."

"That's no problem at all." He smiled, and looked at Miss Janz. "Do you think we can do that for the lieutenant and the doctor?"

"Yes, sir." Her eyes darted between the policeman and the coroner. "Right away, sir." She hurried away to her work station. "No problem at all, Mr. Calabrese."

The three men followed the director of medical records over to her computer terminal.

She called up the search function. A menu appeared, demanding prompts. She carefully typed them in, checking with the lieutenant to see if they were what he wanted.

When all the parameters on the menu were filled and confirmed, Malloy said, "This looks like it."

Miss Janz said, "Here we go."

Four faces drew closer to the screen. She pushed the enter button. The menu disappeared, replaced by a list. The onlookers were silent, mesmerized.

Names of thirty-four children who had ceased to exist on the face of this earth sprang to electronic life on the screen. Names like Michael Anthony, Eric Asala, Gilda Gold, Janet Platzer and Christopher Charles Spekkens. A testament to their passage.

After a pause, Doctor Attersly said, "May we have a print of that?"

Miss Janz's eyes glanced momentarily towards Calabrese before she answered. "Certainly." A quick prompt from a few keys and the printer behind her spat out one sheet.

"Now could we print each file this way?" said Attersly. "Hospital face sheet with diagnosis, etcetera. Then the last three days of biochemistry results appended in order, followed by the med sheets. The same for each file, in series from one to thirty-four."

She looked surprised at the coroner.

"Miss Janz." Calabrese urged her.

"Yes, sir," she shot back, as she entered more codes into a menu. In a few minutes she had the batch ready to process. "Here we go," she said, as she pushed enter.

The printer immediately began spewing forth a steady stream of paper.

Attersly watched the feed of sheets as it poured into a box. He picked up the lead sheets and quickly thumbed through them. His eyes widened.

Within two minutes the printer had stopped.

Attersly gathered up the paper in his arms. He thumbed through the pile for a few minutes, absorbed in the details.

"Doctor Attersly," said Malloy finally. "Will that be all?"

"I ... I think this is all we need for now," he said feebly.

"Good. In that case we can leave these people to their business—let them do what they do best—take care of other people's problems. I'd like to thank you both."

"If there's anything we can do, Lieutenant," said Calabrese, "let us know."

"You've both done plenty already. Thanks very much."

"May I show you out?" said Calabrese, looking a bit more relaxed.

"That's not necessary," said Malloy, wondering what the hurry was. "We'll be fine. Thanks."

"You're very welcome, gentlemen." Calabrese sounding conciliatory.

Malloy, who was on his way out the security door, picked up on that. He stopped dead in his tracks, turned, and squarely faced the administrator. Attersly bumped to a stop behind him, fumbling the sheaf of papers into his valise.

"Mr. Calabrese." He emphasized the "Calabrayzay." "Are you?"

"Emmm ... In the ancestral sense. But I was born and raised in New York City."

"Right." That word again.

Later, Jim Malloy backed the unmarked police car out of its spot in the covered hospital entry. The area that was a no parking zone. No parking for everybody but the administrator, a well known surgeon on call, or even an unmarked police car.

Lieutenant Malloy steered out the bottom of the L, onto a narrow side street which ran beside a steam generating plant with huge plate glass windows along its sides. Brightly coloured pipes were visible inside. Across the street was another well-placed landmark made of dark wood with upper windows looking like an old time caboose. The vendor was selling someone a hot dog.

Malloy pulled out onto Brookline Street, heading back to town in the mid morning traffic. He made a mental note to avoid the pothole on Newbury Street, the massive one in the curb lane just past the bear right that had been there forever.

The day was bright and hot. He was glad the car had air conditioning. They plodded through the cluttered urban sprawl of warehouses, gas stations and service businesses that was Lower Roxbury.

He looked at Attersly poring over the papers. He had started to pull the top pages out of his valise, and flipped them over his left arm, allowing them to fold onto the grey vinyl floor of the car.

Finally, after he had crossed the tracks and gone right onto Newbury Street, Malloy said. "Whad 'ju find?" He looked ahead at the traffic, not believing that anonymous tips ever led to anything but wild goose chases.

"Rick," Attersly said, sounding disturbed. "It's all here. Just like they said it would be. It's all here!"

Malloy looked at Attersly in shocked disbelief. "You're kidding!"

The right front wheel slammed into the huge pothole and jarred the lieutenant's teeth, almost hard enough to loosen a filling.

TEN

Doctor Attersly was as prepared as he could be for his meeting. He had spent the better part of two hours poring over the data he and Lieutenant Malloy had gathered at the Massachusetts Heart Institute after the files had been copied at police headquarters. The originals had gone into safe keeping as evidence. Both he and the lieutenant had received a copy.

Attersly couldn't understand Malloy's skepticism right from the start. On the drive over to the hospital, Malloy had said several times that these sort of people didn't kill. Told him he could remember case reports of individuals killing one or two people in hospital, but never any great number. Killings were the subjects of mob hit men, jealous spouses, jilted lovers, and so on. But there was no precedent for a mass murderer in a hospital setting—except of course in fiction.

After the information had been gathered at the hospital and the sight of the serum digoxin levels had scorched his eyes, he had explained the science to Malloy.

"The serum digoxin levels were two to six times normal in the post-mortems," he had said. "Digoxin is a drug used to strengthen the muscle of any failing heart. Once the surgery is done though, the drug is normally withdrawn when the mechanics of normal heart function return and the child becomes stable. These poor kids had serum digoxin levels which were way too high. They'd been overdosed. An overdose of this magnitude did not occur accidentally at an institution of Mass Heart's calibre. Not thirty-four separate times. Argument, if not, case closed."

So Malloy had agreed with him and thanked him for the medical lesson. He had driven on for some time, and then, like Attersly had seen him do before, Malloy had turned to him and smiled, saying, "I still don't buy it." Not in a malevolent or a teasing tone ... Not to get him going ... Not to pass the time.

What was missing was the scary part. The part that Malloy had missed too.

All of which had taken Attersly to the seventh floor of the east block at Government Centre, to the chief coroner's office.

He sat in a modern furnished anteroom. The walls were pastel, the prints nondescript. Somehow clean and efficient looking even if it wasn't.

Doctor Richard Cummings was the chief coroner for The Commonwealth of Massachusetts. The last time Attersly had met him at his office was four years earlier. It was over a matter he would rather have forgotten.

When Doctor Cummings had called him the night before and asked him to take the case, he had known. He knew right away that the matter was delicate. He knew why Cummings had asked instead of assigning him the case. Cummings needed a man who was thorough. He needed a man who would keep him abreast of every development and every nuance. Cummings needed a man who was discreet. And he needed him on his side.

In fact, it was easy for Attersly to be discreet. He was physically underdeveloped. People hardly noticed him. He spoke softly, walked quietly, and asked politely. So people tended to ignore him. In short, he was the Trojan horse of medical examiners.

"Doctor Cummings will see you now," said the plump secretary, as she stepped out of the chief coroner's office.

"Thank you, June," said Attersly, as he got up clutching his valise and walked through the open door.

She closed the door slowly behind him.

Doctor Richard Cummings turned around from the expanse of windows behind him. "Thank you for taking the case." A slight man in his late forties with wavy black hair, Cummings stretched out his hand, and they shook politely. His pointed face was thin and framed by dimpled cheeks and a pursed mouth. He too was small, in a plain charcoal suit that showed a gold watch chain as his only adornment.

The walls of Cummings's office were laboured with books, journals, and a wall of diplomas and certificates arranged around a shrunken human skull. His desk was a massive dark unit bereft of anything but a phone, a fossilized bone pen holder, and a lexan cube.

"And thank you for calling in your preliminary report," Cummings said, as he walked with a stoop over to his desk. "Now, shall we get down to business?"

"Of course."

Cummings cleared the objects over beside the phone. Attersly took the sheaf of papers out of his brown leather valise, laid them on the desk, and glanced for a moment at the nine deformed .45 caliber bullets in the cube.

"Let's begin at number one," said Attersly. "Michel Anthony. Age at death as you can see, one year, three months. Admitting diagnosis: patent ductus arteriosus. Operative procedure: open ligation of patent ductus arteriosus. Discharge diagnosis: same. Complications: death. Serial laboratory work normal, except for serum digoxin which climbs steadily starting on the first post-operative day until it is 8.7 on the day of death, three days later." Cummings leaned in closer. "Massive overdose. Medication sheet, as you can see, no change in indicated standard dosage. No adjustment made for high levels of drug. Surgeon: A. Roy Purvis."

"Interesting, Sam." Cummings stroked his moustache thoughtfully.

"Take Gilda Gold. Age two. Admitting diagnosis: destabilized intra-ventricular shunt secondary to influenza. In other words, she coughed and reversed her shunt."

"I'm familiar."

"Of course. Pardon me. Operative procedure: closure of ventricular septal defect. Labs all normal except that the serum digoxin climbs on day one of post-op and terminates at 7.5, literally. Post-operative diagnosis: same. Complications: death. Surgeon: A. Roy Purvis."

"Are there any cases that were not done by Doctor Purvis?"

"Only one. A three-year-old by the name of Williamson. Ventricular septal defect done by a surgeon named Voorman." He shuffled through the stack of pages. "Here it is. Same scenario. High serum digoxin, as you can see."

"Yes. Yes, indeed." Cummings satisfied himself. "Of course, all these cases have high terminal digoxin levels, because that's what the computer was asked to find."

"Yes."

"What kind of system?"

"Rantech. Does the medical records and everything."

"That's good reliable equipment. I would expect no less of our friends at Massachusetts Heart Institute." Cummings thought for a moment. "You can leave a copy of this with me. There's no need for us to go over every case now. Time is of the essence. I'll review everything myself later. What's important now is that you get down to police headquarters. I've already spoken with Inspector Dugan. He's the chief detective. He plans to take on this investigation personally and, of course, he expects us to be a part of it for the obvious reason. I informed him that you would head up the investigation for us, and that you would give him and his men complete cooperation."

"Of course."

"Now, I do want you to stay in close touch with me on every aspect of this case."

"I will. You can count on that."

Cummings paused a moment, looking at Attersly. "Have you given this case much thought yet?"

"Yes. Some."

"I'd appreciate your comments."

"Well," Attersly said. "There are obviously high digoxin levels in all these kids. The majority of these children were operated on by Doctor A Roy Purvis. That doesn't make him a criminal. On the other hand it makes you wonder. I've done a number of investigations with Lieutenant Rick Malloy, who's also on this case. Now he has a high degree of suspicion that there was no wrongdoing here."

"Correct me on this one Samuel—he has a high degree of suspicion that nothing happened. Isn't that an oxymoron?"

"I'm not sure."

"On what does he base his so called suspicion? Gut feeling?"

"In part, I think that's it. But he swears up and down that this kind of case isn't reported by anonymous tippers. He's convinced of that. He figures that mass murder is uncovered one piece at a time through routine police work."

"Ah, well." Cummings shook his finger at Attersly, "Perhaps that's why he's a lieutenant and not an inspector."

Samuel Attersly remained silent.

Cummings turned to the window and gave a throwaway gesture. "The fact remains that we have thirty-four dead children at one hospital. I think we have to be very careful with this investigation. We must pick up every detail. We should get the pre-morbid ECGs to look for digoxin toxicity. We need to know who the nurses were who took care of the children post-op. We need to know a lot. There's one other thing we need, and this worries me the most—"

"I think I know what you're going to say," said Attersly wringing his hands slowly.

Cummings turned back to Attersly, "We need to know why the coroner's office missed these."

Attersly waited for the confirmation of his worst fear to hit home. "Yes. I know." He could only imagine how Cummings must feel.

"Dugan has scheduled his rap session for seven this evening, in his office at police headquarters. I want you to be there. You've got time to get dinner. Make sure you save your receipts." He became somber. "I need you there as part of the team. Turn over all your other cases to June, tomorrow, and I'll reassign them. Stay in close touch with me, and if you think of anything or find anything, anything at all, let me know."

"I will. You can count on me."

"Excellent. I will, of course, bring in an out-of-state expert on pediatric cardiac surgery. But we'll discuss that tomorrow." He extended his hand. "Goodbye Samuel. And, thanks."

"Goodbye, sir." Attersly left with the disheveled mound of paper clutched tightly in his left arm, along with his valise. He would get June to make the copies and go to dinner. He looked back and caught Cummings staring at the floor. For a moment he felt sorry for him.

ELEVEN

Judge David Loewenstein was waiting for Lieutenant Malloy in his antique oak chambers, at a Louis XIVth desk, drinking coffee. He had tried to absorb himself in the newspaper but couldn't. Even the sports pages couldn't get his mind off the day. The appeal he had heard was a complete and total waste of time, run by a slimy defence attorney, who had managed to shave one month off a sentence after six days in court. No wonder the State couldn't afford to fix the roads.

Three light raps sounded on the door.

Loewenstein looked up. "Come in."

The door opened silently, allowing Malloy entry. He closed it quietly.

"Your Honor." He bowed his head slightly and walked over to the desk carrying a large sheaf of loose pages.

"Rick, sit down."

"Thank you, Your Honor." He placed the sheaf on the table and sat in the arm chair opposite the judge.

Loewenstein had taken his robe off, and sat in black trousers and suspenders over a white roll collar shirt. His hair was close cropped and white. He was lean and his cheeks were deeply dimpled. On top of his large ethnic nose rested a pair of fine gold-rimmed semi-lunar glasses.

Malloy cleared his throat.

"Would you like a cup of coffee, Rick?"

"Yes. Thank you."

Loewenstein turned to get up, but looked back with a squint. "Black, no sugar, isn't it?"

"Yes."

The judge walked to the far corner of the chamber, opened an elaborately paneled door, and poured coffee from a pot into a white mug. "So, tell me already," he said as he walked back with the mug in hand.

"Our preliminary investigation, which was executed on your warrant, revealed some interesting facts. I have here the original printout from Mass Heart's computer, which gave us thirty-four names. These are the records of infants and children, all under five years of age, who had various heart surgeries at the hospital, and died within one week of operation of massive digoxin overdose. What I have here is simply the charts' cover sheet setting out diagnosis, operation, complications, which in these cases were all death; and the surgeon's name. Also, serial laboratory records showing the rise in blood digoxin up to lethal levels, and the medication sheets."

"How do you interpret this?" He rubbed the side of his nose.

"I have here, the computer-generated, incomplete charts of thirty-four children who died post-operatively with what appear to be high digoxin levels. Ditto etc, etc."

"I see." Loewenstein gazed at the tiled ceiling for a moment. "I'm already getting the feeling that you have ... reservations."

Malloy leaned forward on the desk and said, "Your Honor, I'm not sure."

"Are you giving me the old data processing saw—bullshit in equals bullshit out?"

"Well, we did set the parameters according to the informant's specifications. Age: less than five years ... Heart surgery ... High digoxin level ... Death within one week post-operatively."

"You didn't set any time frames in the historical sense?"

"No."

"And how far back do these cases go?"

"Seven years." Loewenstein was leaning so far forward that Malloy could smell his breath.

"Only seven years." He leaned back in his chair. "These operations and these tests have been done for a lot longer than seven years. And Purvis, who figures into all this somehow, has been doing these sorts of operations for well over twenty years at Mass Heart. Explain, please."

"I can't," said Malloy, turning up his palms. "There are simply too many possibilities. The poisoning may have been done by someone who has only been there for seven years or so. The test that picked up these results may have been a new version of some other test, some improvement. Or, maybe, just maybe, A. Roy Purvis has cracked."

"Hmm." Judge Loewenstein snorted the word through his nose. "This is all very speculative. And this from an anonymous informant. Some case." He waved his finger at Malloy. "You are telling me that there is a mass murderer of children on the loose in the premier heart hospital of the United States. A murderer who gets his jollies from killing little children in the post-operative period with lethal doses of heart medication. A murderer who has gone undetected for seven, or who knows how many years. And all of a sudden, an anonymous tipper calls and tells the police where to look for one major, scandalous, ruinous case." He had raised his voice almost to a shout. "Has anybody considered the possibility that the killer is now sick for attention—wants to show off his handiwork?" He reflected for a moment. "Or is he a crank? Do you have any idea what this could do to the reputation of the hospital and its staff? Do you have any idea what might happen to members of your department if this thing turns out to be a hoax?"

"Sir, I've thought about that."

"I hope the hell Dugan has." Loewenstein pounded the table once with his fist. "This strikes me as tentative at best."

"I agree. But we won't know until we look. Your Honor, can we afford not to?"

A silence infected the room.

"So what does Dugan need from me?" Loewenstein realized the chief detective's wisdom in sending Malloy, the diplomat, on this mission. Had Dugan come along, he might not have been as receptive.

"We need a search warrant, to re-enter the computer files as well as the hard copy files in medical archives. The warrant should be without restriction. After all, there may be other cases in other age groups, and so on. We need entry to the staff employment records of the hospital. We need entry to the pharmacy records of the hospital. And last, we need entry to the personal files on the physicians, surgeons, and administrators of the hospital. We need these with respect to the Massachusetts Heart Institute. We need to be able to restrict any unauthorized entry to these areas, by any and all hospital personnel while we undertake our search."

"Is that all?" His nose twitched. "You are going to lay bare the personal and highly confidential files of hundreds, if not thousands, of people, in order to affect your investigation?"

"We can't think of any other way. We don't want to miss anything,"

"Hell of a thing to do for an anonymous tip." The judge's nose twitched.

Malloy leaned to his left and forward, with his mouth slightly ajar, to look closely at Judge Loewenstein's nose. The judge's eyes widened as he turned an embarrassed shade of red.

"I'm so sorry Judge Loew—"

"Never mind," the judge said. "Comes from hearing too many lies." He waved it off with the stroke of his hand and Malloy sat back. "You tell Dugan, if he messes this up, he'll have to answer to me, personally."

TWELVE

Inspector Roger Dugan sat at the head of the large oak table in the detectives' conference room. The room was bereft of adornments except for an American and a state flag, standing crossed in the corner. A large blackboard was stationed behind him. To his left were some oak shelves, supporting audiovisual equipment. Large loudspeakers stood in the far corner.

What had been the lanky Dugan of youth had given way to a less sculpted physique. The angular chin and nose had taken on a rounded shape topped with partly grey hair. Nobody would call it salt and pepper. To do so would have insulted his ancestors, and his temperament which were better described as salt and cayenne.

To his credit, however, Dugan had managed for the last thirty years to hold the reins in on his temper in the interest of political expedience. And so he had risen to his present post, one he had held for nine years.

Everybody who knew him understood the color of his hair.

Dugan had prepared the blackboard behind him with an array of team functions. There was a table to the left of the blackboard, which held a copy of the computer documents taken from the Massachusetts Heart Institute.

The chief detective surveyed his assembled task force and opened the discussion. "Gentlemen, you all know Assistant District Attorney Geoffrey Walters. He has been assigned to this case on a full time basis. You will give him your complete attention and assistance. He and I will command this task force into the investigation of the multiple infanticides at the Massachusetts Heart Institute."

Walters nodded, a thin young man with straight black hair parted to the left. He stood proudly erect in a navy blue suit.

Dugan saw Rick Malloy's expression change when he said infanticide. Malloy looking at Walters now. *What's he thinking?*

Dugan went on quite animated, giving up only the slightest hint of a first generation accent. "Lieutenant Rick Malloy of Homicide and Doctor Samuel Attersly of the state examiner's office paid a visit to the Massachusetts Heart Institute yesterday morning. This was in response to an anonymous call, phoned into the main switchboard at 2:15 Monday afternoon. The call was traced to a pay phone in Lower Roxbury. This is the entire call." Dugan leaned back to the left in his chair to push a button on an electronic recorder.

The blue digital readout counted forward. Then, two JBL reference loudspeakers spoke, slowly, evenly.

"Thirty-four children less than five years old. All operated at Mass Heart in the last seven years. All had lethal levels of digoxin. All died within one week of operation. All died at the hands of one man ... Can you find him?" The dispatcher's voice came on. "Identi—" The recording went silent.

Dugan switched the recorder off and pushed reset. He turned to the officers. "Forty-two seconds exactly." He emphasized the point with a finger. "Let's listen again."

He pushed the button, and the voice started again. Dugan looked at the expressions each of his officers gave up, until the anxious dispatcher's voice came on, just in time to cover the sound of the phone hanging up.

"Gentlemen, listen to that voice one more time." He spoke slowly. "Get to know this person. You may run into him or her in your travels through the hospital." Dugan played it again.

The voice was muffled. It was impossible to tell the sex. Some traffic came through in the background, between phrases. The voice was even, no accent, nothing, just empty.

Dugan continued. "This is the only reference made to the murders in question. At no other time have we received any information regarding this matter. Feel free to listen to this recording at your leisure. The original is in the archives, and a copy has been sent to the FBI for forensic analysis. We expect an answer within one week. I was advised of this call immediately, and conferred with Chief Hawkins. We involved the district attorney's office right away. Mr. Walters ..."

"Thank you, Inspector Dugan." Standing, he paused for a moment to collect his audience. "We have chosen to look upon this call as genuine for a number of reasons." He began to pace slowly back and forth, behind Dugan. "In the first place, the caller sounds serious. There is no hint of tension or humour detectable in the voice." He looked at the floor. "Second. The sex of the caller cannot be identified by non-scientific means. That's very important. Third. The caller has given very specific information on how to locate the bodies." He caught himself. "Or what have you. Fourth. The caller is not threatening to do any harm. The caller is informing of past events—a *fait accompli*. Fifth. The caller did not wait for the duty officer on the phone to answer, to speak to him, or to try to intervene in any way. The message was clearly over, and the caller hung up." He faced the crowded room. "In short, this forty-two second call has every hallmark of a genuine report of mass murder." He turned to Dugan. "Inspector ..."

"Doctor Attersly of the coroner's office accompanied Lieutenant Malloy from Homicide Division to the hospital," said Dugan. "Together they executed a search warrant involving the Massachusetts Heart Institute's medical records computer. The computer was given the same parameters specified by the caller. The computer gave us thirty-four names." He looked at Attersly. "Would you care to tell us what *you found*, Doctor?"

Attersly stood up looking a little uneasy. He motioned at the easel. "What the records seem to show is that all of these infants and young children came to Mass Heart for corrective surgery of birth defects of their hearts. The records indicate that within one week of operation these children all had grossly elevated serum digoxin levels. The records go on to show that these children died. One surgeon did all operations except for one."

"Who might that be?" asked Lieutenant Frank Daley of the Fraud Squad. He bore a heavy Bostonian accent, like a Kennedy.

"The surgeon is Doctor A Roy Purvis." Attersly looked around the table to let the fact take hold. There couldn't be a person in Boston who hadn't heard of Doctor Purvis. "Might I remind everybody in this room that Doctor Purvis is the preeminent heart surgeon in this country, if not the world."

"Nobody here is accusing Doctor Purvis of any wrong doing," said Dugan. He smiled widely at Attersly. He might as well have told him, *and we know that doctors cover for each other.* His smile went deadpan. "And then what did you do?"

"After obtaining a copy of the data, I went to Chief Coroner Richard Cummings's office and discussed the matter with him." Attersly was beginning to look uneasy. "We came to the conclusion that the matter couldn't be ignored."

"Nothing more?" Dugan waved deferentially with his hand.

"No. Nothing more." He looked away.

"Very well then." Dugan leaned back in his chair and propped his elbows on the table, holding his hands with fingers intertwined. "Lieutenant Malloy."

"Yes, sir." Malloy jumped to his feet. "My preliminary findings concur with Doctor Attersly." He shot a glance at the coroner. "Since returning to police headquarters and conferring with you, I have been to see Superior Court Judge Loewenstein. I explained the findings in light of the coroner's explanation and requested a further search warrant. To make a long story short, Judge Loewenstein has given us the search warrant we requested. This warrant," he held it up, "enables us to enter the Massachusetts Heart Institute. It enables us to enter their medical records and other information systems, obtain passwords etcetera, and pull whatever data we see fit."

Frank Daley jumped in. "Wouldn't that be unconstitutional? Violate people's right to privacy?"

"Well, yes and no." Malloy went on, "My discussions with the judge were roughly as follows. A person could claim violation of civil liberties if he could show that his records were being scrutinized for some purpose not in keeping with the due process of law. That is to say, if we were looking into their records for our own amusement, or, for the possible needless dissemination of information. However, our argument is that the information we have obtained was specified by the caller's parameters." He paused a moment. Daley looked back at him poker-faced. "You see, there may be other cases. There may be other cases with different parameters."

Frank Daley exchanged glances with his partners.

Assistant District Attorney Geoffrey Walters intervened.

"There is a point here, in investigations of this type. The state relies on the gathering of information to form an opinion, whether wrong has, or has not, been done. Judge Loewenstein has agreed that we should search for evidence to corroborate the caller. The evidence appears magically, as if it had been there all the time waiting to be discovered, as if it may have been planted." Walters implored with his hands. "We needed to be able to scan other patient files, not to open them up publicly, rather to look over their raw data and determine if they fit any particular pattern. Given the fact that this is a computer search, a patient's name won't come up unless it fits the pattern."

"We have decided to open up the scope of the investigation," said Dugan. "We're going to look for high digoxin levels in all patients who died in any age group, with or without surgery."

"How did you come to these new parameters?" said Daley.

"Entirely arbitrary," said Walters. "We're using this as a starting point to see if there is any evidence to suggest further wrong doing. It is, after all, the duty of this office to protect the citizens of Massachusetts."

"There's going to be a response from Mass Heart about this—and I mean more than outrage," Daley said.

"I think there is the matter of some tactic here too, Frank," said Dugan.

"Yes there is quite clearly," said Walters. "We expect the hospital to counter with an attempted injunction against our investigation. We expect the thrust of their legal effort to center around patient rights to privacy. We'll respond with an argument claiming manipulation of patient data, and not unbridled collection and dissemination. In other words, we are going to take only what we need to make our case, or cases. This is quite different from willy-nilly ransacking of medical records, and we believe this to be a thoroughly plausible and arguable position under the circumstances. But more than that, our search warrant was issued by a superior court judge. That means, getting an injunction against our warrant would require the deliberation of a supreme court justice. That process would not, and could not, occur overnight. By the time such an injunction came through, we would be out of there, and we would have seen what we wanted to see. Either our position would be vindicated and we would show more deaths, or we would simply say, 'sorry,' and put everything back, secure in the knowledge that we have done nothing illegal. I stress, nothing illegal."

"That's one terrific piece of tactic." said Dugan, smiling broadly again. "But let's get back to Lieutenant Malloy."

"And that's one hard act to follow," said Malloy. "But I'll try." He smiled. "Further, the warrant allows us to seize hard copy of the patient records in question. It allows us to enter the personnel office and seize records of employment of all staff at the hospital. After all, we don't know who committed the crimes, if any." Dugan smiled at him. "Further, the warrant allows us to enter administration and seize related documents. And further still, the warrant specifies that we may cordon off any area deemed necessary for the undertaking of this investigation, and bar any and all hospital personnel from the areas of concern."

One of the detectives from Criminal Investigation Division sat up. "Wow. This is the full meal deal. I didn't know the Massachusetts Heart Institute was located in Salem."

There was a round of laughter from the table.

"Good point," Dugan snorted between laughter. "It's a good thing we didn't start this awful mess." He paused a moment, looking around the room. "For this operation we are going to work in teams." He got up and went over to the blackboard. "I've divided you into fairly straightforward groups. Lieutenant Rick Malloy will be in charge of onsite operations. He will be in charge of any, and all, interface with the media. As usual, I expect nobody to speak into a camera, a microphone or a notebook, except of course for Lieutenant Malloy." He scoured the faces in the room for reassurance.

"Doctor Samuel Attersly will be second in command to Lieutenant Malloy. Doctor Attersly will give directives on what information to take, and what to leave behind. Any questions he cannot answer will be addressed by Lieutenant Malloy."

"We will form three teams. Frank." He glowered seriously at Daley.

"Yes, sir."

"I want you, David and Pat Rosen to head up the talent on three teams. I know murder isn't up your alley, but I need you for another reason. You know data systems, and how to examine them for fraud. In this case, simply consider irregularities of the same medical parameters we have already specified."

Daley took out his notebook and pen.

Geoffrey Walters took his cue and stood up from his seat to the right of Dugan.

"The parameters we are looking for: first, death at the institute; second, serum digoxin levels greater than 2.5; third, cardiac surgery; fourth, and not specified, investigator's intuition. We will accept any file that fits any two or more of the above parameters. If they do, you will get a printout of the file, a computer copy of the file, and if possible, the original from medical records. Copies of computer files should be duplicated on diskette and stick."

"Take an information officer from the computer department along for each team," said Dugan. "Organize that tonight. Harry." He looked at Farley and his partners. "You are each assigned to one team. This is after all a criminal matter, and the teams will need all the help they can get."

"Right," answered Farley.

"Each team has been assigned five black and whites from roll call tomorrow morning. In addition, five black and whites will be assigned to the main entrance of the hospital. Remember, if in doubt, defer to Malloy. He has a direct line to D.A. Walters and me."

"You will insure that you have sufficient communicators that everybody can stay in touch." Dugan looked at everybody gravely. "I don't want some situation getting out of hand and then finding out at *our* post-mortem that nobody else knew what was going on."

"The team leaders are Farley, McGuire and Rosen. Farley, you will concentrate on Medical Records."

"McGuire."

"Yes, sir."

"I want you to look into Administration. In particular, look into any actions or discipline that has ever been taken against any medical personnel, nursing personnel, or the cleaning, laundry, and kitchen staff. Anybody. Anything suspicious. Doctor Attersly tells me that sort of thing is usually very well documented. We're looking for minor as well as major misconduct by just about anybody, from the janitor to A. Roy Purvis."

"Got it," said McGuire.

"Knew I could count on you," said Dugan. "Pat Rosen. Hit the Personnel Department. Get a list of names of everybody who has ever worked there as well as their social security numbers and direct banking numbers etc. I want to know when they worked there, when they left, why they left, and where they went. Anything in their file, like unusual donations, receipts etc. I want to know about it. Capiche?"

"Right," she said.

"Take Will Saunders with you, and choose somebody from information services."

Dugan turned to another part of the blackboard. "We'll begin at 7:30 tomorrow morning. Get your cars. You will leave at nine sharp and hit the hospital at 9:30. Malloy will present the warrant to the administrator." He looked puzzled for a moment. "What was his name again?"

"Calabrese," said Malloy.

"Calabrese." He pondered the name with a policeman's wit, and then smiled. "Really?"

That drew another round of laughter.

Dugan went on, shifting a little from side to side. "We will meet back here tomorrow afternoon at the direction of Lieutenant Malloy." Dugan went on in a more somber tone. "I know you're having mixed feelings. But we can't ignore the fact that the information was totally accurate. We must now substantiate that with evidence. Ultimately, we will have to look at the bodies in forensic detail. But that's the next step. The fact that this occurred at the premier heart hospital in the United States, and that it involves thirty-four infants and children, makes this the worst mass murder I've ever heard of." He looked over at Attersly, who seemed quite uneasy. "And this sat undetected for a long time, under everyone's nose."

Dugan was ready for the clincher. He walked over to the recorder. "Let's listen one more time. Remember this voice. Think of the voice every time you speak to someone. Keep it in the back of your mind."

The blue digital counter started its march. Then the voice, droll, almost monosyllabic and empty. "Thirty-four children less than five years old. All operated at Mass Heart in the last seven years. All had lethal levels of digoxin. All died within one week of operation. All died at the hands of one man ... Can you find him?" Then an excited, "Identi—"

Dugan let the experience sink in. The room was silent. He spoke slowly, deliberately, his deep voice almost hypnotic. "The next time you hear that voice may be in the halls of the Massachusetts Heart Institute. At first you won't know what it is about the person you're talking to. It may not even occur to you the first time you speak to him, or her. But eventually, you'll know."

Dugan waited. Then he spoke with much more animation. "When this investigation is over I want a list of names. I want facts. I want charges. I want to convict this bastard! And don't forget to cross all your t's and dot all your i's. I don't want him walking on some slimy technicality." He turned to D.A. Walters. "Did I miss anything?"

Walters discreetly signaled no with his hand.

"In that case, information packages for everybody are on the trolley beside the door. See you at 07:30 hours tomorrow. Goodnight."

The group dispersed rapidly.

Walters was the only other person left in the room as Dugan took the sheaf of papers off the easel and packed it under his arm. "Roger, that was one of your best," he said.

"Thanks Geoff. Didn't think I still had it in me." He smiled.

"You sly dog. You got their adrenalin going. One hell of a show. The Dugan effect!"

"Well." Dugan sighed and glanced at a spot on the ceiling. "A commander has to inspire his troops."

"We're going to get this guy. I know we will."

"Yeah. This guy, or whatever. If we can only follow through, and prove on tissue sample that the digoxin levels were high; that's three quarters of the case. The rest will fall out of the information we're going to cart out o' there tomorrow."

"I'm going to trace the bodies," said Walters. "Make some rumblings about disinterment and get people's thoughts headed in that direction. That'll make the actual jump easier later on. As soon as you can give me something, anything to hang my hat on, I'll be able to proceed with the warrant."

"Right. See you tomorrow, Geoff. Night."

"Goodnight." Walters turned and left.

Roger Dugan carried the large sheaf of papers back to his office and stretched his back as he walked. He sat down in his office without turning on the light and let his thoughts go.

He had a fairly good idea of where he wanted to proceed with the investigation, and he knew how to get there.

He was pleased with the officers he had chosen, but most of all he was happy with Malloy. A perfect diplomat. Had he always been that way, had it come with age, or had it come with his inquiry?

Geoffrey Walters had been a good choice. Ambitious! And his logic in choosing Judge Loewenstein was brilliant. The only thing that had worked better was sending Malloy over to see the judge, alone.

Dugan was happy. He was on track! The black and whites would make it look like an army had invaded the Massachusetts Heart Institute.

Chief Hawkins was sixty-two now. *Well, well, well.*

Roger Dugan stood up, unlocked the bottom drawer of his desk and took out an old leather shoulder holster. The elastic fit snugly across his back. He retrieved his Colt Python .357 magnum from the drawer. After breaking the cylinder out to ensure it contained five rounds, he put the hammer down on the empty cylinder, and holstered the gun.

THIRTEEN

Peter Martins wasn't sure when he first heard the words. They weren't Ian's words and he didn't know where they had come from. The only thing he was sure of was that he had heard them.

The words were, "Cops upstairs ... Murders ..." It shook him.

Peter and Ian had been working on their coronary bypass for almost two hours.

Earlier, Ian Scott had elevated the tip of the vein he held with a fine forcep, tracting a loop of sutures upward from the vein into the shape of a tent.

Peter passed the needle of his fine stitch through the outside of the vein and pulled the loop of sutures tight.

"I can't believe he did that." muttered Ian, just loud enough for Peter to hear.

As Martins approached the inside of the coronary artery with his needle, the scrub nurse suctioned the last bit of blood away. He drove the stitch through, evenly spaced.

"That sort of behaviour—pulling rank—it's just awful," Ian murmured as Peter placed another stitch through the wall of the coronary artery.

"I think that's it," said Peter. "One point five millimetre probe." He passed the probe up and down the inside of the artery and contemplated his work. "Right."

Peter placed the last stitch on the v-shaped boot of his arteriotomy. He carefully glided the needle over the probe to ensure that he didn't pick up the back wall and obstruct the flow of blood. Satisfied, he removed the probe and snugged down his sutures before carefully tying eleven knots.

Ian kept obligingly quiet during the delicate manoeuvres but then nattered on, "I can't believe that he bumped our cases for two days. I mean what's his hurry? Not like he's leaving town."

"I guess when you're A. Roy Purvis you can do what you want, when you want, especially around here."

"Well it'll be a frosty day in hell before I forget."

"Oh well. We're getting our cases done now." Peter shrugged as he looked at Ian, who was all upset. "Let's test this graft."

They went on with their work. The joint didn't leak.

"Cross-clamp coming off." said Peter. "Pump down."

"Pump pressure down," said the perfusionist as he turned down the main bypass pump.

Peter released the aortic cross-clamp as the great vessel became flaccid. "Clamp off. Pump up."

"Pump back up," said the perfusionist.

The aorta hardened and rounded up.

"If you think of the worry that kind of wait causes a patient." Ian couldn't let go. "I've been apologising to my patients for over a day now. I mean, they don't come here to wait with no decent explanation."

"Agreed."

"These people pay good money and they expect good service."

"Agreed, Ian. And they usually get it."

"Well, this just won't do." He was sweating into his mask and cap.

"Ian," said Peter. "There is no way in hell any patient of yours, or mine, will hold this against us. No way!"

"No? Just wait and see."

"Why don't you do what I do?"

"Being?"

"Think of it this way. Roy is chief of the department. That makes him part of administration. Yes?"

"I can buy that much." The look in Ian's eyes above his mask, incredulous.

"Well, you tell your patients that their operative spot has been changed by administration." Peter Martins held his gloved hand up against the coming protest. "The change has at the very least been sanctioned by administration at some level. And if not, it should have been. Therefore, if any of your patients have anything to quibble with you about their delay, give them Calabrese's name and telephone number."

"You think he's going to bat for us?"

"Hey. He signs everybody's cheque doesn't he? I mean, if he didn't want Roy to bump our patients, he would have told him so. Don't you think?"

"If ... he ... knew!" Ian glared.

"Of course he knows. He's the administrator. Just remember what Calabrese is thinking."

"Which is?"

Peter said with a straight face. "He's thinking shit flows down hill."

Ian mulled over the idea for a moment. "So that's what you learned up in Canada?"

"You catch on quick for a surgeon!"

Those in the operating room, oblivious to the doctor's quiet discussion, had broken into the usual post cross-clamp relaxation, and talk. The rest of the operation would go quickly, routine as a cook book, as long as the patient came off pump. With Martins and Scott, complications were unusual, if not rare.

Peter was in the midst of placing a cobra clamp across the ascending aorta to sew the top portion of his veins into the side of the great artery.

The cobra clamp actually looked like the snake. The semi-lunar pincers on top of a long and slender grip, like the reptile's body. He snapped the clamp home on the flaccid aorta.

"Pump back up," said Peter.

"Pump back up," said the perfusionist.

"Number fifteen knife."

The scrub nurse handed him the pointed blade.

Peter pierced the wall of the aorta.

"I think you missed that calcium plaque in the wall by a sufficient distance that it won't cause any trouble getting the stitches through," Ian said automatically, seeming to echo his thoughts.

"Uh huh," murmured Peter. Then clearly, "Punch."

The nurse passed the device.

He weaseled the punch into the cut he had made in the great arteries wall and pressed the plunger home. With a snick the device cut a perfectly round hole in the area secured by the cobra clamp. "Inside's clean."

The surgeons kept up their subdued banter, being a foil for each other. The system had saved many a patient's life, and many a surgeon's ass.

But then, somewhere between his orders and Ian's talk, he had heard the voice. A subdued female voice, saying, "Cops upstairs ... Murders." It shook him, unbelievably.

He looked up from his work and surveyed the room. Up behind the drapes and beyond the anesthesia machine, near the pump room door, a tall blond nurse from another operating room was talking to his circulating nurse. They saw him staring and immediately fell silent.

"What did you just say?" said Peter.

"Pardon?" said the blond.

"I said, what did you just say?"

"You mean, what were we talking about?"

"Yes." He was becoming impatient.

"Well," she said, appearing relieved. "Mary Stuart says there are cops all over medical records seizing patient files. And upstairs too."

"What's going on?"

"She says they're investigating some murders, thirty-four kids. Imagine!" Her eyes looked bewildered.

The words slipped from Ian Scott's mouth, unfortunately audibly. "What da hell?"

FOURTEEN

Peter Martins stood outside the main entrance of the Massachusetts Heart Institute. A hot, wet breeze gently teased his operating room greens around his legs and curled his hair. The breeze folded itself ever so gently around the concrete pillars of the hospital's covered entry.

He followed the slow descent of a drop of condensation from its origin in the folded brown fascia above to its destination in an irregular puddle, twenty feet below on the driveway. The afternoon sun was just beginning to creep over the covered drive, drying the edges.

From the moment Peter had heard the word, "murder," that familiar feeling had crept under his skin and taken hold of him like a vice. He had finished his case as quickly as he could. The words, "fact finding investigation," rang in him, but he couldn't remember who had said them; he had concentrated on finishing the operation. Of course, the staff had kept quiet, talking mainly about the work at hand. But he had heard!

Once they were done, Peter had escorted the patient to post-operative intensive care and excused himself from Ian Scott. He wandered the halls. The signs were everywhere. Hushed conversations. Dropped heads. Averted gazes. The news, as usual, had traveled fast.

Outside of the administration suite a uniformed officer had asked him his intentions. When he had answered casually, that he wanted to visit a friend who worked in the employee relations office, he was redirected. He was told that the office was closed and off limits.

He didn't want to raise suspicions by going up to the executive suites, certain that he'd get the same reception there. Instead, Peter decided that he would try to complete some charts in medical records. But there too, a pair of droll, uniformed officers had sent him on his way.

His survey had taken him to a point about thirty feet from the glass doors of the main entrance. He had followed the descent of the drop of condensation into the rapidly dissipating puddle at the end of the row of parallel parked motorcycles. He counted twelve, neatly parked on kickstands in military precision. Even the angles of the forks were perfect. The white splash guards over the front wheels with their Police signs. Twelve sets of silent red and blue flashers looked right at him. Behind the great black seats a row of white radio boxes lay cradled in chrome baskets. A line of antennae saluted. A perfect Harley ad.

He paid little attention to the cops standing with their feet apart, hands behind their backs, white helmets on, casually interested in their surroundings. Their presence was unobtrusive, yet, by their number, intimidating. One on either side of the entry tunnel, one over by the emergency entrance. One down at the bend in the far end of the covered entry way. And one standing vigil beside a huge concrete column at the main driveway's entry to the covered area.

Peter's attention wandered to the man sitting in the unmarked squad car. He got out of his car and began speaking into a handheld communicator without taking his gaze off Peter. As he leaned against the unmarked car, Peter noticed that his suit showed no sign of perspiration. Only three car lengths away, yet city noise effectively blanketed his conversation.

The shifting breeze dared his limp greens to flirt with his skin again.

Peter had seen it all before, in Toronto. The hospital was under siege.

FIFTEEN

The first ring caught Peter Martins in a very deep sleep. The second ring clearly registered in consciousness. On the third ring, he sat up in bed, propping himself up to his right. He caught the luminous glow of his alarm clock. Ten past two. He turned on his bed side lamp, which cast a pale golden glow over his telephone. He was on backup call. His heart beat faster. On the next ring he answered. "Hello."

"Peter, here is Eugen Wittman."

He took a deep breath. "Yes, Eugen, what's up?"

"Are you sitting down?"

"You can be sure of that."

"We have a problem. Does the name Randolph Hobbs mean anything to you?"

"Secretary of State for Health, isn't he?"

"Correct. He is our first problem. He is here with a leaking aortic aneurysm. Maranghi has confirmed with angiograms."

"Go on." Peter's interest was wakening.

"He transferred here from the Cape, to be operated on by Roy Purvis. He is our other problem."

"How so?"

"We can't find him! He is on call and we can't find him." Wittman sounded agitated.

"You tried his home?"

"Of course. Patricia denies seeing him for a couple of days. Told us to page him. We did. He doesn't answer."

"Did you explain that to Hobbs?"

"He's out for the count with a Versed injection for his angiograms. But his wife has already said, Roy Purvis is who she expects to do the operation. That much was known before they left the Cape to come here."

Peter's guard went up. "Well you explain to Mr. Hobbs's wife, that at her direction, I would be pleased to come in and do his operation. However, I will not do anything without her express consent." He knew that being second fiddle was the quick way to court. "You're perfectly serious that you can't find Purvis, aren't you?"

"Completely! You're getting this second hand from me but I'm sure Maranghi has tried for him everywhere, even his new girlfriend's place, and she doesn't answer either."

"Maybe with this socialised medicine thing coming down he just figures ... naw."

"What?" said Eugen.

"Maybe he figures, God doesn't operate at night."

"You know him better than I do."

"Call me back if she decides, and if you need me."

"I will. By the way, did you see anything of the investigation on TV tonight?"

"Yeah. Looks awful. Looks like the media will work this one for all its worth."

"That was my biggest fear." Eugen paused a moment. "Good night."

Peter said, "Night," hung up his phone, turned off his light, and fell into a troubled sleep.

***

Eugen Wittman left his office and went to the waiting room to speak to Mrs. Hobbs. He found her sitting in the empty waiting room of the Emergency Department. She was off in the corner alcove, a favorite spot for troubled people that Eugen knew too well.

She was an attractive woman of forty-something, with a generous mouth and proper posture. She wore a starched white blouse and a floral patterned skirt.

He approached. "Mrs. Hobbs, I am Doctor Eugen Wittman. Doctor Maranghi has asked me to speak to you about your husband, Randolph Hobbs." Eugen always greeted people under stress with an intimate friendliness. He had discovered the hard way that it was best for him to announce the relative's name clearly, as well as the ill party's, before proceeding. He took Mrs. Hobbs's right hand in his and placed his left hand on her shoulder, in an almost ministerial way. "Won't you sit down."

"Thank you, Doctor. Please call me Theresa." She also seemed to know this game.

"Mrs. Hobbs, your husband is gravely ill. We have confirmed by angiogram that he has a leaking aneurysm of his thoracic aorta. I will explain."

"Please do." She looked at him intently.

"The heart sits in the chest and gives rise to a great vessel called the aorta. In the case of your husband, this vessel has a weakened wall, and this wall is bulging The blood is being contained there. That is to say, the outside of the artery wall has not ruptured yet. If it had, your husband would be dead. Do you understand what I have said so far?"

"Yes, thank you." She sighed. "Go on."

"In order to save your husband's life, he will require an operation to patch the leak and evacuate the clot of blood that has formed in the aorta's wall. He will need this operation on an emergency basis. We are prepared to carry out this procedure tonight."

"Good." There was relief in her voice, and a trace of a smile formed on her lips.

"Your husband has been given a drug called Versed for the performance of his angiograms. He is unable to consent to the operation."

"Go ahead," she said without hesitation.

"There are formalities, madam ... your signature ... we will need a witness."

"Not now." She placed her hand over his in an earnest show of concern. "Please get things organized as quickly as possible for my husband. There will be plenty of time to sign papers."

Eugen Wittman raised his left eyebrow ever so slightly.

"It's not as if we were average people on the street," she said reassuringly. Theresa Hobbs placed her other hand over Eugen's and squeezed firmly. "Please, get Doctor Purvis in to save my dear husband's life."

Eugen thought her eyes could have drawn tears from a stone.

He approached the topic cautiously. "That may present a problem, madam."

"Why?"

"Doctor Purvis is unable to perform your husband's operation." He paused a moment, assessing her response. "There is however ..."

Theresa Hobbs's grip on Eugen Wittman's hands tightened, a lot. Her pleading, slightly hooded eyes sharpened to an angle and her pupils dilated.

"What do you mean? Doctor Purvis is unavailable to do my husband's surgery?" she said.

"It is just so. I am not sure of the reason, but he is unavailable to do your husband's surgery." He let the fact sink in for a moment. "There is however a peerless surgeon avail—"

"Doctor Wittman," said Mrs. Hobbs. "Do you know who we are? We came here knowing the problem, and with the understanding that Doctor Roy Purvis would perform this emergency surgery on my husband. If I'm not mistaken, you spoke to Doctor Cameron in Provincetown and confirmed that fact." She wrinkled her forehead and squinted at the emergency doctor. "Isn't that so?"

"Yes it is, but—"

"But what?" she said loudly.

He hesitated and said feebly, "That was then, and this is now." He clasped his hands, composed himself, and continued. "We are prepared to get this surgery underway most expeditiously. An excellent cardio-vascular surgeon is standing by, Doctor Peter Martins—"

"Doctor Wittman." Theresa Hobbs withdrew and stood up defiantly. "Nobody but Doctor Purvis touches my husband! *Nobody.* Is that understood?"

Eugen stood up to answer. "I am afraid, madam, that is not possible. That is simply out of the question."

"We'll see about that," she said. "Doctor, may I use a phone? I left my cell in Provincetown."

"But of course. Just follow me." He led the way to the charge nurse's desk, inside the double glass door of the emergency room.

The charge nurse saw the pair coming and quietly left her desk.

"This will only take a moment. This is not a private call," she said, looking at Eugen. She rummaged through her purse, and produced a small leather address book in which she found a number.

"Dial 9-1 to get an outside line," said Eugen. He waited attentively.

She dialed without tremor, waited a moment, and then spoke very clearly and deliberately. "This is Theresa Hobbs, Randolph Hobbs's wife. This is an emergency. May I speak to the governor please?"

Surprised, Eugen swallowed hard. Hard enough he was sure she heard him.

***

The governor awoke to the gentle burbling of the telephone on his bedside table. He picked up the receiver on the first ring without turning the light on. He listened as the switchboard operator explained. He said, "Put her on," as he sat up to put his feet firmly on the area carpet beside his bed, and turned on the light.

"Theresa? This is Willard Duke. What's the matter?"

He listened attentively as she explained the situation. His red hair was disheveled, his freckled jowls on his chin.

"There, there," he said sincerely from time to time. He interlocked his toes completely in a pattern with his feet up on their outer edges as he listened. "Now you say he'll die if he doesn't have the operation shortly." His southern drawl was unmistakable. "And Doctor Purvis is not available for some unknown reason?" He listened for a moment. "I see." He strained his eyes momentarily. "No I'm unaware of any investigation going on there right now. I'm sure that Randolph is perfectly safe in Mass Heart's capable hands." He scratched his privates. "Well of course. I'll tell you what I'm going to do. I'm on very good terms with the chairman of the board of Mass Heart and I know Doctor Purvis and his wife Patricia personally. Why don't you just leave this to little old me, and I'll make sure that this is properly taken care of by Doctor Purvis. Don't you worry about a thing. I'm on the job." He smiled a smile fit for a camera. "Yes. Good night Theresa. I'll get right on it."

He hung up and looked at his alarm clock. A quarter to three. For the first time since sitting up he noticed the chill of the air conditioning.

The governor ruffled up his pillows, turned off his light, lay down under his covers, and quickly fell into a deep sleep.

SIXTEEN

Nothing Peter Martins had heard on the radio had prepared him for what he was about to see.

Driving his dark blue Porsche along the divided, treed boulevard of Commonwealth Avenue Mall and further up the urban clutter of Brookline Ave. into Hospital Centre, he listened for details of the investigation. By the time he arrived at the parking garage he had sampled three news broadcasts and two talk shows. The final word: an important announcement was imminent.

What did that mean? Had a suspect been found, or had someone confessed, or were charges pending. Was it a big red balloon, or was it about Randolph Hobbs's surgery. Any news at this stage was going to be anticlimactic.

On entering the parking garage, he caught his first glimpse of the commotion around the hospital entrance. On leaving the garage and crossing the cobblestone corner, he came to a full appreciation.

The street curbs were lined with parked cars. Some of these were SUVs with media logos emblazoned on their sides, others were full size remote vans with tubular antennae extended into the sky. However, one car looked clearly out of place, a black Mercedes 600 sedan. Its orange and black New York plate read, "PRAY4U2."

Under the covered driveway was a melding mass of people, some medical types, the others obviously with the media. The other presence was the display of police force on the far side of the covered driveway.

Peter noticed the remote van belonging to BOS TV. He had watched their report at eleven the night before. He walked past the front of the van and followed the leash of cables from an opening behind the rear wheel well to a television camera on a tripod surrounded by three huddled men.

He pushed through the throng of people to get close to the BOS TV crew. One of the men leaned on his camera, smoking a cigarette. A second tended a large rack of lights that had been raised eight feet over the camera. The third man, obviously the director, held a clip board, and said to Peter as he approached, "Stay clear of the camera or enter the building quickly." He turned to talk to his crew.

Peter blended as best he could into the crowd of reporters and soon realized that his suit marked him. Given the level of tension of the media types, he could only be an outsider. Smokers greatly outnumbered non-smokers. There were many sideways glances. There was constant fidgeting with clipboards, adjustment and readjustment of camera lenses, repositioning of lights and microphones. More lit matches. More spent butts. This wasn't a battle ground in Afghanistan or the Middle East; this was a quiet, and until recently, a rather safe and respectable hospital in Boston. He almost expected to see sweat running in the cracks of the pavement. But then nobody noticed him. Could they see a tree in a forest, particularly a tree they hadn't focused on? What made them focus on anything in the first place?

The answer appeared. A man ran through the glass exit door into the covered drive of the hospital entrance; the hiss of the hydraulic door announced his coming. Lights went on and he spoke rapidly into a microphone, but he was too far away for Peter to hear.

More reporters followed. Then he saw her, running toward the glass door, on polished blue pumps, wrapped in a dark blue dress of conservative but adherent cut. The same reporter he had watched the night before.

All around, announcers were lining up in front of cameras. The covered driveway was becoming an electrified hive.

The BOS TV reporter ran up in front of the camera and stopped a practised fifteen feet from the lens. She produced a cordless microphone in her left hand. She preened her long black hair with her right hand, not unlike an athlete presented to the camera at the end of a heat.

The man with the clipboard waved her first to the right, then to the left, and inched her left again before giving the roll signal with his right index finger. The lights on the high bar popped to life and cast a surreal blue-white glow that bathed the announcer and extended all the way up to the hospital entrance. The man with the clip board held up his hand with all five fingers extended. He waved his upheld hand in a wide circle and folded his thumb. He circled his hand, folding a finger each time. The cue came when he dropped his hand.

She announced for the camera. "Good morning. This is Anne Maples at the Massachusetts Heart Institute." She paused. "The news is not good today."

Peter Martins moved in closer to the back of the camera and sighted down its view. Anne Maples appeared very direct and unemotional—she also looked very good. Behind her gleamed the chrome, the paint and the lights of a dozen Police Harleys. Behind them was the covered glass entrance of the hospital with motionless uniformed policemen standing on each side. The television lighting was so critical that Peter noticed imperfections in the concrete wall for the first time.

The reporter continued. "In the aftermath of the news of the investigation of thirty-four infant deaths comes news of another death. Late last night, Randolph, Hobbs, the forty-six-year-old Secretary of State for Health for the Commonwealth of Massachusetts, died at Boston's Massachusetts Heart Institute."

Peter's mouth fell open. He took a deep breath.

Anne Maples continued. "Details of Secretary Hobbs illness and death have not yet been released. What is known is that he was transferred to the Mass Heart Institute via helicopter from Provincetown, expecting to have emergency surgery performed last night by Doctor A Roy Purvis, this hospital's distinguished head of Cardiovascular Surgery. That surgery did not take place and no explanation for this has been given."

Peter suddenly needed to find out what had happened the night before. Why hadn't he been called? He wanted to get through those doors and get to the operating room lounge, now. He suddenly felt like an alien intruder at a media and police show, but decided to stay put until the reporter had finished.

She went on. "No further details have been released about the investigation into this institution's thirty-four alleged infanticides. However speculation that Doctor A Roy Purvis is somehow connected to the deaths is strengthened by his apparent disappearance."

With those words, the director pushed his earphone tight to his ear, straining to hear.

Peter looked around.

As Anne Maples prepared to continue speaking, the director glared at her and made an obvious cut sign across his throat. Her eyes acknowledged and she continued. "This is Anne Maples, reporting from the Massachusetts Heart Institute, for BOS TV."

The lights dimmed and Miss Maples walked determined down to the camera crew.

"Anne, honey, what are you doing?" said the director.

"Why was I cut, Phil?" she said with a calculated nonchalance.

Peter stayed a comfortable distance within earshot, but looked at another crew, hoping to remain unnoticed.

The director said, "Ted Weiner cut you himself. He was watching live at the studio."

"The bastard!" Her face turned red.

"Honey, honey, honey," Phil said. "We come here to get some important announcement, thinking that it's something to do with the dead babies. You waltz out in front of the camera and tell us Randolph Hobbs died here last night. Then you tell us that confirms speculation that Doctor A Roy Purvis, one of the best heart surgeons in the world, has disappeared."

"Fact Phil." She pointed her finger at him with contempt.

"Then you insinuate that somehow this whole thing is connected. That's too much fuckin' news all at once." He was breathing down on her. "Why didn't some of us know at least some of these facts before you blurted everything out on the air, live?"

"I have my sources." She was defiant, looking wide-eyed at Phil. "I don't have to explain this to you."

"But you have to explain it to Ted Weiner, honey. He's expecting you at the station right now." He paused a moment. "Take a cab."

SEVENTEEN

Peter Martins finally pushed his way past the throng of reporters and technical staff, and into the hospital lobby. A bewildered mob of hospital staff had been watching the media's high tech feeding frenzy, from behind the glassed entry area. Unlike fish in a restaurant's aquarium, they knew they were the object of the feast.

Peter took the elevator to the only place he wanted to be, the operating room. He changed into greens at his locker and went on to the surgeon's lounge.

Harold Williams, the chief of surgery, was in an animated conversation with Saul Greenberg, one of the other surgeons.

Peter approached Williams. "What the hell happened?" he said, "First this was about thirty-four babies; now there's Randolph Hobbs?"

Williams turned to Peter and said, "Nobody else is here yet. We've been discussing Hobbs. We're not sure."

Greenberg, a heavyset man with wavy hair, said, "Hopefully, we'll get to the bottom of this." He nodded upward, "Before they do."

Williams stroked back his great mane of white hair with his left hand and said, "We're waiting for Fowler to show up; he's in the building. So is Wittman. The real problem," and now he was wringing his hands, "is where the hell was, and is, Roy Purvis? And, if he's not here, then I may have to make another statement."

Peter recognised Williams's ego inflating. And the danger that held for Purvis. But why hadn't one of the administrators made a statement? Probably staying out of the pot?

"We should get the facts straight before we worry about another statement," said Peter. "I was called about this sometime after one this morning. At that time the angios had been done, and neither Maranghi nor Wittman had been able to locate Roy." Greenberg and Williams listened intently. "Seems that Mrs. Hobbs was insisting that Roy do the surgery, come hell or high water. Of course I made myself available, being the backup surgeon, but my offer was not accepted."

Williams nodded reflectively. "We can only wonder what happened after that."

The door at the far end of the OR lounge slammed open against the wall. Ian Scott strode in. "I heard what happened," he said. "So what *really* happened?"

The outside door burst open again. Eugen Wittman walked in looking unusually beaten and tired. He was followed by Grant Fowler, the cardiac surgery resident.

"Am I glad to see you." Eugen sighed with relief. "I have had to deal with that Hobbs woman all night. It was awful! She was so unreasonable. So determined. So convinced that Roy would show up. You must believe me, there was nothing we could do!"

Fowler, who was much younger than the rest of the group, looked especially haggard. Peter knew that he could be taken to task for every treatment decision made the night before. Williams crossed his arms on his chest, lowered his white eyebrows, and asked the inevitable. "So, Eugen, tell us what happened."

He wasted no time and brought everyone up to speed on how Hobbs had arrived, and how he had made the diagnosis.

When Eugen was finished, Williams asked, "Then, at any time prior to Hobbs's arrival, had Roy Purvis agreed to do the surgery?"

"*Nein*. We were waiting for the angiograms! We knew Roy wouldn't even consider operating on this one without angios. The aorta was just too tortuous."

Wittman's explanation seemed satisfactory. The group fell silent for a few moments.

"And what happened next?" said Peter.

"After I explained to the woman that we had another excellent surgeon standing by, she went off the deep end. Told me—Roy Purvis, or nobody."

"Yes? And then?" Peter wanting to look relentless.

"She demanded to make one telephone call," holding up a shaking finger, "vich she did."

"Who did she call?"

"Gentlemen," Eugen looked around, "she called the governor." He almost spat the words. "Governor Willard Duke." All eyes were fixed on him. "And after what seemed like a very appropriate discussion from my end, she told me that Governor Duke was taking charge of the matter *personally*, and *he* would get Doctor Purvis in here, *schnell*."

"Yes." Williams had peeled his great eyebrows up.

Peter could see Harold Williams's arteries pounding in his neck.

"Well, we waited for some time. I informed switchboard to watch for calls in case the governor or Roy Purvis called. I had them document my request! All this time her husband lay there. But—"

"But what?" Williams said, trembling.

Eugen shrugged, perplexed. "No calls ... No cards ... No letters."

"Then what?" Williams's eyebrows twitched uncontrollably.

Peter had learned to live with Harold under strain. But his facial contortions were beginning to wear on him.

"Then, after a time, we went to the ICU. That was well after 3 a.m. Of course we had already lowered his blood pressure with propranalol. We got it to about 90/50 with intravenous nitro, hoping that would keep the aneurysm from rupturing. But you know how that is; might as well pray. Maranghi stayed in the building and helped as much as he could, but he insisted this was a surgical problem, not a medical one."

"And he was bloody well right." said Williams, shaking, surveying the assemblage.

"Nobody can argue with your management," said Ian Scott. "I wish somehow that we could have been in on this much earlier, and that we could have changed the outcome.

Howevah. Every one of us here knows the danger of being second best, especially in the eyes of a relative. I don't think any one of us would'a jumped in on this one, given the mortality rate is about fifty percent. Even if we concede that it's only twenty-five to thirty percent here, that's still a considerable risk of goin' to court."

"Let alone the other complications." said Peter.

"Nobody can blame you for not rushing in, Peter." said Williams. "I hope you understand that."

Peter nodded, after he registered consensus.

Williams turned back to Eugen. "Then what happened?"

"We ran the case by the book. We gave Hobbs both colloid and crystalloid IV. We ran the drugs. We kept the pressure low. We kept him down with Versed, and ventilated him. We waited for Purvis or the governor to show up. We watched Mrs. Hobbs pace."

"And you documented that you had told Mrs. Hobbs another surgeon was available?"

"Of course." Eugen waved off the question.

Williams waited a moment. "When did he die?"

"At precisely 5:17 a.m. His pressure simply went to nothing and his pupils dilated after a brief ventricular tachycardia. There was nothing humanly to be done! Mrs. Hobbs was present. I informed her. Gave her my condolences. Then she went over me in such a rage, as if I was a devil." Eugen wiped his sweating brow with the left arm of his lab coat. "*Mein Gott!* I offered her the services of another fine surgeon." His gaze fell to the floor.

"Yes ...Yes?" Williams all impatient.

Eugen looked up. "And then she stormed the hell out of there, to where—I do not know. I phoned you, Harold, because you are the chief of surgery, and to tell you that I haven't found Roy. The next thing, all these media types who roll up at 7:30 this morning."

"And you tried all night to get Roy?" said Ian.

"Yes."

"Couldn't find him anywhere?"

"Not even at his new girlfriend's! We paged him steadily throughout the night." Eugen was trembling. He shook his finger. "The woman would not budge, I tell you."

"I think we all believe you, Eugen, in fact, I know we do," said Williams. "No one here faults your management. We would all have done the same."

"Right." said Ian. "We're all gonna back you guys."

"The question that is going to plague us to the end is what's happened to Roy? Where the hell is he?" Williams seemed overwhelmed. "And who the hell called the media in this morning?" He panned his colleagues. "I've got work to do. We should get a meeting ready with the chief of staff."

"But Harold," said Greenberg. "The warrant for the investigation forbids organized assembly in groups of three or more."

"That's right. Shit! Bloody legalities."

"We've got work to do, Peter," said Ian. He waited for Peter to nod. "Ah'll check on how my case is going. Fanconi is doing the anaesthesia so we shouldn't be more than twenty minutes or so."

"I'm taking a short walk," said Peter. He pulled on a blue lab coat and walked out the door.

Peter decided to retrace his steps from the day before. He walked over to medical records and found it cordoned off by two policemen. He left to walk up to the general administration offices. The hospital staff was still subdued. Not even a nod. He felt that familiar old anxiety again. Shut in. Hunted. He detested it. At the door to the administrative offices stood two more cops. They glared at Peter as he approached.

Peter looked them over, from their oppressive uniforms to their stern, impenetrable stares. He remembered Toronto, unable to speak out, wondering if his career would end, wondering who would be charged. He heard himself breathe. He knew he should leave now that there was nothing here for him to do. But he couldn't take the officers any longer.

Then he made his mistake.

Peter walked up to the closer of the two officers, who shifted back and forth as he approached, and said. "Who is the officer in charge?"

"Why would you want to know that?" The gaze, fixed and impassive.

"I have a few questions. I have some information."

"Lieutenant Rick Malloy is in charge. You can find him in the entry drive in an unmarked car."

"Big fellow?"

"You got it."

"Thanks." Peter turned and left.

***

When Peter Martins was out of earshot, the officer picked up his communicator from his belt. "Lieutenant Malloy, Lieutenant Malloy. This is Walsh."

The radio crackled. "Go ahead, Walsh."

"Some guy up here, tall, dirty blond hair, lab coat, looks like a doctor, wants to see you."

"Right."

"We sent him down."

"Check. I'll look for him."

"Lieutenant. Just thought I might add—sounds like he knows you."

"Oh." The radio crackled with city static. "That's interesting."

***

Peter Martins surveyed the entry drive, littered with media paraphernalia: cameras, tripods, and lights. The odd technician milling about. Waiting for something to feed on.

Just beside the entry door were the twelve Harleys. Five black and whites stood motionless, dispersed along the sidewalk, a silent, omnipresent vigil.

He immediately spotted the unmarked car among the media vehicles, not far from PRAY4U2, parked along the outside curb. He walked over, determined. Sure he was doing the right thing. As he walked, he focussed his thoughts, and could hear only his footsteps on the pavement. When he was within a car length of the unmarked car, the tall man in a grey suit quickly got out, leaned on the roof of the car, and watched Peter approach.

"Lieutenant Malloy?" said Peter.

"Who's asking?"

"I'm Doctor Peter Martins, Department of Cardiovascular Surgery." Peter extended his hand as he came around the corner of the car.

Malloy stood up straight, and, without accepting his hand, said politely, "May I help you?"

"Well, yes." Peter suddenly felt off guard. "This is a little awkward really."

"Um hmm." Malloy cocked his head.

"We were wondering, that is, the surgical staff and I, with this order contravening meetings of three or more, how are we to piece together this Hobbs thing? How are we supposed to work it out?"

"Well, for starters, Doctor, you should talk to the hospital lawyer. He's the one to advise you on that as long as my investigation's going on."

"That's all?" Peter shrugged feebly.

"That's all." said Malloy with official certainty.

Peter collected his fragmented thoughts. "There's one more thing. This baby thing wasn't a murder you know."

Malloy cocked his head again, not unlike a used car salesman appraising a potential buyer after the test drive and before the signing. "And, are you a forensic expert, Doctor Martins?"

"Well, no. But I'm a qualified cardiac surgeon with prior—"

Malloy interrupted with a wave of his hand. "How long have you been on staff here, Doctor?"

"Less than one year, but I served a fellowship, uh—advanced training here—some two years ago."

Malloy smiled as he looked at the pavement, shaking his head slowly. Then he looked up, dead serious, searching his jacket pockets. He produced a business card and wrote on it, handed it to Peter, and said. "Be at police headquarters tomorrow morning at 10:00 a.m. sharp to speak to Chief Inspector Dugan." He smiled broadly. "I'll tell him to expect you."

EIGHTEEN

Anne Maples looked at the bald spot on the back of Ted Weiner's head as he sat in his roller chair, overlooking a bank of television monitors. Beside him sat the editing technician.

She had taken a cab to the station as she had been told. Not the company car. A ride over some of the worst roads to blight North America in a car with no shock absorbers to speak of. In a cab with broken air conditioning and a wretched smelling back seat, each delightful odour capable of telling its own story of life in the city.

That arrogant son-of-a-bitch himself had probably seen to her getting the most loathsome taxi in Boston. He knew the SUV was there. She could have taken that. But no, Weiner was making a point. Registering his displeasure.

Well, one day soon, she'd do it. She knew the day wasn't far off when she'd go network and rub Ted's nose in the dirt.

And now she stood behind him in the darkened newsroom. Watching the producer monitor and cut his live feeds. She stood behind him, looking at nothing more than the polished bald spot on the back of his head.

"You want to speak to me, Ted?" she said loudly.

Ted Weiner swung around in his chair. He looked somewhat surprised. In fact he looked very surprised. Obviously he hadn't noticed the ghost of his star reporter's reflection in any of the sixteen television screens he had been working with. Weiner's silhouette in front of the wall of colour screens was that of a big man. He wore a black leather vest. He was momentarily speechless.

Anne smiled coyly. "I'm here, Ted. Speak to me."

"I was just waiting for Jim to come on with his live remote on the governor. I'm glad you're here." He turned to the technician. "Excuse us, please."

The technician left without a word.

"What's Jim talking to Duke about?"

"Rumors of a gas tax hike." A pause. "Let's get down to business." He waited for her nod. "I run a tight ship, Anne." He sighed. "To make a long story short, you had no right going live and tying A. Roy Purvis into the killings without talking to me first. You know what could happen to us? Do you want to spend the next five years in court?"

"You'll notice that I said suspected disappearance, Ted. I made no statement of fact."

"That's precisely the point." He glowered. "We're here to report facts not fiction. You start broadcasting assumptions and you know how long you'll have a news show? Which brings me to the next point. Where the be-Jesus did you come up with that in the first place, and why didn't I know? You have any idea the calls we been gettin' over that?" He went on. "You want to sit down at the switchboard and answer those calls yourself?"

"Why don't you just let me do my job?"

Ted Weiner smacked his right fist into his left palm. "Where the hell did Purvis's disappearance come from?" His face was red.

She leaned forward against a chair. "I had him watched."

"You what? Who?"

"Mitch Farber, the gumshoe. But I thought you knew." Sounding a little facetious. "Didn't you sign the requisition with your dailies the other morning?" She knew how carelessly Weiner signed his papers. He had the reputation of Father of the Newsroom. Like nobody had an original idea but him, or they'd speak to him first. What he didn't understand was that Anne Maples had no need for a father figure in her life, at least not a Ted Weiner father figure. Another Ted, perhaps, but not a Ted Weiner.

"Anne, you could have talked to me about this."

"I thought you knew." She threw up her hands. "But honestly, Ted, there just wasn't enough time."

"And you sent Mitch Farber?"

"You know as well as I do that Mitch can talk his way out of anything without being offensive. That's why I used him."

"To spy on a distinguished surgeon who is so far charged with nothing. Probably an infringement of privacy suit in there if you look hard enough. So what exactly did Mitch find?"

"Exactly nothing! Mitch parked in front of Purvis's house for less than two days and took shifts with his partner. Apparently Purvis drives a black Jaguar sedan. You know, one of the old types, real classy. The sort of thing you can't miss. Well, the long and the short of it is that Purvis's wife has been in and out with her Benz sports car. But he hasn't been around since Tuesday."

"And that's your evidence?" he said. "You call Mitch Farber off. Today."

"All right, but look." She was getting bored explaining. Wouldn't Ted have jumped to the obvious conclusion already? "At the news conference this morning, the chief of surgery, some guy named Williams. Hey, you ever want to meet the nutty professor from the *Back To The Future* movies, well that's him. He announces that Purvis wasn't available to do the surgery even though he was on call. I mean, put two and two together, Ted! I wasn't the only reporter saying that this morning. And you know that's true. It's just that I was the only one able to put two and two together, *because I had the other two.*" She smiled victoriously. "Now, what's wrong with that?"

Ted Weiner thought for a moment. "And how did you get onto Purvis in the first place?"

"Ted, don't you remember? That came out at the preliminary press conference that cop, what's his name ... Malloy ... gave when the investigation started. He told us that Roy Purvis was the surgeon in the majority of cases. He also said that was why the investigation was going to look at everybody who could possibly have had access to the kids; they didn't suspect Purvis. And of course, nobody from the press gave that out as a courtesy, to protect him." She smiled a self confident, victorious smile and squealed with delight as she flung her arms up. "I scooped them, Ted! I scooped them! What's wrong with that?"

"Only two things." Weiner looked at her gravely. The animated colour of the screens behind him cast angular shadows over his forehead and cheeks. "First, you didn't speak to me about it. Second, somebody else wants to know how you came to your conclusion. You have a mandatory appointment tomorrow morning at 10:30, with Inspector Roger Dugan at police headquarters. I regret that I have no choice but to take you off this story. As soon as Jim is done with the governor, I'm giving him the Mass Heart investigation, full time."

Anne Maples looked at Ted Weiner with total disbelief. "Oh, shit!"

NINETEEN

Peter Martins had helped Ian Scott with his case. The heart, which had been a straight forward quadruple bypass, had gone without a hitch. He hadn't mentioned his talk with the police. Obviously Lieutenant Malloy had made him nervous. So much so, that he perspired noticeably throughout the operation. He hoped no one had noticed. It seemed that everybody was preoccupied with other things.

Once finished, Peter had volunteered to help take the patient to the post-op ICU. He wasn't being generous. Rather, he wanted to speak to Frank Fanconi privately about a remark Frank had made during the operation.

The perfusionist had gone up in the elevator with them, so Peter had to wait until the care of the patient had been transferred to the intensivist.

When they were finally alone in front of the elevator doors, waiting to go down, Peter took Fanconi by the arm.

"Come over here a moment," he said, and directed him over to a large window looking east. Comfortably out of earshot of the elevator in case anyone should come along. Outside, Boston was brightly lit by the noon sun and the view was clear over the urban hubbub right to the Charles River.

"What's up, pal?" asked Fanconi.

"Do you remember when Ian was sewing the uppers you made a comment about Roy Purvis disappearing?"

"No."

Martins was disappointed. "Well, didn't I hear you say something about him disappearing?"

"No. What I said was that he had gone sailing."

"What?" Peter couldn't help but look perplexed. "Sailing? How do you know?"

"Mel Finegold told me yesterday. In the OR lounge. I thought he said he left the day before."

"How would he know?"

"I thought he and Roy are neighbors. Doesn't he have a telescope?"

Peter left without saying goodbye and quickly ran down the steps back to the operating room. After asking the head nurse, he found Mel Finegold scrubbing at a sink for a laser cone on an Arabian princess.

"You choose your patients well." said Peter.

"Comes with the territory. What can I do for you?"

"Frank Fanconi said you saw Roy Purvis go sailing. Is that true?"

"I saw him leave. Watched him go with the telescope Tuesday afternoon." Finegold looked disappointed. "You remember my telescope don't you?"

"Of course I do. You sure it was him?"

"Yeah." He winced. "Only one Hinckley sets out from Nahant. As a matter of fact, I could almost make him out. There's no doubt it was him. Besides, I've never seen him lend his boat."

Peter pulled him closer and spoke softly into his ear. "You realize that people are starting to think he's disappeared! Where have *you* been?"

"I was off. This is all news to me. I heard about the investigation into the kids, and I gather they're all upset about some Secretary of State who wouldn't have an operation, but that's all I know." Finegold was sounding upbeat. "Actually, I was going to find out more just as soon as we were done. One thing is for certain."

"What?"

"People around here sure are quiet now."

"Did you see the cops and the media out the main entrance this morning?"

Finegold looked surprised. "No. Just one cop. But I came in around seven."

"They must have arrived after you. Let me fill you in."

"Please."

Peter gave the whole story again "Along with the investigation comes a restraining order. Seems they're afraid of a cover-up. I don't know. But they're taking admin medical records and the staff office apart. We have no access." Peter looked around. "And apparently Roy operated on most of the kids."

Finegold turned to Peter and let his palms open in one of his expansive gestures. "That only makes sense, 'cause he's the main man for pediatric cardiac surgery too." The pink scrub solution dripped onto the floor. "So?"

"Well, nothing until last night. Roy was on call when Hobbs, the Secretary of State, came in, and they couldn't find him."

"Now Peter, that's very disappointing." Finegold pointed his foamy finger at Martins nose and said, "Either Roy was on call and he shouldn't have been sailing, or what is much more likely, he was sailing and wasn't really on call. I mean, I've known him for years and he has never, ever, welched on his responsibility. But you know that yourself." Finegold looked dead serious. "I suggest you look for a misprint on the call schedule."

"Good point. But that doesn't explain why Roy bumped everybody's cases for two days to get his own done, and then left, vanished without a trace. I mean he could have told us he needed to leave."

"I didn't know about that either," said Finegold in a defeated tone.

"That's what happens when you're not here full time. But you're absolutely certain he was off sailing the day before yesterday?"

"One hundred per cent!"

"All right then. Let's keep this conversation private, and don't tell anyone else you saw him sailing off," said Peter quietly.

"Fine with me." Finegold continued scrubbing. "I think we should give old Roy the benefit of the doubt."

***

Patricia Purvis was becoming increasingly irritated. Her doorbell had just chimed for the fourth time. She tied her white bath robe firmly with a double knot, unwilling to divulge to anyone the fact that she sunbathed on her sheltered deck, naked. And why should she?

She opened the door on two perspiration soaked men wearing suits. Dark blue suits.

"Good day, uh, Mrs. Purvis?" said the heavier man.

"Yes." Her cautious response was almost a question.

"I'm special agent Wills. My ID." He held up a laminated plastic card with an attached brass shield.

Patricia might as well have been slapped across her face with the shield. She could see only three letters. FBI. She took a deep breath, tightened her waist string even more, and hoped neither of these two, excessively hot men would question her dressing habits. "Yes," she said pleasantly.

Wills continued. "This is Mr. Rokowski of the IRS." He waited a moment, leaning forward like a school boy with his hands clasped, almost apologetic. He smiled. Then he said, "May we speak to your husband?"

The topic of Roy changed her attitude completely. Patricia snapped back. "He's not here." She knew that she had better soften up. "May I help you?"

"Mrs. Purvis." Agent Wills assumed an earnest attitude. "When can we speak to your husband?"

"I don't know. He hasn't been home for days. May I ask what this is all about?" She leaned against the door, holding an edge with one hand.

"Frankly Mrs. Purvis, we're not sure your husband has done anything wrong. We're here on a routine check."

"Then does this have anything to do with the investigation at Massachusetts Heart Institute?"

Wills looked at Rokowski who was clutching his hat. "No, ma'am. What investigation?"

She hesitated. "The infant death thing."

"No, ma'am."

She hesitated again. "Then exactly what is this about?"

"Mrs. Purvis, do you know anything about your husband's investments?"

"Other than the fact that he has a lot of them, nothing."

"I see." Wills paused to consider. "Then you know nothing about his redemption?"

"No, gentlemen." She decided to be bold. "I can only assume you're not talking about his holy redemption." She smiled and folded her arms on her chest.

"Ma'am," Wills said, "your husband sold almost twenty million dollars worth of securities only two days ago."

The hot summer breeze rustled the leaves of the great elms across the street.

"So?"

"We were notified under the mandatory reporting rules."

"So?" Patricia shrugged impatiently. "Is there anything wrong with that?"

"No. Not yet," said Wills. "The problem is that the money was transferred electronically by your husband from his broker to a local bank and from there to a bank in Nassau, Grand Bahamas. From there it was transferred again, we think, to the Caymans."

"Exactly what is the problem with that?"

"Nothing, ma'am, except that certain taxes are due."

"Then I am sure that you will find those taxes paid on my husband's next return. How many months does he have to file, eight?"

"But didn't you say, ma'am, that you haven't seen your husband for days?" said Wills. "And what is this investigation about?"

"Oh look. I'm quite sure it's all about nothing." She paused and reflected for a moment. *Roy may be a lot of things but—*

"So Mrs. Purvis, did your husband keep any other accounts?"

"Just his personal bank account."

"At Bay Bank?" said Wills.

"Yes, I think so."

"Did you keep any joint accounts?" Rokowski asked eagerly.

"No. Of course not." Patricia scowled at the IRS agent. The nerve, thinking that Roy Purvis would have a joint account with anybody.

"Does this house have joint title?" asked Rokowski.

Patricia smiled with satisfaction. "Gentlemen, it's all mine." Then she looked severely at the two sweaty champions of federal responsibility and said, "Good day," and slammed the door.

She leaned her back against the door until she felt certain that the two men had gone. She sighed with relief.

Whatever was going on with Roy, she was sure it wasn't friendly. First the investigation was all over the media. Then he didn't come home. Now this. Her head spun with the possibilities.

Roy certainly wasn't a killer. He was a liar, a cheat, and a philanderer. If hard pressed, she might agree that he was a minor felon, but then after all, he was a surgeon. Roy had always insisted the legal title to the home be hers, and he had made regular deposits to her bank account. She smiled again, secure in the knowledge that Roy had, in his own way, taken care of her very well. She wouldn't change her mind. Roy wasn't a killer.

The thing that she had to do now was to get some of this squared away. There was no telling where Roy had gone. She would call the hospital. And speak to whom? The thought was actually scary. Roy would find in a pinch that he had more enemies than he thought. Who would she call?

The answer came to her. She would call that new surgeon. Roy had liked him. Didn't she remember Roy saying he trusted and respected him? She couldn't be sure, yet somehow felt she was. What was his name? Peter Martins?

TWENTY

Peter left his car curbside in front of police headquarters. He didn't bother with a meter; there weren't any. The irregular streets were littered with police cars of every possible description, abandoned in every known mode of parking disobedience, and some that he didn't know existed. Here in the Mecca of modern medicine there was potential for a meter maid convention!

No yellow wheel clamps here.

From the front steps of police headquarters, Peter's car looked out of place, not because it was a blue Porsche 991, but mainly because it was so neatly parked by a curb. He would probably get a ticket.

Before he turned to climb the wide, concrete steps up to the brass entry doors he caught one more thing.

Across the street was a restaurant. A most unusual looking restaurant situated on a corner with green canvas awnings supported by nothing less than polished brass rails. A brass circle five feet in diameter hung above the door heralding the Round The Clock Restaurant.

What really held his attention was the appearance of two men, who sauntered out the front door with obvious familiarity, and then parted ways. They were as different as night and day! The tall one with black hair was gaunt and carried himself with pride. He wore dark blue trousers and a light blue, long sleeved shirt with gold braid above the shoulders. He quickly picked a path through the dead zone of abandoned cruisers and strode past Peter up the steps to Headquarters. He noted the surgeon's presence, but did not acknowledge him. Peter recognized Chief Hawkins immediately.

The other man was harder to fix because he had turned and walked away after he had shaken the chief's hand. He was much shorter and wore brown pants, and what looked like a brown and beige hounds tooth jacket. He ambled with his head down. What struck Peter was his thinning red hair.

Peter walked up to the station's brass doors and found that they yielded with resistance. Then there was a step and a great oak door with a glass centre. He walked over to a dark podium with an elevated globe light at each end.

The large duty sergeant, with his three stripes and three chins, leaned forward and demanded, "State your business."

"I'm Doctor Peter Martins from the Massachusetts Heart Institute. I have an appointment with Inspector Dugan." He stood tall, but not tall enough for his six-foot frame to get a look at the sergeant's desk.

The sergeant peered down through his wire-rimmed semi-lunars, turning some pages in a large ledger. Peter could hear the stubble on his folded chins chaff his blue collar, even in the busy entry hall.

"Ah yes." he said at last. "Inspector Dugan is expecting you." He looked down his glasses with a certainty that Peter had seen before. "Take the elevator to the third floor. Someone will help you there."

"Thank you."

The sergeant handed a blue badge marked "Visitor" to Martins. "Wear this at all times in the building."

Peter took the laminated tag and pinned it onto his blazer. "I will."

He walked over the dark terrazzo to the brass elevator door. What was imposing was the door's brass frame which had to be six inches wide. Looking closely he noted its elaborate leaf scroll. He pushed the elevator button and fought off the urge to touch the patterned brass. Glancing over his shoulder, he saw the duty sergeant frowning on his interest.

The door opened to let him in. He rode up with a sound he identified with his youth, possibly from an old department store lift.

He thought about the Round The Clock Restaurant. The brass a nod to tradition. What would the restaurant serve? Irish whiskey, of course, around the clock, but only most discreetly. Would the discussions at the table touch on tradition, or on more contemporary concerns?

The elevator door glided open. Time to focus!

On the third floor, the duty desk was more modest and of oak which had turned golden with age. A courteous dark haired female pointed him to a glassed-in office on the opposite side of the large, busy room. Peter passed through a gate in an oak railing and chose a path through the many old desks in the centre of the room. He was afforded the odd glance which was quickly deflected by his blue "Visitor" shield.

The room was an odd mixture of old and new with antique desks and cabinets, shiny computers and an egg crate ceiling. But the smell!

He approached a decrepit, unkempt young man who was handcuffed to a chair beside a desk. His denims looked hard from duty, and his dirty blond hair lay oily and limp past his shoulders. The odour of old booze and excrement strengthened as he neared the pathetic soul. Peter looked back and saw the derelict's vacant eyes track him across the room.

Finally, he stood in front of the glass-in-wood door. "Chief Detective" was etched in white capitals across the middle of the glass.

Peter rapped just loud enough. Roger Dugan looked up and beckoned him to come in. He stood up to meet the doctor, and placed his hands in his pockets. Peter closed the door carefully and turned to meet the chief detective.

Dugan was about an inch taller than himself, and looked fit, if a bit loose around the middle. He had on a short sleeved sport shirt and beige pants. His hair reflected the colour of the fluorescent lighting over head with only a perfunctory glint of red. He peered at Martins intently.

"Please sit down, Doctor Martins," said Dugan, as he gestured to the old leather sofa with his left hand.

Dugan betrayed a bit of surprise on meeting the doctor. The reason wasn't obvious.

Peter sat down. "You wanted to see me."

"That's right."

"May I ask why?"

Dugan sat down in his creaky oak rocker. "We're going to be interviewing a lot of Mass Heart staff. After you spoke to Lieutenant Malloy, you seemed like a good place to start." Dugan opened a notepad, laid it on his desk and placed his pen across the pages. "Your name, place and date of birth, please?"

"Peter Martins. Toronto, Ontario. January 30, 1978."

"Really!" He sounded surprised. "How long have you been here? You're not an American Citizen?"

Peter immediately felt annoyed, but what could he do? He thought he should be completely open. "I grew up in Toronto, went to school, and got my medical degree there. I first came to Boston in June, three years ago, to be Doctor Purvis's fellow. I worked under him for one year." He decided to add, "On an educational visa. I returned to Boston this spring on a work visa. To be precise, I arrived on April 2nd. I am not an American citizen."

"Your occupation?"

"I'm a heart surgeon."

Dugan was noting some details and continued as he wrote. "So you came to Boston to train under Doctor Purvis's supervision?"

"Yes."

"Did you operate with Doctor Purvis?" Dugan looked squarely at Peter. "Did you take care of patients for Doctor Purvis post-operatively?"

"Yes." Peter could feel the tension coming.

"Did you operate on any children with Doctor Purvis?" He seemed to reflect for a moment and continued, "Specifically, did you operate on any children under age five?"

Peter sighed. "Yes."

"Could you speak up please, Doctor?" The discomfort that came with the success of Dugan's questioning brought a trace of a smile to his face.

"Yes," he said aloud.

"And did any of these children die within a week of operation?"

"Yes, of course." Peter leaned forward. "Pediatric cardiac surgery is a very high risk area—"

Dugan held up his hand. He asked calmly and deliberately. "Did any of the children on whom you operated die of digoxin poisoning?"

"Of course not."

Dugan raised his voice. "You're quite sure that none of the children who died in your care died of digoxin overdose? I caution you, Doctor." Dugan lowered his voice. "Nobody is accusing you of wrong doing." He barely smiled. "I'm simply trying to establish what you might say if our investigation uncovered the fact that you and Doctor Purvis had operated on a child who we subsequently showed *had* died of digoxin overdose." He leaned back in his creaky chair and propped his chin pensively on the back of his hands.

Peter chose his words carefully. "In that case, I'd have to talk to a lawyer first." He looked defiantly at the police officer.

Dugan smiled again. "A wise move." He continued after a moment. "How many children did you operate on with Doctor Purvis?"

"I ... I can't recall. Quite a few. That's one of the things I came to Boston for. To work on children with Doctor Purvis. He is a recognized, international authority on pediatric cardiac surgery."

"Yes. So I understand. But tell me, did you call the coroner after any of the children's deaths?"

"I don't recall. Maybe I did."

"Maybe you did." He smiled broadly. "What did you do after your year with Doctor Purvis?"

"I returned to Toronto where I took on a job as a staff cardiac surgeon while working on my research which was in excimer lasers."

"And how did you return to Boston, Doctor?"

"I was asked to join the Massachusetts Heart Institute a little under one year ago by Mr. Abel."

"Oh yeah?"

"I agreed, and a short time later I got a permanent work visa."

"Not happy in Toronto, Doctor?" said Dugan.

"It wasn't that." Peter felt reviled. "The opportunity to become part of a team like Mass Heart's, only comes once in a lifetime. For most doctors it never comes. It was one great step for me."

"You and a few others." Dugan looked apathetic. "It appears that the staff at Mass Heart comes from all over the world."

"Yes they do."

"You wonder why they have to do that when there are so many good American doctors?" Dugan looked perplexed.

"They bring together the best from everywhere, sir. To establish an international centre of excellence." He didn't know why he had to explain this, and hoped his words weren't lost on the inspector. "Like athletes on a sports team, these are now the great American doctors."

"Humph." Dugan shrugged. "Have you operated on any children in the last few months? I mean here in Boston?"

"Yes. Six or seven."

Then the next question.

"Have any of them died?"

"No. Of course not." Peter realized the very moment after he said "not," that Inspector Dugan had known the answer to that question.

Dugan seemed engrossed in his notebook. He slowly looked up at Peter Martins, looking him over.

"Doesn't that somehow strike you as odd?"

Peter was unhappy with the argument's conclusion. "Sometimes, particularly in surgery, luck comes in runs."

"Doctor." Roger Dugan leaned forward with his elbows on his desk and looked severely at Peter. "The concept of luck at an international centre of excellence doesn't impress me."

Peter was silent.

Finally Dugan said, "When did you last see Doctor Purvis?"

Peter thought to get his facts straight. "Tuesday morning."

"What was Doctor Purvis doing?"

"Operating."

"Isn't it true that Doctor Purvis cancelled your cases, as well as the cases of your colleagues, in order to get his operations done? And isn't it true that neither you nor anyone else at Mass Heart has seen him since?"

"The first part is true. I can't vouch for the second."

Dugan raised his brows. "Doesn't it strike you as odd, Doctor, that Secretary of State for Health, Hobbs, died waiting for Doctor Purvis to show up."

"I would have done that operation—"

Dugan cut him off. "But Doctor Purvis was on call! Why didn't he answer his call?"

Peter was overcome with the idea that Roy's fate was sealed and delivered, most likely to the devil. A red haired devil gone grey! "I don't know."

Inspector Dugan smiled at Peter and said reassuringly, "I don't think you need a lawyer, yet."

Peter gathered his thoughts together and remembered suddenly what he had wanted to tell the police. "But, Inspector, those children weren't murdered. They—"

"Doctor Martins." Dugan suddenly seemed angry and impatient. "Are you also an expert in forensic medicine?"

"No. But—"

"You see what the sign says on my door?" Dugan waved toward the door. "It says Chief Detective, Doctor. There was hostility in his voice. "That means *I ask the questions*. I have forensic experts at my disposal who will determine whether or not these children have been murdered. This is my jurisdiction." He drove the words home with a glaring pause. "Do I make myself clear?"

"Yes, Inspector, quite clear."

"Good." Dugan got up and put his hands in his pockets. "You may go. I would caution you not to divulge our conversation to anybody." He looked piercingly at Peter. "I would caution you also that you may be questioned again." He waited a moment for Peter to get up. "You've been most helpful. Goodbye."

There was nothing else to say, except, "Goodbye." He let himself out the door.

As he crossed the large duty room, he was met again with stares. This time at his face. Seeing what Dugan had done to him? Peter ignored them. He had just learned something of the workings of the police mind, and didn't like it. He was glad he hadn't brought up Mel's sighting of Roy's boat. For that matter, he was glad he hadn't brought up Patricia Purvis's telephone call either. But then, if the FBI and the IRS had been to Roy's house, Dugan probably knew about it. He probably knew about the money too. The cascade of events began to look like one massive grave was being dug for Roy.

Peter looked back and saw Roger Dugan watching him cross the room. Probably planning his next line of questions. He pushed the button by the elevator door.

In the lobby, Peter was just removing the visitor badge from his lapel as an attractive woman walked through the inner door and approached the desk sergeant.

"Anne Maples to see Inspector Dugan," she said.

Peter looked at her, surprised.

"Yes," said the sergeant. "Miss Maples, you're a bit early but go upstairs to the third floor. Someone will help you there." He handed her the badge Peter had just returned. "Wear this at all times in the building."

"I will." She turned then to go to the elevator and noticed that Peter was staring at her. "Wait a minute," she said to him, "I know you." She shook her finger at him and smiled. "Yesterday morning at Mass Heart. In the crowd."

"You got it." Peter found her smile luscious.

She offered her hand. "I'm Anne Maples, and you are?"

"Peter Martins. Doctor Peter Martins. I'm a heart surgeon at Mass Heart."

"Really! What brought you here so soon?" The question brought a sparkle to her eyes.

"Same as you," Peter feigned a whisper.

The sergeant raised a brow.

"May we talk?" Peter said, as he gently took her left arm and led her over to the elevator, trying to get out of the sergeant's range of hearing. "May I ask why Dugan has you here? You're a reporter."

"Just routine."

"Nothing Dugan does is routine. If it was, he would have called you on the phone."

"Oh?" She pivoted coyly with her hands clasped behind her back.

"Let's be honest," said Peter. "I'm guessing you got cut yesterday morning when you told people that Doctor Purvis was missing." She blushed. "Only a few people knew that, and I don't think Dugan was one of them, up until that point."

The desk sergeant was leaning forward looking disapproving. He cleared his throat loudly.

Peter leaned close and spoke quietly into her ear. "If I'm right, you're in trouble. I'm in trouble too, and nobody but nobody knows what the hell is going on." He noticed her thick, softly curved ear lobe. Her wavy, jet black hair was draped over back and fell onto her shoulder. Her ear twitched. "I think we better meet and talk things over real soon."

Anne turned to him revealing her full lips as she said, "You're right." She looked at the sergeant who was squinting with his head slightly cocked. "Tonight?"

Peter nodded, affirmative.

"Meet me at Club 53, let's say, 8:30?"

"Sounds good to me," said Peter. "I'll see you there."

Anne turned and walked into the waiting elevator. Peter remarked at the fit of her above-knee, gray, two-piece suit. The brass elevator door closed and she was gone with an old fashioned whir.

Peter suddenly felt lighter. He smiled as he walked past the duty sergeant to the doors. The sergeant held himself leaning forward on his arms, watching him walk out. Peter turned momentarily and waved with his finger tips as he passed through the glass inner door.

He stopped on the outer steps of police headquarters and looked around. Now. Where was his car? Should he expect a ticket or a yellow boot?

TWENTY-ONE

Samuel Attersly sat in front of Richard Cummings's polished mahogany desk. No matter how hard he tried to look away, the lexan cube near the edge of the desk held his eyes captive. Odd, he thought, how a fatigued mind could be captivated by something unrelated to the business at hand.

The investigation was now into its second day and he had been pouring over the charts of the thirty-four dead children at police headquarters. At least that was what he had been doing at night.

Most of his days had been spent over at Massachusetts Heart Institute, sifting through new information on other questionable deaths. In all, eighteen additional cases had shown up. The problem was that the investigative flag would pull up a case that had expired with a high digoxin level. So he'd have to make a judgment call on whether to look at the whole chart or not. The digoxin levels weren't high enough to be lethal, but they were in a range to slow down anybody's heart, even a large healthy man's heart. Attersly had decided to look at these cases carefully, later.

He had shuttled back and forth between Massachusetts Heart Institute and police headquarters several times both days.

Downtown, he had helped the detectives coordinate the medical information on the death charts with the hospital's day to day information. It had become clear that the detectives, no matter what their calibre as police officers, didn't really understand the fundamentals of medicine, or, hospital organization. The cause and effect in medicine weren't always as obvious as the evolution of a patient's illness. He had stretched the analogy of the two birds touching down on a pond. One did so because it was full of lead shot, the other on its own. There was no need to retrieve the latter. Keeping them on track made his job more difficult. But they were eager!

He had gotten little time except at night, to look at the charts of the dead children in detail. However, he was formulating an opinion.

And now he sat hunched over his boss' desk, unable to take his eyes off that cube containing nine spent forty-five calibre bullets. He sat in his wrinkled jacket which had become terminally deformed with Boston's heat and his perspiration. His pants had bagged and lost their shape. At least he had managed to change his shirt and underwear. He had not admitted into consciousness the concept of body odour.

The main door opened quietly and Doctor Richard Cummings walked in. He had each of his index and middle fingers in his trouser pockets, parting his charcoal suit jacket and showing off the gold chain in his vest.

"Samuel, how goes the battle? You look beat."

Attersly had been caught off guard.

"Don't get up," Cummings said. "Save your energy for something useful." He sat down. "Now, tell me about it."

"Well, a lot has happened. First, let me say that Dugan's people are doing a great job. Especially his computer kids. First rate. If we ever have a problem, I hope we can borrow them. The rest of his crew, the detectives, they take direction very well. And so," he nodded, "things are coming together."

"Do say."

Cummings's thin, expectant smile, his moustache and voice reminded Attersly of a forties movie.

"First, I want to consider the cause of death. I've looked at the complete charts of the thirty-four kids in detail. All, except one, had surgery by Doctor Purvis. There's another fellow who was in training at Mass Heart who figures into eleven cases. A surgical fellow named Peter Martins."

"You mean doing a surgical fellowship?"

"Yes. Dugan's people say he's a Canadian. The last death from that group was a patient of a surgeon named Voorman. Now, Roy Purvis is the undisputed king of cardiovascular surgery at Mass Heart. He also holds that title with respect to children's surgery. That much isn't new." Attersly bowed his head slightly, making his tone somber, and whispered to Cummings, "You know he appears to be missing?"

"Um hmm," Cummings nodded slowly, smiled, leaned forward, and rubbed his hands together.

"Well, here's the interesting part. In all the cases, the serum digoxin levels rise post-operatively to high normal. In some cases they become toxic. However, the dates on the lethal reports are all after the date the patient expired. That is, the day they were reported, not the day they were taken."

"Yes?" There was an uncertainty, an uneasiness in Cummings's voice.

"That means two things. First. The report was not available to the attending staff or the pathologist prior to autopsy. The delay was thirty-six to forty-eight hours."

"Why?"

"Because the digoxin levels were done at another lab. That leads me to the second point. The lethal levels were not on the chart yet, in the eight cases that were referred to the coroner's office, that is."

"Isn't that interesting?" Cumming's voice smoothed out and he smiled thinly. "And nobody went back to look?"

"No." He paused. "Strictly speaking, none of these cases were coroner's cases. There was some crossover on the reporting rules and I think those that were reported were done out of a sense of completeness rather than a legal need or perceived urgency. You see?"

Cummings leaned back in his chair. "So the levels wouldn't have been on the chart when they were reviewed by the attending coroner?"

"Right. And Mass Heart is so quick with its autopsies that the pathologist probably wouldn't have seen the late levels either. But I'm looking into that one."

Cummings got it. "So here we have a group of post-op deaths with nothing suspicious on the charts, so they just get rung through as no flag cases."

"Absolutely." said Attersly.

"Then the worst this office can be accused of is not following up on unsuspicious deaths that didn't require reporting in the first place." He thought a moment and rambled on with his head turned to the ceiling. "And in these recessionary times, we could easily make a case for not spending any more money than we had to." Cummings looked back down and smiled broadly. "That is very good news, indeed."

"Now. My understanding is that no post-mortem digoxin levels were taken at autopsy. That might be reason enough to call the D.A. and get orders to exhume the bodies."

"I think that's all he'll need." Cummings's voice rang with satisfaction. "Where are you going from here?"

"Well, I'm back to police headquarters to get down to the nitty-gritty of sorting this thing out."

"Do you need help? You look tired."

Attersly rejected the idea. "Now that the primary sorting of data has been done, things will move at a much more sedate pace. I'll be all right."

"Samuel. I won't forget you." He extended his hand.

Attersly got up. He hesitated a moment, looking at the cube on the desk. "Before I go, would you mind telling me where those bullets came from? I've always wondered."

Cummings picked up the lexan cube. "They came out of a man's head. They have crosses etched in their tips. The defence was that the fellow had been shot from several different directions by more than one assailant. Indeed, he was shot from nine different directions. He was quite a crook." Cummings held the case up to the light. "Anyway. I had the forensic office do detailed ballistics on the bullets. Well, a 45 ACP is a low velocity bullet. Not only did all the bullets remain in the victim's skull, but not a single bullet mushroomed."

Attersly waited patiently for the point.

"Our evidence was accepted in court. All the bullets came from the same pistol. His wife's."

***

Judge David Lowenstein's prominent nose hung over the edge of a cup of coffee and inhaled the soothing vapours. Every cup made the connection to his youth, when as a law student, reading late into the night, coffee had become his friend.

Now he took another whiff of the French roast. But the aroma couldn't draw his attention away from the business at hand; the investigation at Massachusetts Heart Institute.

He had been expecting Mitchell Silver for some time, but due to the late hour, assumed he had become bogged down in traffic. Mitchell Silver represented the hospital by way of the firm of Chow, Low & Spiegel.

In spite of a name that evoked images of a Chinese firm working in the garment district with a token Jew for the shingle, they had excellent credentials. Lowenstein knew that their chief stock in trade was corporate work with Pacific Rim companies. An agenda well served by third and fourth generation American Orientals. However, to legitimize the firm, there came Abe Speigel. He was a distinguished New York City trial lawyer who figured prominently in the courts, and in the social register. Abe Speigel had brought all of his talented people with him and placed the firm squarely at the top of the heap, even in New York City.

Mitchell Silver was one of Abe's younger stars from the medico-legal division of the firm, the division that served U.S. Medical Hospital Enterprises and, by way of extension, the Massachusetts Heart Institute. Silver had already distinguished himself in court on several occasions that Lowenstein knew about.

When the knock finally came on the door, David Lowenstein was relieved to stop his musing. "Come in," he said.

A large man let himself quietly through the door. He walked deliberately and respectfully over to the dark Louis XIV desk where the judge sat.

He was a big man, easily two hundred and forty pounds. His jowls blended into a large double chin that hung over his starched white collar. He wore unflattering black-rimmed glasses and combed his dark wavy hair back. His suit was plain charcoal grey with natural shoulders. Even his tie was understated, a blue floral pattern on dark gray. He was bereft of any adornments.

His appearance was deceiving, but Lowenstein knew instantly, by Silver's obvious deference to tradition and his lack of adornment, that here stood one power house of a lawyer. He stood up and said, "Mr. Silver?"

Mitchell Silver extended his hand. "Judge Lowenstein. I'm so very pleased to meet you."

They shook hands. Silver towered over Loewenstein by at least eight inches.

"Won't you sit down?" The judge motioned to the chair opposite him at the desk. "May I offer you a cup of coffee?"

"Yes, thank you. The coffee smells wonderful." Silver took the chair.

Lowenstein walked over to his paneled cupboard in the corner, opened it, and poured a cup full of coffee.

"How do you take yours?" he asked.

"Black. Thank you."

"Ah, same as me." He walked back with the white cup on a saucer and placed it on the desk in front of Silver. "Now. How may I help you?"

"As you know, I am here on behalf of the Massachusetts Heart Institute by way of U.S. Medical Hospital Enterprises who retain my firm." He took a sip.

"I am aware of that."

"We are having some difficulty Your Honor, with your warrant and the accompanying restraining order." He waited politely for a moment. "The one that forbids meetings of more than three hospital staff or administrators at one time."

"I am familiar with the order." Lowenstein peered over his spectacles with his hooded eyes.

"I assure you that my client is not attempting to obstruct the process of the law, however, we feel that certain needs have to be met."

"Such as?"

"The kind of medicine that goes on at the Massachusetts Heart Institute is often of the most highly specialized nature. This applies to physician and nursing input. Often this level of service requires a consultative process between members of health care teams before the correct course of action can be found."

"And are you suggesting that the restraining order limits the consultative process?"

Mitchell Silver looked relieved. He smiled. "Exactly."

"Let me explain," said Lowenstein. "The restraining order is not intended to hamper patient care at the institute. It is intended to hamper covert meetings that might interfere with the due process of law. For instance, it is intended to prevent meetings of a type that might lead to the removal or erasure of evidence."

"We fully appreciate your intent. However, we feel that the implication is that if indeed there were murders at the hospital, that they were committed by a group of individuals. Frankly Your Honor, we cannot fathom that to be so. If there is a culprit, he or she must surely have been working alone. Therefore, I would suggest that the restraining order might be too severe. In fact it may do little more than hamper patient care."

Judge Lowenstein took a moment to ponder this, but said nothing. He would have to be careful and fair.

"You see, Your Honor, I find it difficult to fathom there being any murders here at all."

"Then just how do you explain the deaths and the digoxin levels?"

"I agree that all of this looks very suspicious. I can only say that there must, there simply *must*, be another explanation."

"Well, when you find another explanation, which you did not see fit to do before this investigation started, will you let me know?"

Silver continued in as conciliatory a manner as he could. "Of course we have no explanation to date. But surely we must ask ourselves what is the possible motive for such a mass murder?"

"Mr. Silver, I am not at that stage of my thinking yet. To be perfectly blunt, I am having great difficulty getting adjusted to the idea of mass murders at the institute. Period! I would go so far as to say that I can't believe it's true."

"Yes." Silver nodded agreement.

"However, I have the unfortunate task of having to explain to the citizens of Massachusetts how thirty-four children ended up dead with severely elevated digoxin levels. That is not easy Mr. Silver. Do you understand my predicament?" Silver nodded acquiescence. "If there was another way to resolve this matter I would entertain it. But, other than having the police get all the facts together, and then turning them over to forensic experts for analysis, I can see no way out of this."

"I see," said Silver, humbly. He sipped his coffee.

Lowenstein continued. "The problem is compounded by the convenient disappearance of the surgeon who operated on most of these children." He waited for a moment to let the gravity of the situation sink in. "I know Doctor Purvis and his wife Patricia, personally. I can't conceive how he might be involved in such a thing. However, stranger things have happened."

Mitchell Silver looked deadpan at the judge. "Then I take it that you will not reverse your order to limit the assembly of hospital staff?"

"Mr. Silver! You have recourse to the Supreme Court. Bear in mind that the fact finding portion of this investigation will be over within one or two days. Remember also the old maxim. Justice must not simply be done. Justice must appear to be done. I am afraid that under the circumstances, I cannot help you."

***

Roger Dugan looked around the third floor meeting room at police headquarters. He was looking at his people, the detectives, the black and whites moving the paper copies. Samuel Attersly interpreting results. Everyone else was huddled around the old oak table with their laptops; Dugan at the head with Walters, the D.A., on his left. He was satisfied he'd got them their own local network. Satisfied with all the resources he'd brought to this investigation in such a short time. Satisfied with his future prospects.

"You know Pat, your sheet shows twenty-six different nurses, twenty-five orderlies and five ward clerks were around those kids," said Frank Daley. "That doesn't really make for pinning anybody to the crime."

"That's what happens when you get an unglamorous place to look, Frank," said Pat Rosen peering, deadpan. "Do you know how many people work at this place?"

"Yeah." He slurped some coffee. "Almost two thousand. Too bad a few of them hadn't spent a little more time with more than one of those kids."

"On the other hand, Frank," Pat Rosen called kitty corner across the table, "your surgeon friend seems to figure very highly in all this."

"That's the thing," said Daley as he put his coffee down. "He figures in too strongly."

"What do you mean?" said Rosen.

Daley sat up and looked at her down the length of his crooked nose. Had his nose been a gun, he would forever have placed his bullets to the right of his target; his nose itself, the object of a right hook. "If this fellow had poisoned the kids, he would have had to do it on many occasions."

"Explain," said Walters. He preened the collar of his suit jacket as he sat beside Dugan.

Daley became contemplative. He pushed his white shirt sleeves up, leaned forward on his elbows, and rambled through his thoughts. "Let's assume this guy killed all the kids." The room fell silent. "Let's assume that all thirty-four deaths are bona-fide homicides."

"Right." said Dugan.

"The average number of days after operation until death is four. What's important in our data, and I think we all agree, is that the levels of digoxin climb steadily over the four days."

"So?" said Walters.

Attersly was smiling to himself. Dugan saw that and thought his officers might be getting it.

"What that means is that the killer didn't walk in there with a needle full of drugs and inject the kids once each. That would have been an obvious overdose." All eyes in the room were on Daley. "It means that the killer went in there approximately four times each, for thirty-four kids, to give minor overdoses and build up to the fatal level. That's one hundred and thirty-six drug doses. One hundred and thirty-six drug doses under what can only be suspicious circumstances."

"But they wouldn't have been suspicious circumstances, Frank," said Rosen. "Nobody suspected the deaths." She sat back in her chair looking satisfied with herself.

Daley pounded his right fist onto the table. "Yes, they would. Have you watched those guys work?" He leaned forward and grinned widely as he looked around the table. "I haven't seen one of those prima donna surgeons say, 'nurse get this patient fifty of super lima bean concentrate,' and then get the needle and stick it in someone's arm themselves. Think about it." He sat back on his creaky oak chair. "Those guys say something, and somebody else does it."

Slowly, heads nodded.

"If you have any surgeon give one hundred and thirty-six shots of anything, even over five years, somebody would have noticed. Especially with those kids popping off. I'm willing to bet." He paused and canvassed the faces around the table, "I bet that the confirmation for those doses will come from one of the twenty-six nurses, or orderlies, or what have you on Pat's hot sheet. And further, I bet that it won't stand up to careful examination."

"Are you suggesting," said Geoffrey Walters, "that a nurse or some other paramedical overdosed those children?"

"No. I'm suggesting that it would be next to impossible for a *surgeon* to give one hundred and thirty-six doses of anything to anybody by himself without getting noticed. I think we should bear in mind that somebody may be trying to frame this guy."

McGuire, the squeaky detective from fraud, in a plain blue suit, said, "But why would they have left it hidden for so long? And who brought it out now, if the killer didn't?"

"Good work, Frank." said Dugan. "The mystery deepens. Did someone breach trust with the call we taped, is it a set-up, or is the killer looking for attention now?" He looked at Detective Rosen, and momentarily had to fight back how he had once felt about her. "Pat, get all the details on every person on your hot sheet. I want to know where they banked, how much is in their accounts, if there were any sudden large deposits within the time frame of the deaths." She nodded. "I want to know where they live and where they lived. I want to know who's gay, who's lesbian, and who's straight. I want to know if any of them ever fucked Roy Purvis or the new whiz, Martins. In short, is somebody trying to screw this guy over?" Dugan's sentences had blended into a blurred string of thought. He paused for a moment. "Incidentally, I got a call from an agent at the FBI. Seems he and a guy from the IRS were over to see Purvis. They heard about the killings from Purvis's wife—seems she volunteered the information somehow—which doesn't make sense either. They were over to see him about a withdrawal he made from his broker. Not a small withdrawal—twenty million dollars—the money left the country without Uncle Sam getting his cut."

"Jesus Christ!" said Rosen.

TWENTY-TWO

Peter stood at the entrance to Club 53, hearing the distant piano music over subdued chatter, clinking glasses, and flatware. He walked in. There were a few couples at small tables adorned with candles. The sloped metallic ceiling reflected the lamps suspended ten feet above him.

Sprawling city lights flickered beyond the tall windows. The red lights of communication towers flashed randomly on the horizon.

Anne wasn't there.

The darkened bar was topped in granite and framed in oak, with a mirrored wall behind that advertised its bottled entertainment. A waiter acknowledged his entry with a nod. The bar wrapped around a corner, and Peter walked past unknown couples at tables to the far window. He saw the shimmering red and silver neon sign at the fork of Commonwealth Avenue. He looked around and still didn't see her.

He stood looking out the window. The idea of meeting Anne Maples one-on-one was a little vexing. He was aware of the double edged sword of the media and cringed at the idea of being misquoted. But there was no other way of looking at it. Should he trust her? Why not? Did she visit police headquarters for her own benefit, or was she summoned there like him? Peter suspected the latter. Otherwise she would have been more composed, less on guard, and surprised by their chance meeting. Wouldn't she have asked him for an interview if she was working? There was nothing secretive or out of the way about Club 53. It was simply not the usual thing for an otherwise busy news person to do. Was she for real, or was she fast on her feet and playing him?

Walking back along the bar, he noticed the elevated grand piano. The player raised his eye brows to him.

Peter went to the position nearest the piano, just on the far side of an older man propped up on a stool, and leaned against the counter. He looked at the man, pin striped suit, leaning on an elbow and nursing a drink. He followed the arch of his back, up to his thin white hair, past the hollow cheek bones; forward, under the profile of his brow was a bulging eye. A red eye, that reminded Peter of a fish, was fixed on a silent television screen above the bar that was reporting a Red Sox game. Peter shivered.

"Hi." A soft female voice invaded.

Peter turned away from the inflamed eye.

"Well, hello." He straightened himself up. "Hello!"

Anne Maples stood before him in a dark blue dress that must have cost a thousand dollars. She was thin and fighting trim. He felt flattered.

"I was afraid you wouldn't come," he said.

"That's funny. I had the same feeling." She looked him over, seeming surprised.

Peter went on. "I didn't know where you were coming from, if you know what I mean."

"Not really."

A waitress in long black pants, rippled tuxedo shirt, and a black bow tie approached them. "Can I get you something?"

Peter glanced at Anne who seemed unable to decide. So, he said, "I'll have Ballantine's and soda." He looked back at her.

"Give me the same, but make it a double."

Hard working girl.

Anne said, "I really don't know what you mean." She looked at him. "I think we should get our cards out on the table, don't you?"

"Absolutely. By the way, have you eaten?"

"Yes, thank you."

"Look at it from my point of view. I saw you at Mass Heart yesterday when you came out and made your announcement. By the way, you should know that I simply couldn't get into the hospital before the broadcasts were complete. I guess that was just professional courtesy, not crossing the line and getting into the way of the cameras."

"Thanks for your consideration."

"No problem. Obviously you noticed me enough to recognize me at the police station. But I also saw you get cut when you announced that Doctor Purvis had disappeared."

"I think I said that I thought he had disappeared, and that his disappearance might be linked. Linked to the killings. He has, after all, not been available for comment."

She held her arms crossed, tightly clutching a black satin evening bag. Peter noticed her full lips, just barely quivering.

The waitress came and gave them their drinks. They touched glasses dispassionately. Peter took a sip, and Anne finished half her glass in one swallow.

Hell of a hard working girl!

"I think you should tell me how you ended up at police headquarters," she said.

"If I do, you should tell me the same thing, and we should agree to a policy of honesty and keep this totally private."

"I can buy into that," she said without hesitation.

"My mistake was talking to that big policeman. I wanted to be up front. I'm a heart surgeon at the institute. I wanted to get the idea across that their order to keep our staff from meeting was causing some problems with patient management. Our work depends on close collaboration between team players, and we need to be able to meet and discuss. That's what we're there for, for patient care. And we do it very well."

"There's also a perception that your people kill very well." She smiled. "And there may have been a cover-up."

"Those kids weren't killed." He regretted the statement immediately.

"How can you say that?" Anne said. "There's a big investigation going on all about thirty-four children dying from digoxin overdose."

Peter pulled himself together and took a sip of scotch. "Let me backtrack a moment. I approached Malloy. I remember his name now. I told him that his policy was disrupting patient care. I mentioned that the kids might not have been killed."

"Then how did they die?" She emptied her glass.

"Wait a second." Peter straightened up. "We agreed to discuss how we got to police headquarters, didn't we?"

"And?"

"That's all I said to the cops. That big guy just pulled a card out of his pocket and told me to go see Inspector Dugan. I swear that's all there was."

She looked at him. Her nose was straight, her eyes were dark, burning with curiosity. "I find that just a bit hard to believe, but at the same time, this *is* Boston. In my business, I hear all kinds of shit before I get to the truth."

Peter looked to the bar after draining his glass and beckoned to the waitress. "Two more of these. Make them doubles." He looked back at her. "So how did you end up at the police station?"

"I really had this guy pegged." She paused and looked at him, as if she was wondering. "I had Doctor Purvis's house watched. I don't do this often, but we're allowed to do investigative reporting. There's a budget, and we have a private eye who's really very good. Ted Weiner, my producer, signed the budget slips without reading what they were for, like he always does. He simply didn't see what I was doing."

"Isn't that illegal?" He shook his head and chuckled.

She shrugged.

The waitress came with the drinks. They both sipped.

"After the first press conference at police headquarters with Malloy, I decided to have Purvis watched. That man hasn't been home. I just put it all together and called it as I saw it. I may be wrong. Or I may have scooped it. I mean, there was so much going on, and I just wanted to get it out. Do you know what I mean?"

"No."

"Well, I realize now that the man may just have been off on vacation, but the whole thing seems to fit together. That's scary."

"And that's why you went down to police headquarters?" He needed an answer.

"Do you know what I think? I think that I pre-empted the police investigation. Not only did Ted Weiner find the thing a surprise, but Roger Dugan was listening, and he found it a bigger surprise."

"Really?"

"Sure." Anne took a big swig. "They had this recording from the informant and decided to act on it. There was no way they couldn't. I mean, they couldn't put it down to a crank call without at least taking a look. So they acted responsibly and reeled the whole thing in, after thinking about the consequences, and, more importantly, after thinking about the consequences of not listening." She paused for a moment. "What would you have done if you had received that call?"

"I don't know. I'm not a cop. I didn't get the call."

"Well, think about it. They couldn't ignore it, could they? I mean, they told us what was on the tape and they even played it back, so we could get an idea what was going on, as long as we didn't play back the tape on air. And we had to keep quiet about it for one day. Anne shrugged her shoulders. "They're good that way."

Peter realized the validity of her argument. His interest was deepening. "But how did *that* get you to case Roy Purvis?"

She admitted, "It was just a fluke."

"What? Explain."

"I'm telling you that I went to the station after the press conference Tuesday evening. This is all completely private, right?"

"Of course."

"Well, we're allowed certain discretion in investigative reporting, and I decided to case Doctor Purvis. It was that simple. He is the chief of heart surgery at the institute, and I dispatched the dick to watch his house."

"Incredible."

"Understand that the dick is on salary no matter what, and we didn't have anything else for him to do, so I put in a chit for him to watch Doctor Purvis's house." She took a long sip. "It just happened that Purvis didn't come home. So there." She looked defiant. "Now I've told you everything."

"Not quite." He looked at her. "Did you get the impression from Dugan that he didn't know about Purvis before you broke the fact on air?"

"I can't answer that. Dugan is one seasoned professional who's given lots of interviews, and in his time, has asked many more questions. He's like a nut you can't crack. But if I was going to bet on it, I'd say he didn't know. That's the only way to explain Weiner instructing me to go see him as soon as I got back to the station."

"As soon as you got back?"

She took another sip and looked critically at Peter before she continued. "He played 'rake Anne Maples over the coals,' for not sharing this with him in advance; then in the next breath he said I had an appointment with Roger Dugan. Surprised the shit out of me."

"I bet." That explained her behaviour at headquarters perfectly. Peter began to feel better.

"Your turn now," she said as she slung her purse over her left shoulder and winced a bit.

"Okay. But I'd like to say something first." She waited with her cynical look on her face again, and Peter continued. "I find your explanation hundred percent satisfactory. I think we can work together." He smiled warmly at her for the first time.

Anne returned the smile. "We'll see. I'll buy your story for now."

Peter could live with that.

"First. Do you know where Doctor Purvis is?" she said.

"No," he said, keeping a straight face.

"Have you seen him?"

"Not since Tuesday. He pushed his cases through the OR because he's the chief of the department. That got the rest of us pretty angry, but there was little we could do about it. By the time we got ready to go see the administrator, nobody could find him."

"Really. Have you talked to his wife?"

"As a matter of fact I have. She hasn't seen him either."

"When did you talk to her?"

"Yesterday."

"She drives the Benz SL and he drives the black Jaguar," said Anne. "Right?"

"You really do your homework, don't you?" He nodded affirmative. He decided to slip her a small fact to save the big one. "I'd like to tell you something in strictest confidence."

"Go ahead," she said.

"Purvis has a girlfriend."

Anne slowly broke a broad smile.

"I'm sure his wife knows. As a matter of fact, I know that she knows."

"You're right, Peter," she said with satisfaction in her voice, "we can work together."

Peter leaned back, relaxing on the bar. He added in hushed tones, "Purvis is on his fourth marriage. You know, once a runner, always a runner. That is exactly how the present Mrs. Purvis got her man from the previous Mrs. Purvis. I can't speak for the earlier ones, though."

"Isn't that interesting? But tell me, has anyone tried to get hold of the girlfriend?"

"Can't find her either."

"The work of an investigative reporter is never easy, but it's never dull." She smiled and stared blankly out the windows. "You know, it's pretty damn obvious that Dugan or one of his lieutenants is watching the news broadcasts. Did you see the way they parked those motorcycles, and those uniforms at the front of the hospital? One big photo op! And of course we lapped it up. I can just imagine Dugan's thinking. There you are Mr. and Mrs. Television Viewer, the police are on the job, led by none other than Chief Detective, Inspector Roger Dugan." She thought for a moment. "You know, I think the chief of police's job is coming up in a few years. I'm willing to bet that just as soon as there's a break in the case, Inspector Roger Dugan's face is going to be all over TV. People will remember those neatly parked bikes. And of course Anne Maples will have done her part to make the thing look better. I get this funny feeling that I'm being used. By Dugan, or somebody."

"He's that ambitious?"

"Ambition is his middle name." she said. "So tell me about yourself."

"Well, I'm Canadian, and I've been here about six months."

"I know that."

"Really? Did you find out that I trained under Doctor Purvis for one year, three years ago?"

"No." She leaned up against the bar and asked, "Did you operate on any kids with Doctor Purvis?"

"Yes."

"Any of them die?"

"Yes."

She looked at him quite seriously. "Are you under investigation for murder?"

"Anne," he said, "they're going to investigate everybody over there for murder. They're going to look at the doctors, the nurses, the cleaning staff, anybody they can place within fifty yards of those kids! And the ones who were there most often are going to get squeezed. They're all going to need lawyers. Good and expensive lawyers if they expect to survive. Watch and see. The cops are going to have one hell of a witch hunt."

"Well," Anne said. "Good part of the country for a witch hunt." She chuckled. "I'm sorry." She put her free hand on his arm for a moment. "It's not really funny, is it?"

Peter was a little angered at first, but he did see the humour. "It's okay. Because if they get their way, they're going to drag all kinds of people down before they find someone to pin it on. And quite frankly, I don't think they'll pin it on anybody."

"Really?"

"Really." he said, and stood up straight.

"You speak with conviction." She poked him on the shoulder.

"The only thing that will be served by this is due process. And that process is going to get some people a lot of mileage as it tears others apart."

"Peter, this is interesting." She smiled warmly at him. "You must tell me more."

"Maybe I should." He raised an eyebrow. "Maybe not."

"Oh no, Peter, you must. We have a policy of honesty and privacy, remember? I want you to know, that whatever we discuss tonight will go nowhere else. But right now I have to go to the little news reporter's room. Back in a few minutes."

"I'll be right here."

As Anne turned and left, Peter observed her light steps, her exercised form, and her interesting profile.

He turned around to look out the window and wanted to lose himself in the vista, but couldn't. Was he being used too? But, by whom, and, for what? The thought hadn't actually crossed his mind before and, he wanted to thank Anne Maples for making him aware of it. Who else could gain from the investigation? Dugan? Sure. The chief of police who was about to retire? How? The D.A? Obviously if he brought down a good case. The state? No. The hospital? Obviously not. Roy Purvis? Definitely not. Insurance companies? He doubted that. Anne Maples? Not if she was off the case. Peter? Time to give his head a shake. This was a sufficiently large dilemma that he decided to wait for his new confederate to return.

He had to admit to himself, that rightly or wrongly, he liked her. He promised himself that he would be careful.

He wandered over to the corner of the bar where he had an unobstructed view to the east.

From fifty-three stories up he could get a good impression of the complex maze of streets that spread out into the distance. Far on the horizon, towns glowed, linked to Boston by faint threads of light traversing the meandering tentacles of New England's roads.

Just to the left, the John Hancock Building, reflected millions of city lights in its grid of glass walls. Beyond that, the void of Boston Harbour, and Logan Airport shining on the other side with four planes approaching in a line.

And further still, somehow sadly positioned and barely visible at the end of its causeway, were the lights of Nahant. Where, if the police cared to look, Peter was certain they would find Roy Purvis's car.

"I thought you weren't going to leave."

Peter swung around, startled from his wandering thoughts, to look at Anne Maples. He smiled and said, "I didn't leave."

"Oh yeah, sure." She took him by the arm and led him back to their drinks. "I come back and find you, clearly fifty feet from where you promised to wait for me. Now, how can we build a foundation of trust here, Peter. I'm disappointed." She giggled.

Peter looked at her with a fond smile.

Anne held up her hand. "I've been thinking too. You've been terrific. You didn't have to be. I expected to come up here and get some cock and bull story from a fresh surgeon. You surprised me." She changed her tone to the flippant. "And now I come back to find you've cheated, leaving me this way. Well! What can I say? My heart's broken. I may cry."

"Really? I didn't mean to." He played along. "It wasn't that important to me."

"Well you did." Anne's tone became serious. "I saw you looking out the window." Then intimate, "You know what I like about Boston?"

"What?"

"I like the way the highways cut up the landscape at night. It's like a—, like a—"

"Galaxy in space. With distant galaxies at the ends of the arms.

"Exactly." She smiled widely.

"May I ask you a personal question?"

"Shoot."

"You attached?" he asked.

"No, sonny, I live my work. My place in the cosmos is to interview the liars, cheats, robbers, murderers, and the other politicians of the world; to bring a bit of honesty, integrity, and accountability to their wretched lives. I do this morning, noon, and night. No sane man would have anything to do with me. The men I meet are either sociopaths or frank psychotics. I live every young girl's fantasy." She raised her eye brows, shrugged her shoulders and took a long sip of the rapidly diluting scotch.

"Sounds camp to me." They looked at each other, and Peter asked, "Are you really off the case? I mean, did your producer—what's his name, Weiner—really take you off the Mass Heart story?"

"Are you really a heart surgeon?"

"Yes."

"He gave it to the pretty boy who cases the governor." She looked down.

"Wow." Peter sighed.

"You still a heart surgeon?"

"Only until I become a witness. Or the accused."

"Sad." She thought for a moment. "Tough holding onto a job any more, no matter what you do."

Peter decided to come clean. "You know what I was saying before, about the kids not having been killed?"

"Uh-huh."

"Well let me back track a moment. I didn't know what to expect from you tonight either. I'm glad we met. So—"

"Get to the point Martins. You're boring me."

"Those kids weren't killed."

"No." Anne sounding surprised now. "They got killed. You're trying to tell me they weren't murdered. There's a difference you know. I'm willing to bet your actions kill people all the time, but it's not murder." She looked at him with mock regret. "Am I coming on too strong?" She took a sip of her scotch.

Peter took a long drink. "No. I can handle it." Maybe he was wrong about her. No. He decided to go on. "Those kids weren't murdered. I can prove it. I tried to tell the police, but they won't listen."

"Hey. They want an investigation. You want to rain on their parade. What else can I say?"

"I'm serious."

"Sure, you are." She pouted. "Are you going to tell me about it?"

"When I was training in Toronto, some time ago, there was an investigation of baby deaths at our hospital. I had trained on some of those kids too. There were twenty-six of them. They all died of digoxin overdose."

Anne snorted into her drink just as she was going to take a sip. "So why aren't you in jail, Peter?"

"They tried to hang it on a nurse. A girl named Frances Wright. Bloody Spanish Inquisition all over again."

"Did she walk?"

"Yes, she did in the end."

"How so? I mean, why did she walk?"

"Because they proved scientifically that kids post-operatively make their own digoxin. It's a substance almost indistinguishable from medical digoxin which they secrete in response to the stress of cardiac surgery. It's a normal, adaptive, bodily response." He waited a moment before continuing. "There's a large body of evidence in heart surgery now that says the human body knows best... Knows what to do. Even in adults on bypass machines, we don't try to outsmart the body as much as we used to."

"You're not kidding?"

"No. That's what I was trying to get across to, what's his name, Malloy? I tried to get it across to Dugan too, but he nixed me. Asked me if I was also a forensic pathologist. I told him, no. He told me he had an army of forensic pathologists on his side and he didn't need my input."

"Jesus Christ, Peter, Mary, and Paul!" Her eyes beamed. "Do you realize what you've just told me?"

"Yes."

"Can you back it up?"

"Sure, given time."

"Peter, do me one big, cosmic favour. Help me run with this. I'll make sure you come out smelling like a rose."

"Why not."

"I think I'm in love," she said, flippant. "We've got to go to my place. I've got to record this. Do you mind? My car's downstairs."

He looked at her and saw the enthusiasm.

"Please."

"Let's go. No point in wasting time."

He called for the tab and settled it momentarily with a note marked one hundred. Before they strode out to the elevator, Peter looked one last time at the vast matrix of flickering lights that was Boston, and wondered where he was in that cosmos.

TWENTY-THREE

Peter walked quickly with Anne beside him across the darkened floor of the underground parking garage. A bare overhead light bulb glared in his eyes and cast a shortening shadow behind them. They passed under the light and the ghost-like followers jumped ahead of them, two fleeing shadows stretching into the darkness.

Once out of the light, the shadows vanished.

The darkness, the organised rows of waiting automobiles, and the sharp echoes of their footsteps could have unsettled anyone.

They didn't speak, except when she pointed him in a new direction to her car.

"Just up here on the left," she said as they turned beneath another large circle of light.

"What do you drive?"

"Benz. 500 E," she said.

"Really?" Peter tried to look at her shadowed face in the dim light, but only saw a silhouette against the grey floor.

"Right up there." She pointed.

Peter saw the outline of the Mercedes about one hundred feet in front of them on the left. Empty spaces flanked the sedan.

Peter was suddenly bothered by something, but he didn't know what. He slowed his walk. An animal? An observer? Then he had it. He knew that he had seen the faint glow of a cigarette coming from the inside of a car somewhere in front of him.

Anne took Peter's left hand. She strained to see ahead, past her car, and drew to a gradual stop. She pulled him close.

Peter could tell her pulse was quickening. Was that sweat?

"What's the matter?"

"That car—"

"What car?"

"Over there on the right, facing us in the corner. Grey." She whispered loudly. She didn't point.

Then he saw the glow of the cigarette become brighter for a moment. His vision was drawn to the black shadow of a head, with copious hair, sitting in a mid size car parked against the far wall.

Anne said quietly, disturbed, "He followed me here."

"Did you see anybody else?"

Peter scoured the patches of light to their left and right. He looked back over his shoulder. He faced the car which was perhaps a hundred and fifty feet away, and he saw the glow again. Over on the left, about two thirds of the way to their observer was the Benz, shining wine red under a light.

"No." Anne paused. "I'm scared! What's happening?"

Instinctively they turned together. Bits of sand grinding under their heels. They started to walk away quickly.

The question uppermost in Peter's mind was what did the observer want? Second, how serious was he about getting it? And third, who?

"We can come back for my car tomorrow." She sounded panicked.

"Sure."

One question was answered by the mechanical whine of a starter motor. They quickened their steps.

The engine didn't catch. The sound of the starter echoing.

"Where's your car?" she said.

"Copley Plaza." he said, as calmly as he could. "Hurry."

They quickened their pace toward a glassed-in stairway as the car's starter tried again. The engine caught under a heavy foot. The headlights sprang to life. The tires chirped. It was in motion and catching up.

The pair sprinted for the glass door of the stairway. They reached the door as the car squealed around the corner fifty feet behind them. Peter plowed his palm into the wire-meshed glass of the door marked "Stairs" and blew it inward with a rush of air.

They ran up the flight under bright fluorescent light. As they rounded the landing and headed up the second flight, Peter ducked down to catch a glimpse of the driver. He couldn't make out the face.

The grey Kia sped past, leaving a cloud of dust.

At the top of the stairs they found themselves in what was a bright glass fish bowl on another level of the garage. They could hear the car's roaring engine and squealing tires getting closer.

Peter went for the door, yanked it open, pulled Anne through quickly, and closed the door.

"Over there, behind that car." he said.

They ran to a group of vehicles in a pool of shadows and ducked behind the closest one.

The Kia racing around.

They peered through the windows of their covering vehicle and suddenly saw the bright lights of the car at the far end of the garage.

"Here." Peter pulled Anne towards him and held her, his hand on her shoulder. "Get right behind the tire." He put his feet behind her as the approaching car cast a long rounded shadow about their legs.

The car squealed past. They gingerly followed the shadow around to the front of the sedan. The speeding car went by. They followed the grill of the Marquis around to its driver side fender.

Anne tripped over a heel. "Shit!"

She righted her aching foot and followed Peter, crouching along the driver's side in the shadows. They rounded the back of the car just as the Kia passed in front.

The driver's gaze was fixed on the glass stairway. He accelerated past the stairs, towards the ramp at the far end of the garage. The car squealed around the corner and the sound hushed as the car disappeared behind a concrete wall.

They stood up.

"You okay?" he said.

"I'll be fine. Who could that—?"

"Shhhh." Peter put his hand to his lip as he motioned to the ceiling. He listened to the heavily muffled sounds of the car careening around the garage above them. "Bastard's really looking for us ... well ... for you."

She looked at him reproachfully.

"You were on P-3, correct?" he asked.

"Yes. Never mind my car; it's insured. Besides, if this guy or these people are serious, they've got a bug on it."

"Right." He listened carefully as he looked at the ceiling, tracing out the imaginary path of the car. "Maybe he'll leave."

"Maybe not," she said. "He knows who he's looking for. What if he waits on the street—or comes back?"

Peter looked at Anne and saw her agitation. "Above this is P-1. Then there's one more flight of stairs to the street?"

"Correct."

"One thing is certain, we can't wait here. This guy is bound to be back. We've got to go up the stairs to the point where we're just barely looking out on P-1. Then—do whatever's necessary."

"Like what?" She looked at him.

"If the guy's gone, we get up and out."

"And what if he's waiting outside? Do we just walk away and say, 'pardon me'?"

"At least there are other people up there."

"At this time of night, off Boylston street?" she said. "Know what you're going to find? Drug pushers and addicts. Which do you prefer?"

Peter ignored the protest. "If he comes back we'll have to break for it."

The sound up above suddenly abated.

"Let's go." He looked at Anne, took her trembling hand, and entered the bright stairwell. They couldn't hear the car.

On the second flight, Peter ducked his head as he came level with the floor above. He turned, surveying P-1.

"He's checking between cars with a flashlight. He's on the far side of the garage." Peter watched for three, maybe four minutes. He sensed he was sweating too. "He's picking up speed now."

Anne stuck her head up.

The car was going for the ramps. It rounded the corner and the tail lights came up like a bobbing duck.

"Now!" Peter said. "He's coming back down."

They bolted upwards, staying out of the driver's sight.

"Keep going."

They ran up the stairs to the outdoor vestibule of the parkade. Peter pulled the door open and they ran out, swallowed by the shadows.

"Over here." He pulled Anne toward the dark wall of the building. They stopped there panting, leaning against the dark brick wall. "Pretend we're making out. You stay on the inside and he won't recognize us."

They embraced. Peter towered over Anne. From the shadows they watched the garage exit.

The car suddenly appeared, its engine straining. The Kia roared out and turned toward the Back Bay.

"He didn't see us," said Peter. "Let's go. Along the wall, in the shadow."

He led her by the hand. The skyscraper towering above them.

They were on a side street. There was no traffic. Only one car stopped up ahead. He didn't see the Kia. Neither did he see a cab.

"Let's get going. We need to get to Boylston Street. It's just a few blocks up here to the right."

"Oh God!" she said.

"Don't worry. I'll protect you. Take my arm and look relaxed."

They walked stiffly, cautiously along the inside of the sidewalk, Peter continuously looking for the Kia. They passed the service entrance to the building, smelling the garbage.

"Do you think we look nonchalant?" said Anne. "My legs are shaking."

"Never mind."

A large, old Chevrolet sedan was parked at the curb just up ahead. An antenna gave it away as an unmarked police car. They drifted toward the curb, toward the car. There were people inside. Two in the back were talking, all animated.

"What do you plan to tell them?" Anne whispered. "'We're Peter Martins and Anne Maples. We just got chased around a parkade by a mysterious car. By the way, we're involved in the Mass Heart investigation. Can you help us?'" She looked at Peter.

They were near the back of the car. The front window was open and Peter could see a man carefully watching their approach in the rear view mirror. They walked past the back door and glanced in. Two men were exchanging something in the back seat. The man on the front curb side watched their passing. A lit butt flew out the driver's window.

As they came alongside the front, the officer slowly turned his head and looked dolefully at the passing couple, his eyes glazed and empty. He sat hunched forward, hands on his lap. His jacket was open, revealing the grip of a large pistol. The police radio on the pedestal crackled with a message.

They drifted stiffly back toward the inside of the sidewalk, sure the observer was watching. The men in the back seat continued their exchange.

Some distance further Peter looked at Anne and said, "Sometimes the cure's worse than the disease."

A yellow cab turned onto the street in front of them.

Peter leapt out past the curb, waived his arm, and shouted. "Taxi!"

The cab accelerated toward them and squealed smartly to the curb. The driver looked them over before unlocking the door.

They slid into the back, behind the plexiglass partition.

"Where to?" asked the driver with his head cocked slightly over his shoulder.

"Fairmont Copley Plaza. Side entrance by the registration desk."

The driver accelerated away from the curb. Peter saw him looking at them in his rear view. Probably wondering what their story was—taking a cab five blocks?

The cab rounded the corner of the ornate public library building.

One block up, across from Saint James Cathedral, the cabby pulled up at the curb opposite the hotel, and Peter slipped a bill through the money window.

"Keep the change." They got out of the car.

"Hey, thanks man." The taxi pulled away.

"Peter! Over there! Don't look." Anne turned her back to the street.

A grey Kia with a hairy driver came to a stop at the corner in front of the Copley Plaza.

"Come on." He took Anne's arm and led her up to the elevated entrance of Boston Fisheries. He held the brass rail and looked over his shoulder to confirm the car was coming their way.

They quickly entered the large glass door into the vestibule and walked past a large group of waiting patrons to the reception desk.

Peter nodded to the Maitre and said, "Hello," as they walked past without stopping, through a milling crowd toward the modern wood and brass bar. He wanted to see out the windows, but be lost in the melee.

"Hey, wait a minute!" The Maitre shouted and chased after them.

Peter pulled Anne along as he glimpsed out the large glass wall from behind huddled people and saw the car passing slowly by. The same car!

"Wait one minute." The Maitre intercepted them.

At the entrance to the darkened dining room, Peter quickly turned left, ignoring the Maitre, and proceeded behind the brass rail of the long bar. The couple forged ahead, through the crowd. People were staring at them.

After a moment, the Maitre adjusted for their new tack and followed them through the eddy of swirling people they left behind. "Pardon me!" He held up his hand, partly in protest and partly for people to give way.

Peter could hear someone say, "Isn't that the newswoman. What's her name?"

Anne ducked her head.

Peter pushed his way to the far end of the bar with Anne in tow.

"Sir!" The Maitre shouted.

Peter turned toward the doors and quickly exited through the same crowd he had already ruffled once. They were equally upset with his departure. One fellow offered some resistance. Peter pushed harder.

They had left a crowd of disheveled guests at Boston Fishery. *Pretty good for less than a minute's work. Teach them not to take reservations.* They exited the swinging doors and he surveyed the street as he walked down the steps. No Kia.

The Maitre arrived at the door and held it open. He yelled haughtily into the street, "And you be sure to come back, sir!"

Peter and Anne walked hand in hand across the four empty lanes of Dartmouth Street. They strode past a dark green Mercedes 600 and up to the large, old brass framed doors of the Copley Plaza Hotel. They went through a set of inner glass doors, past the large reception desk with the clocks high on the wall showing the time around the world, almost oblivious of the high ceiling, a crosshatch of gilded dividers and huge crystal chandeliers, the walls light, and the floor of white and grey marble.

They hurried, turning immediately left into a wide hallway leading to the front.

"I love this place," said Peter as he strode down the hall.

"Me too," said Anne, with relief.

They came to the inner glass door. The uniformed doorman held the door open for them and said, "Yes, Doctah?"

Peter gave him his claim check and a big tip. "Bring the car around right to the door. Leave it running. Don't let it out of your sight."

"Yes, sir." He went to a brass wall cabinet, which he unlocked and gathered a key from, before relocking it. As he walked smartly into the night, Peter pulled Anne back inside.

In a few minutes, the blue Porsche appeared. The valet got out and left the driver's door open before proceeding around to the passenger side. He opened the door and waited attentively.

Peter and Anne hurried out. Peter got in first and closed the door. Everything was in order. The valet gave Anne a hand, and closed the door behind her. Peter hit the red security button in the console and the doors locked. Anne reached for her safety belt and did it up.

"Ready?" Peter engaged forward.

"Ready."

He jabbed the gas and the car surged forward as the doorman saluted their departure. They stopped for a red light at the wide corner of Dartmouth Street. The library was to the right and ahead. When the light turned green they rounded the corner alongside the plaza, and onto the next light at Boylston Street.

As Peter drove, Anne said, "Look over there." She pointed to the left rear corner of the car. "He's seen me."

Peter caught the outline of a Kia, three cars back. "You sure it's the same guy?"

She was looking out the back window. "Of course I'm sure. Same head of hair. Lose him, Peter." Her voice trembled.

He pushed the gas halfway down and the Porsche's soul sang, propelling it to the second light, Berkley Street. He waited for a pedestrian then prodded the car left. They crossed Newburry Street just as the light turned yellow. The Kia had to stop behind another car, but Peter only got as far as the double crossing of the heavily treed Commonwealth Avenue Mall. The Kia was two cars back before the light turned green.

"Jesus Christ, Peter! I can almost make him out through the other car's glass."

"Recognize him?"

"No. Just keep on driving," she said, panic in her voice.

"If you think about it logically, he's not a rapist or he would have taken off as soon as he saw I was with you."

Anne took her gaze off the rear window and turned to Peter. "If he's gauging your fight by your driving ability," she shook her head a little, "he's not going to worry."

Peter looked at her and smashed the accelerator down. The whine tightened up and the car fishtailed slightly across the green lights of Marlborough and Beacon Streets.

A car crossed Back Street, and Peter braked heavily. Anne jerked forward. Peter pressed the pedal to the limit as he turned right across the traffic and entered a lit underpass. Peter and Anne were pinned back in their seats as the car screamed ahead in a gentle left hander that went up and merged with Storrow Drive. At 95 mph he passed everyone in sight. *Pray there are no cops.*

"That should do it," he said, staying in fourth. The engine roared behind them at 4100 rpm.

Anne finally relaxed in her seat. She reclined, folded her hands on her lap, and smiled at Peter.

"There's something I've been meaning to ask you," said Peter. He looked at Anne. "Do you ever drive your Benz backwards down the last entry ramp to Tobin Bridge?"

"Was that you in the white Bimmer?" Her eyes ablaze.

He said, "My buddy was driving."

"Wasn't that great?"

They shot past the Government Centre exit and followed a sweeping left hand turn which had Peter pushing off the console and Anne's knees pinned to the door. The road corrected to come right under the broad, classically lit arch that was Longfellow Bridge. Their bodies swayed to the opposite side of the car.

"Have you ever heard Ian Fleming's maxim?" he asked. "First meeting, happenstance. Second, coincidence. Third, enemy action." He looked over as they took a long left hander past the Massachusetts Eye, Ear, Nose, and Throat Infirmary on the right. "I've got us at encounter number four—likely racing on the streets of Boston to ditch your boy friend—where does that put us?"

"I don't know who that creep is," she said. "All I know is he scares me." Then timidly, "But I guess this makes us friends."

Ahead of them was the problem. A traffic light. A red traffic light. They stopped at the front of the reverse traffic circle and overhead walkway. Signs for the science centre pointed off to the left. Up to the right was the sign for I-93. Beyond that the North End. Peter considered his options.

"Oh my god!" said Anne.

"What?"

"He's right behind us." She was looking toward the rear.

Peter recognized the too familiar silhouette.

"I must admit I'm disappointed, Peter. Heart surgeon drives a hundred thousand dollar Porsche and can't lose a Kia." She shook her head again.

"Is that feedback, Maples? You might try being positive."

Peter held the brake partly down and gunned the gas. The Porsche edged forward each time. The Kia followed suit. He saw a lull in the traffic and accelerated hard right. Peter checked the mirror.

The Kia poked into the traffic, connected with an oncoming car with a muffled crash, and spun around a hundred and eighty degrees.

Anne had been looking back. She put her hand on Peter's shoulder as the steam rose from the cars.

The Porsche screamed up the street. Then Peter slowed down.

"Do you think they got our plate number?" she said.

"We'll know in a few minutes. Won't we?"

"Peter, what *is* going on?"

"I have no bloody idea."

Anne sat back in her seat, folded her arms, and went over the events. "I was on the case. I broke the story on our channel. I figured Purvis out by accident. So I scooped the story. Weiner cut me and I had an interview with Dugan. We met, and met again. I was followed to the Prudential Centre. When we left there, this creep followed us like *his* life depended on it." She thought for a moment and asked, "Do you know why none of this makes sense?"

He looked at her as he drove. "No."

"It doesn't make sense because we're missing something."

"That's obvious."

"I mean, if this was a straightforward murder investigation, people wouldn't be putting a tail on us. Would they?"

Peter wasn't in the mood for analysis. "I think the tail was meant for you," he said. "But we need to figure out what to do next. Go to your place?"

She turned to him. "Obviously not. There's probably somebody there. How about your place?"

"I live right over by the accident."

"Damn! Well, we can't just drive around waiting for the cops to pull us over. Can we?"

"I agree. Let's beat it out of town. Not too hasty mind you, but before they pass out our plate number and our pictures. We should get some rest and pull our thoughts together."

"I'm in complete agreement. Where do we go?"

"Provincetown?"

"Sounds wonderful."

TWENTY-FOUR

Peter looked over at Anne asleep. The whole drive she only awoke as the car's tires hummed across the metal centre of Sagamore Bridge, over Cape Cod Canal. Peter kept the car at an almost even 75 mph; fast enough to go places but not fast enough to attract attention.

Traffic was sparse. The car's high beams illuminated rolling sand dunes capped with stands of tall grass and groves of pines. Walls of half lit dunes crossed with shadows streamed past the windows with the rush of the wind and disappeared, lost in the night with the memory of the car's droning exhaust.

At Dennis Port, Peter stopped at a late night store to buy some refreshments. When they left he reminded himself that the Cape was the only place on earth where the hydrangeas grew naturally blue.

He drove for another three quarters of an hour to Provincetown. Near the tip of the Cape the dunes became taller and the pines stood like black sentinels.

But the beauty of Cape Cod lay not only in its exotic nightscapes and salt box fishing villages. It was close enough to Boston to be accessible, but far enough. That had made the choice easy.

Just outside Provincetown, Peter turned right onto an unlit side road that took them to the shore. Flanks of pines quickly thinned to lone irregular shapes and were finally replaced by tall wisps of grass. By the time they got to Waxman's Inn, even the grass had been reduced to short, infrequent tufts by years of salty winds.

A quiet night in comfort was infinitely preferable to the pressured hubbub of downtown Provincetown.

They got the last, and the farthest, of three cabins, detached from the main lodge. The Inn was located on a solitary portion of east-facing beach. Their cabin was elevated on piers, situated on a slope, with the back of the cabin at the level of the sand. They followed a meandering drive lit with squat mushroom lamps up to the rear. The front had a wide covered porch. Waxman's was quietly discreet, and at this hour, asleep.

The inside of the elegant barn wood cabin, decorated with old American walnut furniture, had a living room with an overly tall fire place adjoined by a small, modern kitchen. There was a sandstone bathroom, and, at Peter's request, their cabin had two bedrooms.

Neither Anne nor Peter had set out for the Prudential Centre with packed bags, so they had arrived in a state best described as, what you see is what you get. They would have their clothes pressed in the morning. The balance of the evening was reserved for the casual, if understated elegance, of the wraparound towel.

Peter tended to the drinks, barefoot in the kitchen. He smeared the lips of two whiskey glasses with the insides of large lemon peels and added ice.

He thought about the Kia. His first impression of the event was not to trust Anne. But he had to admit that she couldn't have faked her pulse and her sweaty palms. Besides, who would have been chasing her, and why? A few new ideas suddenly occurred to him, ideas that had escaped his attention before, in spite of the many he had considered on the way down.

He favored both glasses with a few ounces of Tanqueray, then splashed just enough Noilly Prat onto each to approximate a twelve-to-one mixture, and stirred.

He saw Anne watching quietly from the door of her bedroom, looking shy, and rightfully so, wrapped in her towel. Not the sort of thing her mother would have told her to do on a first date. Looking a little wary, and yet, somehow comfortable, she walked toward the kitchen.

Peter smiled. "I was just thinking of you." She looked good in a bath towel, maybe better than in a dress.

"Wicked things no doubt?"

"On the contrary. I have an idea. Let's turn the lights off, sit on the porch, and talk." He held up the glasses. "I've mixed us some drinks." He added reassuringly, "nobody should bother us here."

She smiled and said, "Why not."

They left the light on over the kitchen range and went out. Anne sat on a wood rocking chair and Peter perched himself on the balcony railing. They sat absorbed in their senses for a few moments.

The black sky looked alive with millions of stars that seemed close enough to touch. The sand of the beach formed a broad ill defined crescent, bordering the black, slowly heaving surf. There was no wind to speak of. Sea salt hung in the warm air, clinging to skin like damp silk. Quiet. A silver blue glow hung on the horizon, expecting the ascent of the moon. Under the roof of the porch, sat two almost invisible figures sipping their drinks.

Peter finally said, "I've always liked being by the sea. You?"

Anne leaned against the back of her rocker, causing it to creak. "Only when the crowds disappear. But nights, on a deserted beach like this. Wow!" She leaned forward and scanned the water front from left to right. The chair protested again, slightly. "I don't see any light. Except up there."

"It's quiet. We might as well be here alone." He decided to broach the subject. "You know, I never thought I'd trust a media person. But somehow, tonight ..."

"Don't get sentimental on me," she said in a friendly tone. "Understand that I feel the same. The way you got me out of there. I wouldn't have made it alone."

"Not necessarily! You got lots of smarts, and don't forget, I've seen you drive *backwards*. Besides, who says that fellow was going to do anything to you? The question is, who is he?"

"Hmm, I've tried to figure that out. I can't." She paused. "I keep thinking that Ted Weiner sent him, but he's not our man."

"That doesn't mean Weiner couldn't send somebody else." He decided to let her finish her train of thought.

"True. But what's Ted got to gain by watching me? He kicked me off the job."

"Maybe he thinks you'll lead him to Roy Purvis. After all, you figured out that he was gone."

"I don't think so. It's unlike him. He'd grill it out of me, or at least he'd try. Obviously, that didn't happen or I would have told you so."

"Right." Peter gave Anne a moment. "What if someone else wants you to lead them to Purvis?"

"Like who?" She seemed puzzled.

"Like the police."

"No! Dugan would simply hash it out with me too. We have that much respect for each other."

"I don't mean that police. I mean the income tax police, the IRS."

"Peter, you've lost me."

"I had a telephone conversation with Mrs. Purvis," he said. "The other day, two men came to her house. One was from the FBI and the other from the IRS."

"So?"

"They were inquiring as to Purvis's whereabouts too."

That perked Anne up. "Those must have been the two that my man saw at the house just when I called him off the case! That much makes sense."

"What your man didn't tell you was the reason for their visit. But he couldn't have known, he was too far away to hear."

"Go on."

"It seems that our friend Doctor A Roy Purvis made a substantial withdrawal from his investment broker earlier this week. I think on Monday. But the crux of the matter is that he wired the money to the Caribbean, to a tax haven."

"Oh really?" She sat forward. The chair protested. "How much?"

"A lot of money. More than we could count." He decided to be honest. "Nearly twenty million."

"Wow!"

"Now, I gather Mrs. Purvis let slip that there was an ongoing investigation at Mass Heart. That seemed to interest those boys."

"You don't say!"

"So let's put two and two together."

"Right. They check with Dugan about the investigation, and he tells them the spiel—I catch on quick you know—then they find out about my scoop and, voila!"

"Exactly. They tail you thinking you'll lead them to Purvis."

"I never thought of that! But you told me Purvis had a girlfriend. You didn't tell me about this before." Anne took a big drink from her martini and let her chin fall into her left palm.

"You didn't let me! We got onto that drug thing. Then the chase was on. I'm leveling with you now."

"So the way things happened," Anne said, "was like this. On Monday Purvis cashes in his chips. He works all day Monday and part of Tuesday. You and your buddies sit around on your hands. Monday evening the cops get the call and tape it. They scramble. Tuesday, Malloy and the coroner pay the hospital a visit. They consider the evidence and Dugan decides to go for broke. They clue us in as long as we keep quiet, and Wednesday the hospital gets torn apart. Coincidentally, Secretary of State for Health Hobbs bites the dust. Thursday, Anne Maples scoops Purvis's disappearance and gets cut. Yes indeed folks, she catches two levels of police with their pants down, and guess who they want to rake over for it? Who knows who else has a stake in this that we haven't figured out yet."

"Exactly." Peter swirled his drink, rattling the ice cubes before taking a swallow. "If you're asking me, I'd say the chief coroner."

"Oh yeah." She sipped. "Why?"

"Well, if any kid died under mysterious circumstances, don't you think the coroner's office should have figured it out and investigated the thing before it went this far?"

"Holy shit! The coroner's office could be in on this too." Anne bowed her head momentarily, looking overwhelmed.

Peter looked to the horizon, noting the silver glow just above the water. "Moon's coming up," he said without ceremony.

Anne looked at the horizon. "You know what Peter? Even if Purvis is innocent, he's got a lot o' shit to pay."

"That's what I'm afraid of." Anne's face suddenly became light with detail and Peter followed her gaze. "Oh, look at that!"

The cap of the moon slowly rose out of the sea, paving the water with a broad, silver highway that ended in front of their cabin. The moon was about seven eighths full and large on the horizon, revealing its acne complexion. They watched, silently, in awe.

The shoreline took on exaggerated detail. The sand shone with a silver iridescence and was randomly marked in the way nature does with such uniformity, with black crescents of wavy sand and strings of footsteps. The cedar shakes of the next cabin's roof were immediately obvious. Almost fluorescent, the bare sand dunes rose high at both ends of the bay, their back sides black in shadow against the living night sky.

"Want to go for a walk?" said Peter.

"Love to."

"Won't need to lock up. Leave your drink."

They put their glasses down and walked out into the bright moonlight. Peter took Anne's hand and they walked to the edge of the sea. They walked south on that dark part of the beach that was close to the water, that part that was cool and firm yet which gave away slightly under their feet.

They said nothing for a while, savoring the heavy salt air, revelling in the texture of the sand, flirting with the myriad silver reflections, and witnessing the full ascent of the moon.

There came a moment as they walked, a moment when Peter looked at Anne's face to see what that might reveal. She was silhouetted against the sea, but her lips were full and pouted. Her nose was not overly long but was matched almost perfectly by her brow. Her dark long hair flowed down behind her and glanced off her shoulders onto her white towel wrap. Curled wisps trapped moon light in their maze. Her eyes remained dark.

Anne stopped walking and looked at Peter. He wondered what she saw and felt.

Anne wrapped her arms around Peter's waist and looked up. "Come here." She kissed him on the lips, cautiously at first, but then with urgency. Not a long kiss, just enough. She withdrew slightly, smiled so that there was a twinkle in her eyes, laughed hoarsely, and then pulled her towel off and held it to her side for Peter to see.

She had on a black strapless bra and briefs.

She dropped the towel on the sand, laughed again, and ran splashing into the ocean. She dove in, disappearing for a moment, and came up in an effervescent silver pool.

Peter dropped his towel beside hers in the sand and ran after her into the sea in his grey briefs. Half way out to her he dove, keeping an eye on the shimmering surface above. The moon stayed ahead, a quivering silver ball just out of reach above the water. Even the water looked alive with faintly shimmering particulate matter. Faint patterns of waves flowed silently over the rippled bottom. The light bottom and suspended ocean silt coalesced into a watery horizon that was first blue, then black, and ultimately silent. Finally, he saw the blurry outline of her pale body in her dark underwear. He extended his hands to hold her, letting his hands slide up over her thighs, her thin waist, and up her torso.

She leaned forward and they kissed the salty brine off each other's lips. They entangled themselves in each other's arms and fell over into the sea, not breaking apart until they had to come up for air.

Peter cleared his throat and dove out to sea. He did eighteen breast strokes and came up about fifty feet away. He couldn't stand.

"Wait," Anne shouted and started a crawl out to him.

He took a breath and let his head slip without a ripple beneath the surface and swam silently toward her departure point until he saw her form breaking the surface above. He tucked his arms against his sides, took aim on her waist, and ascended slowly to intercept the approaching form. Without surfacing, he nipped her waist with his teeth on the crest of her hip. She froze, and Peter could hear her scream even under water.

He surfaced to hold her. They treaded water, kissing fervently.

Hearts pounded.

"God, I hope nobody heard that," said Anne.

"Never mind," Peter said. He felt her body against his; he felt her warmth, her shape, her movement, her underclothes. He felt her excitement and recognized it as his own. Then he felt the caress of the cool ocean on that vignette of his abdomen that wasn't touching her.

They spent a few more moments treading water to stay together.

"Go back?" said Peter, and they swam toward shore.

When their feet met the sandy bottom, they ran, splashing toward shore, breathing hard.

On shore they quickly spread out their towels on the warm sand and fell to their knees.

They pulled off their wet underwear and quickly rubbed away any traces of sand. In the moonlight they fell onto the towels in a fevered embrace, and found each other's arms, legs, and lips.

Finally spent, they ran to their cabin, letting the door slam behind, and showered together.

They got into bed and Peter lay on his back with Anne nuzzled into the left side of his neck. He felt her warm breath on his ear. His hand on her waist. He felt warm again.

She propped herself up on her elbows and looked at Peter.

He ran his finger nails lightly up and down the small of her back.

"Mmmm. You could do that forever." Anne murmured like a purr.

She rested her head on his chest and Peter smelled the sea in that part of her long, damp hair that fell over his nose. He didn't try to move, revelling in the scent.

"Anne. May I ask you a personal question?"

"Only if you promise never to tell." She didn't take her head off his chest.

"What's your background? Where did your family come from?"

She propped herself up on her elbows again and smiled in the half darkness. She said slowly, quietly, as if betraying some secret, "My father was first generation Greek from Athens." She paused, expectantly. "My mother was the daughter of a second generation Italian. I was born and raised in Boston."

Peter propped his head up by putting his hands behind his head. He asked shamelessly, "Then how did you ever end up with a name like Anne Maples?"

"Shhhh." She had her finger over his lips. "Not so loud."

"Who's going to hear?"

"Shhhh."

"All right." he whispered.

She continued quietly. "My real name is Anna Metzonopoulos. I changed it years ago. After all who'd want to listen to a news caster named Anna Metzonopoulos?"

"I don't know. You look pretty good from here."

"That's 'cause you're horny, honey."

"Anna Metzonopoulos." He contemplated for a moment. "That explains a lot of things."

"Oh! Like what?"

"Your temper. Don't deny it. I've known you one day and I've already seen traces of steam."

"One day? God!" She paused, maybe thinking about the cataclysmic chain of events that had delivered her into bed with this man. "What about you?"

"Oh, I'm Canadian for generations. Family came from Europe decades ago. I grew up in Toronto, got educated there, the whole nine yards."

"Then how did you end up at a place like Mass Heart?"

"They asked me."

"No."

"Yeah." He was a little taken aback until he realized she was kidding. He had to get this feeling of being a foreigner out of his system. His defensiveness had to show. "In case you don't know, that place is a United Nations of medical talent. The people come from around the world."

"Really!"

"Yeah," he said. "The concept's as American as apple pie. Take for example, the American space program, brought to you by a good ol' boy named Werner von Braun. Where you suppose he came from. No guessing please. You only get one chance."

"Quit it already." She laughed quietly and looked him in the eye. She punched him on the chest. "Let's get serious." She began to gently caress his abdomen, letting her fingers follow the curve of every muscle.

"There's something I haven't told you," Peter said after a few moments.

"What?"

"Roy Purvis is gone." She stopped her caressing, but restarted as he continued. "One of the guys saw him sail off on his boat. Likely with his girlfriend."

"He saw this first hand?"

"Yeah."

"How far away was he? Did he identify Purvis?"

"I don't know. Five or six miles."

"Give your head a shake, Peter." She pressed her fist against his chin.

"This guy has a bird's eye view of Nahant and Purvis's slip. He has a telescope, a sixteen-inch Mead reflector. Believe me, at five miles he can tell how many strings are on a bikini, let alone if one of them is mismatched or untied. There's no doubt he saw Purvis sailing out. This fellow keeps records."

"You're serious?"

"Absolutely."

"Who is this guy?"

"A gynecologist named Finegold. He's got a place on the Winthrop coast with a view of Revere and Nahant. He uses his telescope every morning and every night. And as I said, he keeps notes."

"He keeps notes? Really?"

"He does everything seriously," said Peter.

"And he saw Purvis sail out?" She sounded incredulous. "How did he recognise his boat?"

"I gather there's only one Hinckley 47 moored at Nahant. Mel saw him leave Tuesday, after work. Told me about it yesterday, after a case."

"Hmm," she said. "How far could Purvis get in a day?"

"Hey. I've never been on board, but he should be able to do a hundred miles a day. On auto-pilot, in open waters going all night, he could conceivably do fifty per cent more."

"So he's three hundred miles away now." She chuckled. "In international waters with no hope of bringing him back, on his way to an offshore haven."

"With his dolly."

"Yeah. With his dolly." Chuckling again. "And he'll be in Bermuda by Monday night."

"Sounds about right to me."

She continued caressing him and said, "I'm glad we talked. Things are really beginning to make sense." Then she kissed him and held her hand firmly over his pubic bone.

Peter's body immediately responded to the prodding. "Glad I could help," he said.

He rolled Anne off his chest, onto the bed beside him. She was smiling impishly. He pulled her close by the back of her neck, still intoxicated by the scent of her hair.

Anne seemed to sense that and pushed him flat onto his back again, smothering him under her hair. Rubbing her cheeks against his chest.

Peter buried his face in her neck.

Anne said softly, "Here we go again ..."

When they were done, they lay there for some time, entangled in each other's hold, luxuriating in the contact of skin on skin, intruding wisps of soft, pungent-smelling hair, the exquisite excitement of a soft hand, the warmth of another's breath, and in the silence, the comfort of hearing another's heart beat next to their own.

Outside, the moon cast its iridescent spell on the sea shore. The slow waves played gently up onto the sand; fingers of water drew a lazy, silvered retreat. A gentle southern breeze bore pine scents. A night hawk screeched and darted, hiding its silhouette from the moon.

TWENTY-FIVE

Morning came as it usually did, with its lack of concern for the living; that is, too soon. The rush of a shower brought refreshment and the realization that some housekeeping needed to be done.

Peter and Anne recapped their discussion from the night before and made a plan. That included a call to Ian Scott about Peter's patients, as well as a call to Grant Sardis, the biochemist and pathologist in Toronto, who had blown the Frances Wright Trial wide open. Scott was in, but Sardis was not.

Peter was dispatched to Provincetown on a buying trip. After he dropped off Anne's dress for pressing, he bought blue jeans, tee-shirts, and sport shoes for both of them. Some toiletries were necessary as well.

Anne attended to her hair and makeup rather efficiently. A surprise to Peter, but a necessary reality in her business. The unexpected bonus was how good she looked in Levis, Adidas, and a Kliban Tee. They could have been a married couple if anybody in Provincetown paid attention to that sort of thing anymore. They drove to town and dropped Peter's suit at the same cleaners to have it pressed. After parking the Porsche they walked down a treed knoll into the center of the seaside town.

Pastel salt boxes lined the streets, giving the commercial core a quaintness.

They needed lunch, or more specifically, brunch. They looked into a number of restaurants and saloons along the main street. Tex-Mex wasn't for them. One saloon was crowded with rough looking bikers, which didn't appeal to Anne. Peter tried to explain that they were probably just vacationing university professors, lawyers, and businessmen, living out their fantasies—albeit a bit late. Anne on the other hand said she didn't care to be part of that fantasy, let alone anywhere near.

Peter was beginning to see a different side of Anne, a side that wasn't dressed to the nines and making social comment into a microphone, a side that looked at life's uncertainty and unpleasantness and said, "Personally, I don't give a shit."

Brunch was to be at a place called Bill's Restaurant. Anne felt it represented the cleanest and most straightforward approach. The Maitre led the couple through the entrance to the restaurant which was done in the local de rigueur—colonial barn wood. Past a dark wooden bar, the restaurant opened into a large square room, glassed-in on three sides. There was bric-a-brac everywhere. Tables covered with checkered table cloths. Peter and Anne got a table by a window nearest the ocean. The problem was that the Maitre pulled out and offered Peter a chair. Not Anne.

"Feeling jealous?" he asked.

"Hardly." She answered in hushed tones as she folded her arms on her chest. "I know what makes you tick."

Peter looked at her and smiled.

The clientele of the restaurant reflected Provincetown's mix. Nearly half the tables were occupied.

"We better order before things get hot," said Peter as he picked up his menu and perused the offerings. "I think I'll have the lobster sandwich, a house salad, and some zinfandel blush."

"Peter! It's hardly noon."

"Charlotte, it's Saturday," he said. "And quite frankly, I don't give a damn."

The waiter returned and asked, "Are you ready?"

Peter and Anne both looked at him. Anne shrugged her shoulders and said, "Quite," and deferred to Peter with a wave of her hand.

"I'll have house salad, the lobster sandwich, and a glass of zinfandel blush." Looking straight at the waiter.

"Thank you." The waiter turned to Anne. "And you, miss?"

"I'll have what he's having."

"Very well." He put away his pad. "I'll be right back with your wine." He departed hurriedly, scanning other tables.

Listen. I appreciate your openness about your mother and father last night."

"A weak moment, Peter," Anne said as she leaned forward taking his left hand in hers and stroking him reflectively. "You won't talk about that. Will you?" She kept her eyes on his hands.

Peter tipped her chin up with his right hand. "Never."

The wine came. They touched glasses and sipped.

Anne held her glass up before her eyes, looking at Peter's distorted face through the blush wine. "The dilemma, as I see it, is when do we talk to Sardis?"

Peter answered without hesitation. "Today, if he'll see us."

"And if he *will* see us."

"Then we buy what we need and go. Put our little unplanned weekend getaway on Visa Gold, as it was intended. No reason to miss the opportunity just because we hadn't pre-booked. And above all do not stop at home, do not bump into police, and do not go to jail."

Anne held his gaze for a moment like she was thinking about him, about the situation, and their half baked plan. Then she grinned broadly and said, "Let's do it."

Peter suddenly felt at risk of becoming maudlin. He changed the subject as he saw the waiter reappear. "As soon as we're done I'll try Sardis again."

The waiter brought two huge tossed green salads and placed them on the table. "The lobster sandwiches will be ready in a moment."

"Oh good. I'm hungry." said Anne.

The waiter looked at her as if he had been wounded.

There seemed little point in further discussion, and after last night's activities, there were other needs to be met. They lit into their salads and wine.

The waiter returned with the sandwiches.

Peter said, "Two more blush," taking the time to look at him.

"Of course, sir."

The lobster sandwiches were divine.

"Hope you don't eat like this all the time, Peter. The cholesterol..."

Peter shrugged and took a big bite with a smile and a wink.

The waiter shortly returned with two more glasses of wine. He placed them on the table and looked at the plates, especially Anne's.

Peter looked at him and figured he was thinking, *That bitch can eat!* He sat upright and stared at the man in a way that could only mean, "That will be all."

He spun on his heels and left.

"Got to hand it to you Peter. You know how to impress people." Anne smiled.

Peter finished the last corner of his sandwich. After he gulped it down, he said, "I'm going to try Sardis again." He took a large swallow of zin from his second glass and pulled out his cell phone. "Gotta find some bars." Then he added, "I'll be right back." He got up, throwing his napkin carelessly onto his plate, and strode off toward the restaurant entrance.

The best reception was just outside on the street. He dialed the number.

"Hello."

"Grant Sardis?"

"Yes."

"This is Peter Martins."

"Peter, how are you?" There was pleasant surprise in the voice.

"I'm very well, thanks. I'm calling from Boston."

"Yes. So I heard. Congratulations!"

"Thanks, Grant. But I'm not sure that's in order. To be precise, and honest, I'm calling from Provincetown."

"I see. What's troubling you?"

He explained the situation at Massachusetts Heart Institute, and how it mirrored the Frances Wright Case in Toronto. And how the police weren't listening.

He went on. "Well I'm with a TV reporter, a girl named Anne Maples. She would love to do an interview with you in Toronto and blow this thing wide open."

"Oh?" Sardis paused. "You know they'll get it eventually."

"I know, but in the meantime? You should see the crap that's going on. Anyway. Just the science you understand, open people's eyes to the fact that this may well be a wild goose chase."

"If that's all you want, just name the time."

"I'll call you back. Likely this evening or tomorrow morning. Anne knows somebody at CBTV, and she told me that was an option. Is that okay with you?"

"I'll be expecting your call."

Peter looked up the number for Porter Airlines and momentarily had reservations to Toronto at four in the afternoon, returning late the next morning.

He bounded through the dining room. There was satisfaction in his steps, even though he knew he had not yet arrived. Just the sort of feeling that a player had when he knew he was going to score, that a surgeon had when he finally knew he was going to pull the patient through, the sort of feeling that told Peter he was going to get his message through to the cops this time.

"You look like the cat that swallowed the canary," said Anne.

He smiled. "We can see Sardis this afternoon or tomorrow morning. I have seats booked on the four o'clock flight to Toronto."

"Peter, that's fabulous," said Anne as she sat up straight.

"I suggest we pay the bill and get out of here. We'll need to find a small suitcase and get our clothes from the cleaners. It's only twelve, so we should make Logan Airport by three, easily. You can make your arrangements from the plane. Okay?"

"Let's go."

"Waiter!" said Peter as he waved. "The bill."

He finished the last of his zin in two large swallows after paying cash.

They were walking back to the car, arm in arm, when a woman approached them.

She was older, at first indistinct from the crowd, wearing a brightly flowered sun dress with broad shoulder straps. Her hair, obviously dyed, and her mouth open as wide as the lenses of her large glasses. She approached the couple at a tangent, toting her straw hand bag and holding her head cocked like a young school girl spellbound with curiosity. Her path cut through the crowd straight at Peter and Anne.

She came up right in front and stopped them. Her head remained cocked and she looked out from behind the large frames embossed in a red and black checker board. Her mouth remained agape.

She said with amazement, "My god, Miss Maples, it is you."

Anne didn't speak.

She said discreetly, "Well, Herb and I sure enjoyed your show on the beach last night."

TWENTY-SIX

The flight to Toronto was a short hop, lasting an hour and a half. Peter read a magazine while Anne made her Toronto arrangements with the television station by Airfone. She talked almost the entire length of the trip, inquiring about things like recording format, studio costs, lighting, times and so on. Peter was relieved she had her own gold card.

They landed downtown at the island airport. The cab ride to the hotel brought out the city's other side. Tips insufficient to help with a mortgage weren't appreciated. The cabbie made a remark about a twenty percent tip, so, in the end, Peter kept it.

Their room, however, was great. They were on the twenty-seventh floor looking south over Centre Island. They had an anteroom with a makeup table outside a marble bathroom. Beyond there was a king size bed, two couches, and an armchair. Sheers hung over the wide windows with matching blackout curtains to the sides.

Peter called Sardis to arrange for a 7:30 p.m. meeting at the studio. He introduced Anne to Sardis, and she fielded a discussion with him punctuated with the expected questions.

In the hour that she talked to Sardis on the phone she managed to dress in her blue number from the night before and apply makeup.

They barely managed a cab by 7:15 and were let out in the entertainment district.

It occurred to him as he walked across the street toward the historic building that housed the studio, that he was either becoming jaded, tired, or bored with this problem—or worse still, all of the above.

They entered the glass swinging doors and approached a broad reception desk.

A chic young oriental asked, "May I help you?"

"Anne Maples to see Mr. Lowry."

"He's expecting you," she said. "You can find him by turning right behind these doors and taking the elevator to the third floor. When you get off the elevator, turn left and go to Studio C. Just go in. I'll let him know you're coming."

"Thank you," said Anne.

They passed executive offices, partitioned from each other and the outside world by veils of Venetian shades on glass. On the right, beyond the elevator and behind dark smoked glass, was what appeared to be a radio studio with several booths, and on the far left, a music library.

They entered a plain stainless steel elevator.

Third floor was claustrophobic by comparison. A long narrow hallway faced in heavy dark cloth ran in both directions over a carpet of thick deep blue. Indirect lighting filtered in between ceiling tiles which hung at various heights. Studio C was clearly marked on a shingle.

Anne rapped lightly and they entered.

She was greeted by two men and two women.

A short fellow in a rolled up white shirt offered his hand. "Hello. I'm Ed Lowry. You must be Anne Maples."

"Yes I am," said Anne, taking his hand. "This is Doctor Peter Martins, who made the other half of this possible."

"A pleasure to meet you, Mr. Lowry." Peter shook his hand and turned to face his old friend. "Grant. Good to see you! You're looking well." He pumped his hand and held his forearm.

"And you, Peter," said the grey haired gentleman in the olive green summer suit.

"May I introduce my friend, Anne Maples."

"At last, Miss Maples, charmed," said Sardis.

Anne blushed. "Thank you for coming."

"Watch it, Grant, she's got a bite." said Peter.

"Well one would hope so, wouldn't one."

That got polite laughter.

"This is Carrey, said Lowry. "She'll be operating the camera tonight and she's very good with lighting."

They exchanged greetings.

"May will operate the other camera." A young little oriental woman in blue jeans and a tee-shirt nodded at them. "I'll operate the console and call the shots." Lowry turned to Peter. "Doctor, you of course may remain in the studio."

"Thanks."

"Now, Anne, I've thought over the financial arrangements."

"Yes." Anne seemed to brace herself.

"I know Ted Weiner in a peripheral sort of way. I haven't called him. That may surprise you."

"It does."

Peter looked at her. He hadn't expected that she might need permission to do this sort of thing. What hoops would they have to jump through now?

"To be frank, I thought about this and decided to let you use the facilities on us. Two things helped me make that decision. First is Doctor Sardis's reputation. He's legit. He was pivotal in the Wright thing. I won't even call that an investigation—witch hunt would be more appropriate. I'd like to think we're giving Boston a helping hand. Second. I think you may well scoop something here, and charging for the use would only rub salt into Ted's wound. Besides, he might return the favor in the future."

"You can count on my help," Anne said. "Thank you so much."

"Right. Let's get on with it then. Do you two know what you want to do?"

Anne and Grant both nodded.

"Let's get rolling." Ed walked over to the control monitor, threw some switches, and lights in the studio went on. Monitor screens came to life and took on the colours of the small stage. "All right, Miss Maples, if you'll sit here on the left." Anne walked onto the stage and took the blue swivel chair on the left. "And, Doctor, if you would sit here."

Carrey was already busy aligning the lights. She said, "Miss Maples, if I could get you to turn to the right a bit more." She was immediately pleased. "That's better. Now, I can eliminate more shadow if I lower these—"

"Shadows?" said Anne. "What shadows?" She looked at Peter.

Peter gave her an exaggerated shrug of his shoulders. *Stick around. Just stick around.*

"There. I've got it," said Carrey. She turned her attention to Doctor Sardis, who actually seemed quite compliant.

"Alight everybody, listen up!" said Lowry. "Whatever you do, don't look into the camera when you're talking to each other. Are you ready Miss Maples?"

"Ready. I'll need an ID and a mark."

Lowry pushed some buttons. The lights on top of the cameras glowed red. "Rolling!" Lowry said.

Anne faced the camera and said, "Anne Maples interviewing Doctor Grant Sardis, in Toronto, August 25, 2014. CBTV studios. I'm ready for mark."

Lowry held up his left hand with four outstretched fingers and counted down, "Four, three, two, one, and mark."

Anne sat erect. "Good evening. This is Anne Maples in Toronto. Tonight I'm interviewing Doctor Grant Sardis."

"Doctor Sardis has agreed to speak to us on the matter of the multiple infant deaths at the Massachusetts Heart Institute." She turned to Sardis and said, "Good evening, Doctor Sardis."

"Good evening," he answered.

"Doctor, what can you tell us about digoxin overdose in infants and young children. Let me be more specific—in ill infants and young children who were taking the drug therapeutically prior to death."

"That's a difficult question to answer, Miss Maples."

"Why?"

"In the first place, it is very difficult to overdose children with the drug. It has been scientifically shown that children tolerate much higher tissue levels of the drug than adults do. Secondly, it has been reliably shown that tissue drug levels and blood drug levels have absolutely no correlation with time of administration of the drug prior to death. Third, and most important, other drugs and altered body chemistry appear to have a totally unpredictable effect on the drug level in the body."

Peter saw from the monitor that Grant hadn't lost his touch with the camera.

"Can you elaborate on these points for us, Doctor?"

"Well simply put, there's no reliable predictor of serum digoxin levels in children. My research group showed in 1998 that serum digoxin levels in children continued to climb to high levels even long after drug therapy was stopped. I could cite a variety of other studies dealing with differences in blood levels and various tissue levels. What is important is that the rise in blood levels of digoxin prior to death, even in the absence of drug administration, is a common pathophysiological pathway. Or in lay terms, it is a common event prior to death."

Sardis continued. "It is important to note that infants who have never received the drug test positive for it. I am even speaking of well children just after birth."

"Doctor," asked Anne in her most earnest and concerned manner, "How do you account for this?"

"We showed that other digoxin-like factors cross react with digoxin tests. We also gave evidence then of an endoxin, that is a normal bodily hormone similar to digoxin, that is present at the time of birth and is believed to increase in certain disease states, like heart defects at birth. This is a normal bodily response. In one study, up to fifty per cent of the digoxin found in sick children's blood was determined to be endoxin or similar compounds."

"Doctor, why is so little of this known publicly?"

"Well, we're actually speaking of the cutting edge of modern medical research. As you know, this exact issue was the cornerstone of evidence that acquitted nurse Frances Wright of mass infanticide here in Toronto. Of course, in these times of fiscal restraint, research has been cut back. But most of all, research that concerns the dead has been lifted off the back burner and placed on the cooling rack. In other words, everybody forgets about it after the rush."

"How do you see this influencing the investigation at the Massachusetts Heart Institute?"

"Understand that I am not familiar with the facts surrounding the Boston investigation. However, if the matter is as I suspect, that being a progressive rise in digoxin levels in infants prior to death." He shook his head apologetically. "Then they will find elevated digoxin levels in children who never even received the drug. The simple fact is that a lot of these kids secreted their own endoxin through a perfectly natural process."

"Doctor, what was your role in the Wright trial?"

"I was the chief scientific witness surrounding the issue of blood and tissue digoxin levels."

Anne looking at him seriously. "Doctor, have you been contacted by the authorities in Boston?"

"No."

"Just one more question, Doctor." She paused a moment for effect. "If you were asked to look at the Massachusetts Heart Institute data, would you?"

"I would of course, be pleased to help."

Peter watched Anne lean forward and say, in heart rendering sincerity, "Thank you, Doctor."

"You're very welcome, Miss Maples."

She turned to the camera. "This is Anne Maples in Toronto for BOS TV, Boston."

Lowry said, "Cut," and dimmed the lights.

Anne and Doctor Sardis walked over to the console.

"Care to see a replay?" said Lowry.

Anne eagerly said, "Yes."

"Here we go." Lowry pushed a button on the console and the screen came to life.

"Anne Maples in Toronto, interviewing Doctor Grant Sardis in Toronto, August 25, 2014 ..."

Peter watched Anne's face from the end of the console. He saw her smile, and then he saw her smile fade. He witnessed the faces of satisfaction and sufficiency, the self criticism that had to be going on, the ultimate approval of her work. Would she want to do it over? He thought not. When she cocked her head in self satisfaction over her perfectly engaging, "Thank you, Doctor Sardis," Peter knew it was over.

Sardis's face wasn't nearly as animated over his review. He looked honest on television—very believable. His voice never wavered. He never hesitated, never held back an answer. The question came, then the answer, this was the way it was! Bingo. Over. Done. He even quoted scientific references, so his answers would satisfy the scientific community and the viewer at large. *A polished act.*

But seeing Anne in the studio and on the screen, he recognised something deeper. She approached her subject with knowledge, followed it with objectivity, allowed the subject its dignity, and polished her interview with a chutzpah so subtle, yet so convincing, that Peter was sure that if she was a surgeon she could convince a Jehovah's Witness to accept blood.

"Very nice interview!" said Lowry to Anne. "If you ever want a job—"

"Thanks. And thank you, Doctor Sardis."

"My pleasure. I hope this sheds some light on the matter, and helps you."

"You can be sure of that." she said.

"I suppose then, that there's no reason for a re-tape," said Lowry.

"None as far as I can see," said Anne. "I'm happy."

"Good. I'll make a few copies." Lowrey said as he handed the pack to May.

She left quickly.

Grant Sardis looked at Peter and Anne. "I've got some prior commitments, so I won't be staying any longer."

"You could join us for a drink," said Peter.

"I'd love to, but I really should go. My wife is waiting, you see."

"I hope we haven't inconvenienced you too much, Doctor," said Anne.

"Not at all. I'm always glad to help." He paused a moment, but getting no response, he added, "Very well then. I'll be on my way."

As he went toward the door, Anne stopped him, pumped his hand, and said, "Thanks again, Doctor Sardis. Goodbye."

"Goodbye, Miss Maples."

"Grant, let's meet again when we can talk," said Peter.

"That would be nice. Next time you'll have to give me more notice. Bye!" He nodded. "Mr. Lowry. Miss Gove." He walked out the door.

"May should be back with the disk any moment," said Lowry as he leaned back on the monitor console and folded his arms. "Now, Miss Maples, what are you going to do next?"

"We're spending the night and returning to Boston around noon tomorrow. Right Peter?"

"Right."

She continued as she leaned forward on the console chair, supporting herself on her outstretched arms, "I plan to call Weiner just before we get back, from the plane. I'm going to make him an offer he can't refuse."

"Oh?" said Peter.

"I can imagine," said Lowry. "Think I'd do the same."

Peter remembered that Anne had basically levelled with Lowry on her long talk from the plane.

May came in the door with four studio disks and handed them to Lowry before leaving.

Lowry said, "Thanks," and turned to Anne. "I'm keeping the original and one copy. Consider it a form of safe keeping. The other two are yours. That fair?"

"More than fair," said Anne as she accepted the disks. "I guess we can be going then." She looked at Peter.

"I can't see why not."

"That's what I like," said Lowry. "Good encounters of the fast kind—get lots done with a minimum of fuss. It's been a pleasure to meet you both." He extended his hand and shook in turn.

Anne shook Lowry's hand very slowly, "I owe you big time. Thank you very much."

"You're right, and you're welcome. Goodbye."

Outside, they hailed a taxi.

"Where are we going?" asked Anne.

"Hungry?"

"Yeah." Her response was quick.

"Let me take you to the best kept secret in Toronto."

"Sounds charming."

"It is, in a way."

The cab let them off on Dundas Street East, at an old office building from the forties. They entered the plain glass door which led up a flight of stairs. On the door was a marquee for Danny's.

Inside, the place was noisy and dim, requiring some getting used to. A long bar stretched along the left wall with all manner of people on stools propped up against it. The bar was mirrored at both ends and littered with liquor bottles. An island of oyster crates stood in the middle, and a black board announced the varieties available and their prices.

To the right of the room were giant bubbling fish tanks full of edible crustaceans. Behind, in dark alcoves, people huddled around small tables eating.

Anne and Peter were greeted by a thin young man carrying a tray of drinks over his head. "Wait here," he said.

They stood by the bare metal support that had a lectern welded to its side to hold a writing pad and a telephone.

Peter could finally make out the look in Anne's eyes as she looked around the room. She was squinting at the bare reflector bulbs suspended by wires from the ceiling, then at the walls of the alcoves covered in graffiti.

Anne stared at Peter until she got his attention. She said, "Charming place."

"Isn't it?"

She looked at him reproachfully.

The thin boy came back. He looked at Anne and Peter. "How many?" he asked.

"Oh brother!" said Anne.

Peter obliged, "Two."

"I've got room for you at the end of the bar."

"That'll be good." Peter smiled at Anne and motioned she should follow the waiter.

They followed their man down to the end of the bar. He motioned to their seats. Peter helped Anne with her chair.

"I guess they don't help a lady with her seat any more either."

"Oh, they still do in the better places," said Peter.

"What do you call this?"

Peter looked at her seriously. "The best kept secret in Toronto."

"Really?"

He patted her on the hand with an exaggerated motion. "Just relax, Anne, and you'll be having fun in no time." He motioned to a man wearing a baseball hat who was leaning against a cooler, swilling a beer.

The slight man came over. "You looked after?"

"No," said Anne.

"That important?" He pointed at the two videos on the bar. "I could put it away for you somewhere safe."

"No thanks." Anne drew them close.

"Got any Veuve Cliquot?" asked Peter.

"Yeah."

"How much?"

"Few bucks." The guy bobbed his head from side to side. "Just something to drink before dinner, you know."

"We'll have one."

"Sure." He disappeared into a cold room and came out with the orange labelled champagne bottle. He uncorked the bottle without losing a drop and poured two full glasses, offered them, and leaned against the bar. "So." He looked at Anne. "You been here before?"

"No." She took a sip.

"He has." The man motioned to Peter.

"Anne, this is Danny. He owns the place." He didn't look at her sipping champagne.

"Oh Danny, a pleasure to meet you." She offered her hand. "Nice place. I've heard so much about it."

"Well, thanks." He dropped his gaze to the bar. "Just like home you know."

"And where is home, Danny?" asking in her most sincere, practiced form.

"Nanaimo." He looked at her a moment. "British Columbia."

"Cool," she said.

Danny looked at Peter. "Know what you want?"

"Dozen oysters to start. Malpeques."

"I'll get 'em." Danny ambled down the bar.

"Peter, are you a partner?"

He looked at her and smiled. "I knew you'd be impressed." She didn't respond. "Just wait 'till you try the food."

She looked around the room. "I'm so excited I can't wait."

"Now, Anne. Tell me. What do you plan to do with the tape?"

"Obvious really." She tapped the disks. "I'm going to call that bastard Weiner from the plane, just before we get to Logan. I'm going to tell him what I've got, and I'm going to offer it to him."

"What if he doesn't bite?"

"Peter." She turned toward him, leaning on the bar. "I'll remind him that he kicked me off the job and that this interview didn't cost him a plug nickel." She held up the disks. Fire in her eyes. "I'll simply tell him that I freelanced this one and the tape is available to the network that makes me the best offer." She shrugged her shoulders and smiled.

"Knew I could count on you," said Peter.

"No way are they keeping me out of this one. No, sir. They can grovel for dirt all they want, the cops and the coroners, trying to blame someone." She paused reflectively and looked at the disks in her left hand. "But I'm going to pre-empt them! And I did it with your help."

"We made a good team, Anne. But Dugan won't back off that easily. I mean, justice must not only be served ..."

Danny brought the oysters on an iced platter. "Enjoy. And don't forget the vodka sauce."

Peter took an oyster on the shell, freed it up, squirted on some lemon from a wedge, and took a brown vinegar shaker from the bar. He sprinkled some on the oyster. "Peppered vodka." He put the oyster up to Anne's lips and tipped it back for her.

She slurped back the mollusk. "Mmmm, that's great. Let me have another."

He did.

"You know, some people think these are aphrodisiacs," Anne said.

Danny reappeared. "Know what you're having for dinner?"

"Make mine the Texas rib," said Peter. "Medium rare with mashed potatoes. Got any fiddleheads?"

"Yup."

"That's for me." He turned to Anne. "Want to see a menu?"

"Actually that sounds real good."

"Give the lady a princess cut," said Peter.

"Pardon me," she said.

"Guess she'll have the regular then." Peter raised his eyebrows to Danny and continued. "Got any red wine?"

"You know nobody drinks that shit around here anymore. They all want what the ad man tells them. You know white wine, rose, craft beer, coolers. I only got one bottle of red wine left." He walked down the bar, looked underneath, and came back with a bottle that had a black and gold crest on a rectangular beige label. "Chateau Gruaud Larose 1982." He contemplated the bottle and said, "Got it years ago for fifty-eight bucks; price is still on it. I'll open it for the same. Hell. I only sold five in ten years."

"Pop it, and I'll pay you fifty-nine," said Peter. "Everybody's entitled to a profit."

Danny poured a bit into a broad-rimmed glass and offered it to Peter.

Peter tasted the wine. Swirling the Bordeaux around his mouth for a moment and smiled. "A trifle young," he said, "but it'll do."

Danny smiled and poured two large glasses. He said, "Glad to get rid of this one."

"Isn't Gruaud Larose one of those famous French wines that people pay a fortune for," said Anne.

"It is," said Peter. "In the right kind of places you can pay a lot. Danny just saves the stuff for special occasions." He sipped some wine. "So you have to tell me, seriously now, about your boyfriend."

"I told you last night—haven't got one." She took more oysters with peppered vodka.

"That's hard to believe," said Peter. "A good looking woman like you with a great job. Must be a line of guys at your door."

"Can I tell you something?" He nodded, and Anne said. "This is the new century. Men don't want women who can talk, at least, not intelligently. Uh, can I get you a beer honey? That they appreciate. Not, let's talk about the Mass Heart investigation. Most of the guys I've dated don't like me taking off in the middle of dinner to cover the fire in Quincy. They don't like my salary or my car for that matter, because it might be nicer than theirs—unless of course they're driving. In short, things haven't changed much."

"I have some of those problems," said Peter.

"So I had to make a decision. Putting up with all of that male shit, or getting on with my career." She paused, took a long drink of her Veuve Cliquot, and looked at Peter. "My choice was easy." She took another drink. "I do date selectively."

"One hell of a date we had last night," said Peter.

She turned to him. "That was no date."

"What was it then?"

Anne hesitated. "A chance string of events."

"Even after the swim?" Peter asked.

She smiled impishly. "For your information buster, I'm not on the pill," and pecked him on the cheek.

"Doesn't worry me," he said. "I'd welcome that."

"However, the timing isn't right. So ..." She shrugged.

They ate and drank quietly for a few minutes.

Peter broke the silence. "So, are you going to make network?"

Anne's pupils dilated ever so slightly. "Damn right, I am."

"Will you have time to see me in Boston?"

"You mean between operations?"

"No, I mean between chasing news stories," said Peter. "If I get home first, I'll chill the wine."

"Sounds like an offer I can't refuse."

The food came soon after they had finished the last Malpeque and the Veuve Cliquot. Anne was looking at her regular cut of beef. The piece was larger than her arm and perfectly done. Peter caught her looking at her waist.

"So, Peter," asked Anne between mouthfuls, "what do you think really made Purvis go if he didn't kill the kids?"

"I haven't the foggiest, but he didn't kill them. As sure as I didn't kill them. Maybe he had some personal problems. I don't know. He was on his fourth wife."

"But the whole thing just came together so perfectly," said Anne. "I mean the call, him disappearing; it all seems like too much of a coincidence. Even if Dugan believes Sardis's explanation he won't let up on the investigation because of the caller."

"Unless they can establish the call as a crank," said Peter.

"But that's just it," said Anne after taking a bite. "They found everything the caller said they would." She wiped the corner of her mouth. "I mean, the caller had to know exactly."

Peter answered after a long sip of red wine, "That's why I think there's something we're missing, the cops are missing. There had to be a motive for making the call, even if Sardis is correct and this is bogus just like the Wright thing."

"But the caller didn't make any demands. Up until now he hasn't called back to say, 'Give me a million bucks or I'll kill thirty-four more kids.' " She waited for a response. Getting none, she looked frustrated, waving her hands. "So where's the motive?"

"I don't know. As far as I know, the hospital corporation and its parent company are fully solvent. I'm not aware of any politicians coming around, except Hobbs."

"And you guys fixed him up real good."

"That's not funny. True. But not funny." Then it occurred to him. He leaned over to whisper in Anne's ear. "The morning after Hobbs died and they couldn't find Purvis, our emergency guy told me something. He said that Hobbs's widow called Governor Duke in front of him. And he said that she told him that the governor himself would get Purvis down there. Or something like that."

"Can you trust the emergency guy?" she said.

"Eugen Wittman? Sure. But he didn't speak to the governor himself, as I recall."

"What kind of name is Eugen?"

"German. I told you we got the United Nations down there."

Then Anne asked the clincher. "Do you think she bluffed?"

Peter thought for some time. "People do the strangest things under pressure. But I can't remember anybody pulling that kind of shit before."

"On the other hand, politicians are what they are, and she was married to one. That sort of thing rubs off." she said as she cocked her head.

"We're missing something big." said Peter.

"You think it has something to do with the National Health Bill?"

"They're not threatening hospitals. They're opening up insurance as I understand the thing. You know what, Anne?" He looked at her squarely again. "I sure wish I knew what the governor really told Mrs. Hobbs."

"Unfortunately, there's no polite or ethical way to ask," she said.

"Well, he didn't exactly come through for her, if Eugen's version is correct." Peter thought a moment. "What if Duke's connected to this somehow, really deep? That's big."

Anne shrugged her shoulders. "Tell me about it later."

Two hours after they came in, after Peter got the cheque, they swaggered out.

Back on the street, Peter hailed a cab. The West Indian driver soon had them at the door of their hotel. Peter tipped well before the doorman opened his door.

They skirted through the revolving doors and traversed the lofty lobby which was decorated chinois, with brass bird cages and cockatoos.

In the room, Peter left the light off and Anne didn't seem to mind.

She put her disks on a bedside table, walked over to the window, and whisked the curtains aside.

Lake Ontario was alive with the silvery light of the moon, occasionally dotted with the lights of boats, some moving, some not. The air was clear and there were lights on the horizon fifty or sixty miles away.

Peter watched Anne silhouetted against the window; she slowly unzipped her dress and let it fall to the floor. She stood there, black against the reflections on the lake.

Peter approached and embraced her gently, his left arm around her shoulders and his right hand stroking her flat stomach for a few moments. He rested his chin on her right shoulder.

"Look out there," she said. "What are those lights on the horizon?"

"That cluster over there on the right is Buffalo."

"Isn't it a fabulous night?" She rubbed her buttocks gently across Peter's thighs. "Oh!" She took his right hand in hers and guided it down, slowly over her stomach, past her navel.

They turned to look at each other in the moon light.

Anne said, "I guess we didn't need the oysters."

TWENTY-SEVEN

From the moment Peter woke up Monday morning, he knew the situation at the Massachusetts Heart Institute had changed, for the better.

He had tended to some chores after dropping Anne off. Then he caught up on his sleep. But he did manage to see Anne's reports on TV, Sunday night.

Her report from Toronto had aired on BOS TV on the evening news as well as on the late report. There was more hubbub on the late edition. She had created a stir, even though there were no reports from other experts or from the authorities.

And she'd had her day with Ted Weiner!

On Monday morning, Peter caught the 7:30 news driving to work.

The newscaster indicated that investigative reporter Anne Maples had gone to Toronto to interview an international expert in the field of digoxin overdose in children, Doctor Grant Sardis. He indicated that the high levels of digoxin found in the dead children were part of a normal series of events in terminally ill children. The announcer commented that Doctor Sardis was the eminent scientist who had testified in Toronto in a remarkably similar case involving twenty-six deaths. The result of the months-long trial was to acquit the accused, a nurse named Frances Wright, for lack of evidence.

Just as Peter was driving across Kenmore Square, Chief Detective, Inspector Roger Dugan commented on air. "We are, of course, aware of this information, and we plan to contact Doctor Sardis in the very near future." When asked about the status of the investigation at Massachusetts Heart Institute, he had said, "The investigation is still ongoing."

Neither the coroner's office nor the district attorney had been available for comment.

Leaving the heavy lifting to Dugan.

As Peter had walked across the cobblestone corner between the parking garage and the hospital, he saw neither reporters nor police.

In the building, the easing of tension was palpable. Smiles all around.

Peter hadn't told anyone of his involvement with Anne Maples's report. He had only told Ian Scott that he would be away.

The surgical lounge teemed with discussion about the matter. Harold Williams in the rare company of Aldo Calabrese had espoused his own theory of how the digoxin elevations had occurred. A good theory, but incorrect. The development, which signaled the end of the inquisition in Peter's mind, was the phone call from Assistant District Attorney Geoffrey Walters at 7:30 a.m., which Calabrese recounted. The ban on association between physicians and all hospital staff had been lifted without explanation. In fact, a literature search for information on digoxin overdose in children was under way. The emphasis was on Sardis's research. An emergency meeting of the board of directors together with the medical advisory committee had been scheduled for ten that morning.

The only person who looked unimpressed was Ian Scott. Peter thought he looked preoccupied. But he had a case to do that morning, and Peter was to assist him.

Ian's case entered the operating room at 7:55, and, thanks to Frank Fanconi the anesthetist, the patient was ready for the surgeons at 8:25.

The normally jovial Ian, was strangely quiet at the scrub sink. The best he had done was to mutter words that Peter couldn't make out.

The case started routinely. They had cracked the chest, taken down the internal mammary artery, and Peter had harvested the long saphenous vein. The first real problem occurred at cannulation of the aorta. Ian only got the tube partly in, which resulted in a huge spray of blood, until the site was controlled and the tube was sutured in.

Peter thought that he was the only one to notice Ian's slightly erratic movements. Not that he wasn't doing the job, he just wasn't as smooth and sure as he normally was. This hadn't started with the cannulation mishap; Ian had been shaky sawing through the chest and had almost lacerated the innominate vein. Peter made no comment but did catch a very concerned look from Mary, their scrub nurse.

They proceeded in silence. The chatty team. This was one very unusual morning. Especially considering all the good news.

Even Frank Fanconi peered over the curtain to observe the unusually silent surgeon.

Ian suddenly became fidgety as he was half way through sewing in his first vein graft. He started to mutter again, and in spite of their heads being only inches apart, Peter only thought he heard, "I can do?"

"What's wrong?" asked Peter.

Ian looked up. He was sweating. He stammered, "Just help me ... help me."

"All right Ian. Everything's going well. Let's be calm."

The black surgeon looked pasty. He was soaking his hat and mask. "Can't you see, it's not okay! Goddamn it, help me!"

"I'm right here. What do you want me to do?"

Ian looked up sharply as he shouted, "Just help me!" Which broke the fine blue suture at the sight of the anastomosis. He stared at Peter, looking wild. "Now look." He threw the armed needle holder onto the instrument table.

"All right. Calm down." said Peter, trying to stabilize the situation. "The surgery is going well. Is something else wrong? Do you want me to take over?"

Ian stood defiant. Hyperventilating. He said, "New needle driver and suture." He held out his right hand for the instrument.

Mary, who normally addressed him by his first name, handed him the armed driver. "Here you are, Doctor." She looked to Peter with worry in her eyes and sighed.

"All right," Ian shouted. "Now everybody just give me a chance to get this done and everything'll be all right." He bent down to get back to his sutures and Peter could hear him mutter, "Can't believe it. All gone."

"Ian, do you mind if we turn on the radio?" asked Peter.

"That would be nice. Just give me some space to work." After a minute he added, "That's better. Lots of light."

The worst seemed to be over.

Frank tuned in a soft rock station on the radio and returned to look over the curtain.

Ian Scott had joined the broken end of his suture to a new length and was feverishly working to complete the union of vein to coronary artery. He completed the task, tested the junction, and finding it satisfactory, proceeded on to the next lower anastomosis.

Peter was just in the process of easing the vein down, when the ten o'clock news started. Frank, maybe expecting more good news about the hospital, turned the volume up.

The announcer said, "While officials deny the possibility of wrong doing in the Massachusetts Heart Institute investigation, news has come from New York of new problems for the beleaguered institution. With a report, here is John Davidson at the New York Stock Exchange."

Davidson stated, "While news surrounding the Massachusetts Heart Institute has concerned the possibility of criminal charges in the deaths of thirty-four infants at the nation's leading heart hospital, other developments have gone by unnoticed. With me is Jeremy Hechler of New World Investment Bank. Jeremy, what can you tell us?"

Hechler commented, "In the past few days we have seen tremendous fluctuations in price, as well as a large volume of trading in Mass Heart stock. The shares which opened this morning at three dollars and twenty-three cents—"

"Ugh!" The announcement was overwhelmed by Ian's moan. Then he cried, "I'm ruined. I'm ruined!" He dropped his needle driver onto the floor, clutched his chest, and sighed inward as he took one huge breath, "Uhhhhh!" He teetered and groped for Mary before falling sideways onto her. Mary tried to steady herself on the large instrument tray, but they teetered onto it, and fell with it clattering onto the floor in a metallic shower.

Glass shattered. Metal pans clanged. People were shouting. Instruments crunched beneath the two writhing bodies. Then Mary was on her knees, and luckily she wasn't cut. Ian wasn't getting up. He lay sweating and silent on the floor, clutching his heaving chest.

"Holy shit!" shouted Frank, coming around the table. "Get someone in here fast! Call a code. Call Cardiology." He turned to Peter as he bent down over Ian. "Are you okay to continue?"

"Yeah. Get Voorman or someone in here." Peter, shouting to the nurses. "Get a new setup! Perfusion, run cardioplegia now! Vent closed! Cardioplegia line open!"

"Cardioplegia running," said the perfusionist. "Do you want a full dose?"

"Absolutely. We'll have to wait for a fresh setup." He turned to Frank who had pounded Ian's chest twice and had started external cardiac massage. "How's he look?"

Frank breathed into Ian, mouth to mouth, before answering. "Not good! I'm not getting a pulse. Obviously arrested. His pupils are responsive and he's groping." He sounded anguished, shouting, "Christ, get a team! Get T.P.A! Get a stretcher! Get oxygen—"

Mary handed him an oxygen cylinder and an ambubag.

"Pump his chest, Mary. I'll ventilate," said Frank, as he sealed the ambubag around Ian's face with his hand. "Call Charlie from the next room to help out."

But Charles Piper, the anesthetist from the next room, was already beside him, cutting Ian's operating gown off and putting an intravenous into his arm.

"Thanks, Charlie," said Peter from beside the patient. He couldn't leave the patient while he was on bypass with his chest cranked wide open.

"Didn't see you, Charlie," said Frank.

"No problem. I've got a number twelve in," said Charlie. "Somebody get me an IV line of anything. Get a monitor. Get a stretcher!"

The circulating nurse pushed the mess of instruments out of the way with a wide broom and motioned to some other nurses to bring the stretcher through.

The perfusionist pulled the running bypass pump back at an angle to clear a space for the stretcher.

"Frank. Mary. Get ready to heave him onto the stretcher with me. On the count." Mary continued to pump his chest. Frank ventilated Ian by mask. "One. Two. Three, and now!"

They barely got him onto the stretcher. Frank grabbing the shoulders and neck, Charlie the torso, and Mary the legs.

Once on the stretcher, Charlie emptied the syringes of drugs into the IV that the circulating nurse was taping down. He said, "Let's roll him out of here and get the defibrillator ready at 350. Wheel it out with us."

Maranghi stuck his head into the OR just as the stretcher was getting to the door. "What happened?"

Frank Fanconi left the room with Charles Piper to explain the chain of events to Maranghi.

Peter was alone in the room with the perfusionist, a tall girl, and the circulating nurse who was out of scrub. Mary was back at the sink rescrubbing. Circulators from other rooms were busily wheeling in new trays of instruments.

When Mary finally re-entered the operating suite, she helped Peter redrape the lower half of the patient. She said, "Voorman's on his way. He's not far."

"Good," said Peter. "The patient's stable. We can wait a few minutes. Nobody else available?"

"Everybody's tied up. And there's some meeting in the board room."

"Yeah. Some stuff about the investigation." But Peter already knew what would be said; the results of the literature search. "Think we'll be getting off pretty light by the look of it."

Mary said, "You mean lady luck was on our side?"

"No, not really." He looked at her, not saying anything more.

Voorman peered into the room, tying an operating mask around his face. "I came as quick as I could. Be right in."

When he finally got up to the table, Voorman asked, "So, what happened?"

Peter explained, as they settled into the job of completing the operation.

***

Two hours later, Frank and Peter wheeled their patient into the post-op intensive care unit. They settled him in quickly and turned him over to Samuel Cohen, who reviewed the procedure and the operative stats with them.

"Nothing fazes you guys?" Cohen said. "One of your own goes down during the case and you still turn in routine numbers. Not even a long pump run."

"Maybe it was a simple case." said Peter.

"I tell you, Peter," said Cohen, "your own mother could die at the dinner table and you wouldn't notice."

"Yeah, yeah, yeah." Peter let it go.

"When was the last time you were in Toronto?" Cohen wasn't letting go.

"Not long ago."

"When was the last time you had dinner with your mother?"

Peter thought for a moment. "A few months ago."

"You see?" Cohen shrugged. "I have dinner with mother every other week as a bare minimum."

"That's just your guilt, Sammy."

"Of course, I'd feel guilty," he said quietly. "But you oversexed, BMW driving, lying sons of bitches called surgeons—"

"Porsche driving, Sammy. Porsche driving." Peter stretched his hands out.

"But seriously, Peter, the numbers are good. You did your usual great job."

"Thanks, Sammy. Coming from you, that's a real compliment."

Frank had just put a phone down. "Ian's in a coma. Maranghi's down there with him now. Doesn't look good. Thinks that he may have had a stroke as well as a massive heart attack. Shit! And nobody's told Jenny yet."

"I'm going down there," said Peter. He quickly turned and left.

Frank followed.

They got to the small alcove beside the elevators, and Peter pulled Frank aside. He spoke softly, but there was no one near to hear. "You see what set him off?"

"Yeah pal. The stock report. He must have lost a fortune."

"Frank?" Peter wasn't sure he wanted to ask.

"Yeah."

"How come you're not worried?"

"I only had one full year's worth of options. That's a loss of about sixty thousand, but I figure it's not like Ian who's been here over fifteen years and must have had a huge packet." Frank paused. "Besides, I'm still young."

"Right," said Peter. "Well, I didn't have any. So, there it goes. And speaking of going, I better talk to his wife."

In the cardiac intensive care unit, Peter found Maranghi at Ian Scott's bedside, staring at the monitor above the bed.

"Hello, Peter," said Maranghi. "That must have been scary."

"Yeah." He was at a loss, looking at Ian lying motionless, connected to a ventilator.

"I've decided to paralyze and ventilate him for now. He wasn't breathing and his pupils were sluggish; he might have had a stroke. He came back from the arrest in fibrillation, and I finally got him stabilised with amniodarone. His pressures have been a little on the low side, but I'll buy that for now. We can always balloon him. I think this represents the best treatment under the circumstances. He has a monitor line in so we can follow the heart very closely. There's no point in operating on a fresh heart attack. Besides, he's had tissue plasminogen activator, so he may come back with good coronaries." He looked at Peter for a moment. "I hope all this meets with your approval?"

"Yes, thanks." He wiped tears from his eyes. "I'm sorry. We were close. I don't mean to embarrass you. Guess I'll call his wife."

"No worries. Look. Do you want me to call her? I don't think she knows."

"That's all right." Peter put his arm over Maranghi's shoulder. "I'll manage it. You've done enough." He knew this was the moment.

"Very well then. I'll be seeing you." Maranghi started to walk away.

"Oh, one other thing." Maranghi turned back to face Peter from a few feet away. "How long have you been here, at Mass Heart, I mean?"

"You can tell Mrs. Scott I've been here fifteen years, and I've been the chief of cardiology for the past three years now." Maranghi looked eager to turn and go.

Peter asked clearly and distinctly. "How come you're not worried?"

The smile vanished from Maranghi's face. "Pardon?"

"The stock price has fallen from over twenty dollars to a couple of bucks. How come you're not worried?"

Peter watched Maranghi's adam's apple bob noticeably as he slowly, silently, backed away. He walked backwards to the end of the short hall and let himself out the door.

Peter went downstairs to his office, locked himself in, and phoned Jenny Scott.

"Hello." A soft voice.

"Jenny? Peter Martins here."

"Oh hello, Peter. This is a pleasure."

"I have some bad news. Are you sitting down?"

"It's about Ian?"

"Yes."

She sniffled once. "I thought there'd be something."

"Oh. Why?"

Jenny was slow to answer. "He wasn't himself over the weekend. We went out. He didn't talk to people. Didn't even talk to me. He slept poorly and talked in his sleep. He kept mumbling in his sleep, 'Help me, help me, I'm ruined.' "

"Really?"

"It started on Wednesday, actually. You know, the day the investigation started." She sniffled again. "Did he have something to do with it, Peter?"

"To do with what?"

"The killings?"

"No, Jenny. There were no killings. It's all a big mistake, or a cruel hoax."

"Then, how is he, Peter?"

"Do you want to come down to the hospital?"

She spoke softly, but with clear intent. "Tell me now."

"He had a heart attack." Peter waited some moments, leaning back in his chair. Looking up at his surgical diploma, he was suddenly filled with despair, a consummate impuissance. "He's in poor shape, Jenny. He's on a ventilator."

Jenny Scott cried softly at the other end of the line. Peter wished he could be with her.

He interrupted. "I have to tell you more."

She stifled her crying and said, "Go on."

"I'm afraid we also think he had a stroke."

"Yes."

"Do you want me to come and get you?"

"No." Still crying softly. "I'll get my friend to drive me down."

"I'll be here," he said. "You know where to find me. My office is next to Ian's."

"Thank you, Peter. You've been a good friend. Bye."

"Goodbye."

The phone line went to dial tone. Peter held the receiver in his hand, looking at it. Feeling hollow. Wondering if he'd be able to help Jenny. Wondering how she'd clean up Ian's financial mess. Wondering ...

TWENTY-EIGHT

Governor Willard Duke walked down the lower corridor of the State House. He would stride if he could, so confident that he would avoid most of the press. He was satisfied with the increase in the gasoline tax. But he was happy with his capture of the flailing Massachusetts Heart Institute. That was going to be his triumph. Putting it into the State's portfolio of hospitals. Now he was going to collect the taxes *and* the profits that place generated.

He had shown them. No other governor had done anything like it—and the president—well didn't this look good on him. *That's for not even talking to me.*

His bodyguards separated as he approached the doors to the back entry.

Looking out he saw a wall of reporters and cameramen. He swallowed hard.

***

Anne Maples sat carefully on a blanket with her microphone in hand. She had been waiting for the governor for almost two hours. The shade of the drive-through behind the State House was the most comfortable place to be. She sat on the curb just in front of the house leader's car, looking at the state troopers assembled around the stone arches. Their broad-rimmed hats looked excessive in the heat and silly in the shade. But there was strength in the uniform.

Anne sat there, thinking about the interview she expected with the governor. She was careful not to wrinkle or soil her new, summer dress, one she had chosen for its fit and conservative look.

The State House sitting had been an emergency. Most noteworthy representatives had left some time ago, and the debate which had ended two hours earlier, had been handily won by the majority. But Governor Willard Duke was keeping the press waiting. Frigging politicians, as Peter had called them. His words had actually been more colorful. Anne had to lock that kind of thought out of her mind if she was going to score this.

She had interviewed Duke before, and knew that describing him as cagey was an understatement. She wasn't going to blow it.

But Peter had told her about his confrontation with Maranghi a few days earlier. He wouldn't have lied. And the tumbling stock price was common knowledge. So, she could only hope that her questions were cogent and she'd catch him unsuspecting. Maybe she'd prove their theory—about Duke— maybe to the nation.

Most of all, Anne recognized that she had arrived at a crossroad in her career. She had spoken to a network vice president yesterday and made a deal. *To hell with Ted Weiner.* Today she'd put out, or be wiped off the national landscape of broadcasting, forever.

She realized she had to have every cognitive faculty ready for the governor. The next few minutes were a little bit like the shootout at the OK Corral, no holds barred, no rules apply, except for one: appear believable for the viewer. Everything she had ever done before had prepared her for this moment. Anne looked at the microphone in her hands. The letters were black on a white shield, NBS.

As she sat pondering her future, she was oblivious to the singing of the birds in the courtyard, behind the State House. She was oblivious to the distant sound of traffic. In fact, she almost missed the governor.

The doors at the back of the State House burst open. The governor's bodyguards preceded him, looking left and right.

Reporters were already circling. *They're swarming him like flies.* Her cameraman and soundman were running across the covered drive to get near Governor Duke. *Shit!* She jumped up off the blanket, forgetting it entirely as she raced across the drive, smoothing the front of her dress.

She got to the back of the group of reporters and found them like a wall of locusts, constantly moving.

"Governor!" shouted one.

"Yes, sir," he said with a look of accommodating interest.

"Is it true that the House Majority passed a rise in the State Gasoline Tax today?"

"We didn't want to do it, but yes, it's true."

"And is the rise five cents a gallon?" shouted the same man.

The crowd fell silent for the reply. Anne wasn't having any luck bullying her way through the undulating wall of bodies, the wall that swayed from left to right, as heads turned to hear questions and answers. But as the crowd fell silent to hear Duke's answer, the solution to her dilemma came to mind.

She kneed the reporter in front of her in the calves. He turned around several inches shorter, wincing.

Anne told him, "Yell, and I'll brain ya!" and pushed her way past. She saw her camera man was on the far side of the governor, on his left. She couldn't see her audio technician.

Governor Duke answered with a smile, "No, that's not true at all." He emphasized with his index finger. "That's what was suggested."

The same reporter said, "Would you care to elaborate on the actual amount of the rise?"

As the crowd fell still again, Anne kneed the next man, gaining a further advantage. She was now one row away from the governor.

"Well I can assure you, that the Government had the welfare of the public in mind when they voted on this rise. And we debated ceaselessly, in the summer, to come to a liveable consensus."

"And what is the rise, Governor?"

He turned to gain better advantage of the many lights and cameras, and smiled benevolently, "It's only four point two cents a gallon. You don't think this administration would have allowed anything close to five cents a gallon to get through the legislature, do you? Personally, I think that would have been grossly unfair and an affront to the people of this state."

"Governor!" A reporter, far over on the right, who shouted above the excited murmur of the crowd, held up and waved his hand. "Governor!"

"Yes, sir." Willard Duke pointed at him.

"Is it true that this debate, and in fact, the vote, was called as an emergency?"

"Not at all," said Duke. "It is our policy to deal with matters, especially those of finance, on an ongoing basis." He paused for emphasis, and raised his hands with palms outstretched. "Now I will admit that this administration didn't know the exact date on which we would deal with the issue. However, we did deal with the matter in as orderly and timely a fashion as we could."

Anne pushed her way through two reporters and shouted, "Governor Duke. Anne Maples. NBS TV News."

"Let the lady through," said the governor, and the reporters cleared a path for her.

"Thank you, Governor," she said politely and smiled, letting Duke dwell on her face for a moment.

Anne wasn't sure where to start, so she decided to go for the jugular. She asked demurely. "May I change the subject slightly?"

The governor looked ruffled. "Why, certainly."

"Governor Duke," Anne said, as she made certain she looked benevolently honest for the camera. "Who owns the majority of Massachusetts Heart Institute Common Stock?" She didn't realize, but she was tapping her left foot.

"I don't believe I know the answer to that question."

"Is it not true," she said, "that the State bought massive amounts of Massachusetts Heart Institute Common Shares last week?"

"Well." Willard Duke swallowed almost imperceptibly. "We did buy common shares of Mass Heart last week, but only in an effort to shore up the institution in its time of need! I might add that the average price per share paid by the State was very low."

"Was this under your knowledge, or on your order?"

"We shored up the Massachusetts Heart Institute. At my order."

"Is it the normal business of State government to buy shares of businesses in the State, for any purpose, at all?" she said.

He had only hesitated slightly, but she knew it had been immortalized by the camera, just like his uncomfortable swallow.

He said, "Miss Maples, it has become common practice in France, and especially in Japan, for governments to intervene in the marketplace to smooth transitions in tough economic times."

"But, sir," she said, "this is neither France nor Japan, and these were not financially troubled times for the Massachusetts Heart Institute."

"That all depends on your perspective," said the governor as he smiled uncomfortably. "I'd say that anybody, whose shares started at over twenty dollars and who watched them plummet to near two dollars within one week, would interpret his or her company to be in trouble, or at least under pressure." He showed a defiant smile.

Anne knew she had him now. She said, "Will this mean the departure of distinguished doctors from the State? For example, I have heard that Doctor Maranghi is leaving the Massachusetts Heart Institute."

"Miss Maples. Let me break the good news to you. Doctor Maranghi is not leaving the State." He looked more upbeat. "In fact, I'm pleased to announce that he is becoming the new Undersecretary of State for Health, effective September 10."

"Thank you, Governor Duke," said Anne.

"Not at all." Duke smiled at her. "That's all for today folks."

Anne hit him again. "But isn't it true that Representative Richard Farber argued that the Gasoline Tax hike was solely for the purpose of paying for the Massachusetts Heart Institute takeover?" Anne noticed for the first time that her knees were really trembling. "Governor?" She was sure nobody had noticed her shaking. "Governor?" Now she also knew that Peter's theory was correct!

Reporters were mobbing the governor with questions.

Governor Willard Duke's bodyguards broke a path for him through the reporters. He didn't answer. He was flushed and sweating..

Duke stormed past Anne, looking straight ahead as he hurried to his waiting Cadillac Limo. A grey State Police cruiser with dark blue fenders and doors led the way. The police car had ramming bumpers.

Anne thought that the last time she had seen the governor his eyes looked blue. Perhaps it was just the greyness of the covered entryway. But he did look washed out, his hair was mostly grey and his eyes appeared brown.

She signed off her report sincerely and dispassionately. Knowing her camera had captured every nuance of his discomfort. "Anne Maples, NBS News, reporting from Boston."

She looked back at the site of the interview once her crew had left. Without the governor and the crowd of reporters, the covered drive at the back of the State House looked cavernous and empty. The stippled bracing atop numerous circular pillars and the stone arches were all that was left of the old architecture. There were modern doors and stainless steel railings where fittings more appropriate to this historic site used to be. Bright yellow paint marked official parking spots. Suddenly, she felt let down, sad.

She wrestled with her thoughts, and after a few minutes, Anne knew she had clinched it. She would add the rest of the story later! *Might be the beginning of the end for old Willard!*

One hell of a business she was in. But somebody had to keep these crooks called politicians honest—otherwise they'd desecrate this great nation.

She walked proudly to her car and drove down past Fifty-two Precinct to the corner of Sudbury and State streets. Behind wire mesh fencing stood a child care facility with an outdoor sand lot, a low wood house on stilts, and an activity centre. About thirty children were screaming with delight, playing inside the compound located beside the busy intersection.

She crossed State Street to approach the Callahan Tunnel. A car in front of her had a bumper sticker that depicted a red stop sign with a red slash across the profile of the governor. The logo read, "Stop Duke."

TWENTY-NINE

Peter drained the rest of his Ballantine's and soda, rattled the cubes, and set it down on the bar. He turned to look at her.

"Personally," he paused, "I find it incomprehensible."

"It's going to be all right." Anne got up off her barstool, came over, and wrapped her arms around Peter, kissing him in the nape of the neck. "It'll work out." She looked at him, pleading in her eyes. "Let's change the subject." She looked at the bartender who was coming over, extended her arm, and said, "Ah-ha."

The black man said to Peter, "Will you have another, sir?"

"I've been looking up there, with the scotches, there's a dark one."

"Yes, sir. Black scotch. Many of our patrons prefer it. Would you like to try?"

Peter nodded, and the bartender poured some into a glass and set it before him. He tasted the single malt.

"Very nice. What is it?"

"Loch Dhu. They only make it certain years."

"I'll have a double." Peter turned back to Anne.

She said, "I agree, a lot has happened this last month. I'm not happy with everything either." She pumped Peter on the chest. "The way the trail's gone dead."

"Roy's gone," said Peter, grabbing her hand. "People have spotted him in the Caymans with his girl."

"Have they really? You're sure?"

"Yeah."

"So he's not to blame?" Anne thought a moment. "All of Mass Heart's management is gone. All of them." She started to chortle. "Calabrese, Abel, Van Boren." She laughed, and caught herself. "Have you ever seen anything so ridiculous come of a murder investigation?" She shook her head slowly.

"Well the big boys have all gone. No million dollar salaries means, no management. No stocks means no Fanconi, no Wittman. Just think of how much they lost." Peter took a long sip and looked into his glass. "God, I'm going to miss those guys. Only one left is Mel Finegold, 'cause he's married to his research. But now the State owns the place and the university runs it." He looked at her. "And Williams, the fossil, is head of everything. But he's all right." He looked around the oak-paneled room. "I'll bet Dugan wishes he'd stayed home. So why do you figure Malloy's doing all the interviews now?"

"Dugan's not on the short list since Chief Hawkins died. You know, he would have been a contender if he hadn't gone ahead and exhumed those kids." Anne took a drink. She looked at the bartender. "Get me one of those black ones too." She winked at him. "Double."

"Yes, Miss Maples."

"But, we still haven't answered the question." She sat on his lap and cocked her head, looking at Peter with her arms around his neck. "Who made the phone call?"

"Was it Maranghi, or was it Roy Purvis? Maranghi is the only one who gained anything," said Peter. "Undersecretary of State for Health. That's where I'd place my bet. If you could look, I bet you'd find he also cashed his shares before they tanked." He paused. "Don't forget though that U.S. Medical Hospital Enterprises didn't raise a finger to help Mass Heart when the shares fell. They just seemed to hand it to Duke. I think he's the only one who knows the truth, but he'll just stick to his story." He touched glasses with Anne and they both drank. "So, we'll never know."

"One thing's certain," said Anne. "After this fiasco, The D.A. won't want to go after wily old Willie. They'll be happy if the whole thing just disappears."

"The other certainty's that Governor Duke will never get elected again. Not after you ferreted him out like that. Better not even try."

"I did pretty good, huh?" she said. "I love holding those bastard's feet to the fire."

"Just don't do it to me."

"Hey, why so glum?"

" 'Cause you're moving to New York tomorrow."

"So?" She waved her arm out widely. "It's just down the coast." Pouting. "You can come visit."

"You're really going to do it."

"I'm going to host the morning news on NBS, and I'll get to guest anchor. Then the sky's the limit. Besides, when you get tired of Boston, and this health care upheaval settles down, you might find something real comfortable down there too."

"Oh yeah?"

"Yeah. Seriously." Anne waited a moment and pulled him close. "Know what I want?"

Peter shook his head. "No."

She let him wait a moment. "Go to your place."

THIRTY

Roy Purvis walked knee deep in the water, looking at the shoreline of Five Mile Beach, the warm water and soft sand caressing his feet. He had gotten used to life on Grand Cayman. Lazy days, wonderful nights, and Janet. She was walking just ahead of him on a narrow stretch of beach by some palm trees.

She turned to him. "Roy, look—" Pointing at the colorful umbrella over the wagon of a drink vendor. "Come on, let's get one."

He walked out of the water and took her hand. They went to the stand and got a strawberry Pina Colada.

After walking off together for a few minutes, Janet looked at him. "Everything all right?"

"Yes, dear." He turned and gazed into her clear blue eyes. "Why?"

"You seem preoccupied."

"Oh well, I'm just thinking how lucky we are here." They started to walk again, in the shade of the palms. "This beautiful place. Everything really."

"The condo. What a treat that is."

"Yes." He shook his head. "You know, if I had waited just a few more days I could have lost everything when the institute tanked."

Janet nudged him. "You're a very bright man, Roy."

"You're biased. But the investments are going well, and no taxes. Things couldn't really be much better."

She stopped him. "I'm just so happy you're sharing all this with me." After a moment she said, "You're not getting bored with me, are you?"

"Nonsense." He chuckled. "How could I possibly?"

"Guess I'm just a little insecure."

Janet hugged him and walked off ahead of him, having her drink.

Roy remarked at how good she looked in her tiny bikini. A great figure, if a little fuller than when they had arrived.

But his thoughts wandered off her form, one that he had become completely familiar with. For some reason he was thinking about Massachusetts Heart Institute.

Why had he panicked that way? He didn't even know any more. Was it Van Boren and Abel pushing Peter Martins at him? Was it Patricia's revelation? *I don't know.*

He had nothing against Peter—Loved the guy. Could have worked with him. Would have done well with him. *Did my ego get in the way?*

And that investigation—if that's what you called it. *Crap.* Why hadn't anybody looked up digoxin overdose in children. Peter had told him about the investigation in Toronto. That one had been a wild goose chase too, only to find that the evidence didn't support the charges. They had even looked up the science together. *Those cops were dead wrong.* He could have told anybody about that. But then, he had already left. Now Mass Heart was gone, and all Americans paid the same fees, and only foreigners paid full tilt. The profits ...

So, he thanked his lucky stars that he had cashed out early. Some things are just fate.

Janet was approaching their condo. Just then he smelled something, burnt. Like on a barbeque. Roy slowed down. For a moment he thought it was like the smell of electro-cautery on human flesh. Like he used to do to a sternum after the saw cut through, when he was cracking a chest. He could sense the vibrations of the saw and the feel of the instruments he hadn't used in months. The click of a clamp tightening down on an aorta.

Roy stopped walking and slowly looked down at his hands, palms upturned.

THIRTY-ONE

A damp heat hung in the Louisiana air. A heat that even October had failed to extinguish.

Peter was sitting in the window seat of this plane on the first leg of his journey home. There had been moments, but on balance, he was glad he'd come.

As he sat staring out the portal with the drone of jet engines behind him, his attention drifted over the purple hues of distant hills, vibrant under the pink and orange afterglow of the mackerel sky. Drifting over the bowed trees painted in Shenandoah greens crossed with evening streaks of purple and grey, and settling on a few drops of condensation trapped between the portal's window panes.

His thoughts were trapped, as surely as the drops between the glass panes separating him from the world outside.

The engines revved and the plane rolled smoothly forward, one position closer to takeoff.

***

He might have chosen better clothes to wear. But he hadn't. He had arrived in his jeans and shirt. He'd carried his jacket all day. What was appropriate in Boston late in October was not the thing for Baton Rouge.

The moment Peter deplaned, he found the first eager looking black cabby that he could.

"I'm going sightseeing. I need all day," he said in the open window.

The pleasant man in the blue striped shirt said, "That'll be two-fifty."

"I want to see Hornsby," he said. "Here's three hundred." He doled out the money. "Keep the change." He got in the back of the dark cab and noted that the picture in the folio matched the driver.

The driver looking in the rear view seemed to notice Peter's interest in his license. He soon had the cab at the outskirts of Baton Rouge, heading north on Nineteen, to Scotland and beyond to Clinton where he would turn right on State Highway Ten to get to Hornsby on the Amite River.

"Gonna take an hour and a half to two hours," the driver said to the man in back who had let his head fall comfortably to rest on the seat back of the meandering taxi.

"That's fine," Peter answered without opening his eyes, tired from the heart he had operated on the night before. "Just stick with me. I'm on a friendly mission. But, you know ..."

"Ah unnastand, suh." The driver looked the man over in his mirror. His jacket lying flat on the seat without any bulge.

Peter watched as the cab drove beneath a canopy of bent sycamore and pecan trees. Gentle grassed land rolled out into the distance, occasionally punctuated by a swamp. The bayous marked with tall stands of grass and the grey, dead trunks of trees. He saw more orchids high in the trees. Flowers of violet and pink. Spots of bright life against a dusky green background.

"What kinna business yu in, suh? If yu don' mind me askin'."

"I'm a surgeon. A heart surgeon."

"That's why yu tired. Yu the workin' kind. Not the big shot kind."

"Maybe you're right."

"Um hmm. I take yu to Hornsby. Don' yu worry."

Peter laid his head against the seat back and nodded off to the rhythm of the cab's undulating tires treading a path over the repaired roadway.

Some time later, the driver said, "Suh. We's in Hornsby."

Peter awoke. He let his eyes adjust to the bright light and sat up. He checked his watch. One-thirty.

"Where to, suh?"

"Twenty-two River."

"Uh huh." The driver executed a left turn. "This is River."

The street, wide and unpaved, ran beside the Amite River. On the left, old houses that could best be described as run down cottages, many without front yards, stood in a long, dusty row. Their wood shingle or metal roofs got shade from an occasional tree. Windows were open. Folks congregated out of the sun, on porches with swings and chairs.

On the right side of the street, cottages stood beside the Amite, on stilts. The dusty road approached the doors and windows, and porches hung out over the gently rolling river.

The cab crept slowly north on River to avoid making dust.

Black folk of all ages followed the path of the cab from their perches in the shade. Men of all sizes without shirts. Women of all shapes in bright cotton dresses, some without underclothes. Young children in shorts, their tops bare or covered in tees. Teens conspicuously absent. The dark centres of saucer eyes following the path of the white man in the dark cab.

"This is twenty-two on the right," the driver said, as he turned to Peter.

The house was little more than a single-storey shanty with tar paper bricking and a tin roof. There was a door at the front, flanked by two single-paned windows.

Peter got out of the cab and threw his herringbone jacket in the back seat. He approached the front door and knocked.

The driver got out of the cab and stood leaning against the fender, deflecting the many curious looks from the other side of the street.

A little woman answered the door—no taller than five feet. Her hair, a one-inch Afro of the purest white. Her eyes, coloured with many tiny blood vessels, peering from a deeply wrinkled face, punctuated by a mouth full of pearly false teeth. Ninety, if she was a day.

She looked at Peter and took the cigarette out of her mouth. "Uh hunh."

"I'm Doctor Peter Martins. I'm here to see Ian Scott."

The old woman raised her gaunt arm out straight, pointing to the corner of the house. "Yo find him on the veranda. We expectin' yo. Follow me." She let the jerry-built front door slam shut with its squeaky spring and walked to the corner of the house. She marched ahead in her pink sleeveless dress with the stiff gait of the old but independent.

Peter followed her onto the wood-planked creaking porch which was stilted out over the river. The porch, which had a modest railing of heavy tree boughs, was covered with an extension of the tin roof and ran around the corner of the house.

Peter felt his heart in his throat as he saw him for the first time. He was in a rocking chair, hunched slightly forward, propped on his elbows. He looked like he had lost weight, dressed in green work pants and a blue plaid shirt. He stared out at the gently moving river.

The old black woman approached and put her arm on his shoulder. "Peter Martins here, Ian." She patted him twice as she passed and took up a position leaning against the cottage. She puffed leisurely on her home-rolled cigarette as she watched Peter.

The surgeon crouched at his friend's side and looked at his face.

He slowly said, "Ian. It's me, Peter ... Peter Martins to see you. How are you, Ian?"

The man looked dispassionately out at the river. He didn't answer. He didn't wink the way he used to. He didn't even wince.

Peter tried again. He put his arm on Ian's shoulder. "It's me, Peter Martins."

The man looked straight ahead.

Peter shifted around to his front and stared straight into his eyes.

"Ian. It's me, Peter."

The man's eyes did not move. He might have been looking straight through Peter, or been in a trance. His skin was smooth, almost wrinkle free. His eyes were clear, white, and unwavering.

The old woman said, "Been like that since he got home." Peter looked at her. She finished her cigarette and threw the butt into the river. She walked over to his side. "Ah talk to him all the time. Sometimes Ah think he hears me." Her voice was positive. "Most o' the time he just watch the river go by. Oh yeah, Ah take care o' him now. Ah feed him, clothe him, change him. He walk if yo guide him, yo know."

Peter got up and stroked Ian's short, curly white hair. He didn't stir. Peter watched as he drooled onto his pants, and he turned to the old woman, perplexed.

"My name's Aida, "she said without extending her hand. "Aida Scott. Ah'm Ian's momma."

"I'm—"

"Ah know, boy. Ah know."

"Aida," said Peter. "Where's Jenny?"

"Now that's an interesting question, son." She looked squarely at Peter and said. "Jenny is one good woman. Um hmm. She came down here with Ian after the hospital in ... where was it?"

"Boston."

"In Boston, let him go." She paused to light another cigarette with a match that she got out of her pocket. "Ma boy was a high roller. Lost most o' his money an' got sick. Jenny came down here with what was left of their savin's and stayed a few weeks. We had some good talks." Aida looked out over the river. "We talk long and hard, right here, with Ian listening. Though he don' say much."

"And?"

"Well, Doctuh Peter." She squinted as she looked up at him. "Ah tol' Jenny she was a good girl. Wanted to stay by his side. Honest too." She took a deep puff. "Ah tol' her this no place for a beauty like her be taking care of Ian. If she did, she'd live to resent ma boy, an' Ah don' want that. Ah tol' her, leave him here with me, live her life, find a new man, and maybe come see us once in a while. We split the money down the middle. She left three weeks ago. Cryin'."

"I understand."

"Good. Not like a white man to unastan'." She paused, waiting for a reply, but getting none, she said, "Ma boy back with his momma, and she gonna take care o' him." Aida hugged Ian with her left arm.

He didn't stir.

Peter bent down and looked into the clear brown eyes. "Goodbye, Ian." He stroked his soft hair.

The man looked through him.

It didn't matter.

Peter left after saying goodbye to Aida and giving her his card. He told her to call him if they ever needed anything extra or anything special. She watched him drive off, and Peter knew that he would never hear from her again.

They drove away and Peter couldn't think of anything other than the look on Ian's face. Was it an accepting dispassion? Was it a catatonia, a depression? Peter knew better. He knew that his friend had lost his mind in a stroke that morning at the hospital. Anything else would have been more acceptable to Peter. It would have been treatable.

But Peter had needed to satisfy himself. And now that he had seen the empty shell of his friend, he felt like crawling into some black hole until he had dealt with his grief and had learned to accept Ian's fate.

The driver asked, "Yu feel better, Doc?"

"No." He sat back in the seat. "Did you know where I was going this morning?"

"Yes, suh. Yu said yu wanted to go to Hornsby, and yu said yu was a heart surgeon. Hell. Ian Scott's a celebrity to us folk down here. He one of us."

"Of course, he is." Peter thought for a moment. "I need to be at the airport for six o'clock. Can we drive 'till then?"

"Ma pleasure, suh."

Peter rolled the window partly down, rested his head on the seat back, and shut his eyes as he breathed in the late summer. He smelled the leaves of the trees, touched the scent of the swaying grass, felt the aroma of orchids. And he tasted the brackish droplets of bayou before he fell asleep.

***

The ping pong of the plane's intercom plucked him from his thoughts. The pilot announced, "Flight attendants, prepare for takeoff."

Outside a droning continuous boom started and shook the side of the aircraft until the plane's taking-off receded into the distance.

The airliner's engines revved up momentarily and settled down, as the plane crept forward and stopped again.

So, what about his new position? Since the demise of the investigation, and the institution it centred on, Peter had taken a much less egocentric view of himself. He had become entirely more circumspect. In the long run, few people would be able to take advantage of the scam. So he had decided to just roll with it and continue to practice some of the best medicine in the world. And now, Doctor Peter Martins, the new chief of cardiac surgery, was going back to Boston.

Peter never did understand Abel. But his appointment had gone full circle—perhaps he had known all along that Peter would be the new chief! Maybe it had been planned that way. After all, at the university, chiefs of departments were only appointed from outside the system.

The plane's intercom sounded "ping pong." The jet engines whined harder and the plane edged forward, executing a slow left hand turn. Half way through the turn, the engines accelerated to a scream, and a droning hum pinned the passengers back in their seats. The airliner shook a rapidly quickening line down the runway.

Peter felt his sweaty fingers dig into the arm rests.

The plane punctuated its departure from the earth with two thumps as the main wheels left the tarmac.

As the plane droned steadily upward out of the pastel horizons of the Louisiana sky, Peter knew that he had left behind his good friend for the last time.

He watched in the window, a few drops of condensation slowly tracing a diagonal trail toward the rear of the plane.

Klaus Jakelski

The plane banked left, and as it did, the color of the sky took on a dark, inscrutable, eastern blue.

Acknowledgements

I want to thank my wife, Cathy, and my children, Natasha and Nicholas, for their support, encouragement, and patience. Kudos to my editors, Sharon Crawford and Shane Joseph, for setting me straight. For Sean Costello's guidance, I can't say enough. To Dr. Jim Strong for his help with the science. Special thanks to Gregory Phillips (Philips Ryther and Winchester) for all his sage advice. And thanks to Dr. Vern Dennis Gugino, for grounding me in Boston.

And of course, my dogs, Asti and Tito, for always agreeing with me.

Klaus Jakelski
2014

Author Biography

Klaus Jakelski started writing poetry in high school. He got diverted into photography and enjoyed some real success. Film school tugged on his shirt sleeves, but academia reigned him in. The young man aspired to Aerospace Engineering, but didn't have the eyesight to fly the planes. Somehow he ended up in Biological Sciences.

He graduated from The University of Western Ontario and went on to University of Toronto Medical School. A practising physician since 1979, he's worked everywhere: from the emergency room to the operating room, from the hospital floor to the office floor. Klaus has done his time in administration and on public boards. He has also written columns for a local paper.

He lives with his patient and forgiving wife, Cathy, and their children, Natasha and Nicholas, in Sudbury, Ontario, where he still practices the best medicine he knows.

Klaus is an avid sportsman, equally at home on and in the water. An avid hunter, he haunts McGregor Bay and the North Channel of Georgian Bay with his dogs, Asti and Tito.

He is a renaissance man who is equally at home on the streets of his favorite big cities, Toronto, Boston, and Berlin, where he regularly annoys waiters.

On a good day, Klaus does everything full bore. On any other day, he plans his next move.

Dead Wrong is the embodiment of years of passion for writing. With so much lifetime experience to borrow on, there has to be more.

CPSIA information can be obtained at www.ICGtesting.com
Printed in the USA
LVOW10s1607171214

419285LV00018B/1037/P